Science and Technology of Thermal Barrier Coatings

Science and Technology of Thermal Barrier Coatings

Editor

Yeon-Gil Jung

MDPI

Editor
Yeon-Gil Jung
School of Materials Science and
Engineering, Colleage of
Mechatronics Engineering,
Changwon National University
Korea

Editorial Office
MDPI
St. Alban-Anlage 66
4052 Basel, Switzerland

This is a reprint of articles from the Special Issue published online in the open access journal *Coatings* (ISSN 2079-6412) (available at: https://www.mdpi.com/journal/coatings/special_issues/ Sci_Technol_TBCs).

For citation purposes, cite each article independently as indicated on the article page online and as indicated below:

LastName, A.A.; LastName, B.B.; LastName, C.C. Article Title. *Journal Name* **Year**, *Volume Number*, Page Range.

ISBN 978-3-0365-0318-9 (Hbk)
ISBN 978-3-0365-0319-6 (PDF)

Contents

About the Editor

Preface to "Science and Technology of Thermal Barrier Coatings"

thermal insulation in gas turbine engine blades and vanes in the aviation industry [ ]. Generally, a TBC system consists of a metallic bond coat (MCrAlY; M = Co, Ni or Co/Ni), a ceramic top coat (YSZ, yttria stabilized zirconia), and a thermally grown oxide layer (TGO). The ceramic top coat has an essentially low thermal conductivity and low thermal expansion and the metallic bond coat is deposited between the metallic substrate and ceramic top coat for developing the adherence of the ceramic top coating to the substrate alloy [ ]. The basic purpose of CoNiCrAlY layer is the adhesion of ceramic top coating with base surface and these alloys help chemical stability which ceramic top coating cannot provide due to the porous surface [ ].

Improving high performance wear resistant coating materials to protect the metallic substrate is an efficient approach to reducing wear. MCrAlY overlay coating is used as a protective coating against high temperature oxidation and corrosion. Due to the sufficient amount of Al in the coatings during service life is the main degradation factor in conventional MCrAlY coatings. The performance of a metallic bond coat can be improved by applying Al and Cr gradient MCrAlY coatings [ ]. Plasma spray, HVOF and CGDS coating techniques are used producing of CoNiCrAlY containing bond coating structure [ ]. Materials processed by the detonation gun (D gun) and supersonic plasma spraying (SSPS) techniques are used to display alternative characteristics/qualities for the production of coatings. The SSPS process enables the production of coatings cheaper, faster and easier. The D gun technique also enables the production of hard and denser coating structure [ ]. It's expected from CoNiCrAlY metallic bond coating structure to be dense, to have low porosity and crack due to primary role on TGO forming and growing [ ]. D gun spraying is a thermal spray coating process that creates a coating surface with extremely hard, wear resistance, good adhesion strength, dense structure, low porosity and compressive residual stresses [ ]. Additionally, due to D gun spraying being an intermittent coating process, very few pores and blanks appear in the sprayed coatings [ ]. It is preferred for protecting gas turbine engine parts and increasing material life against various types of wear at high temperatures. Unlike the D gun technique, SSPS technique enables the production of coatings more efficiently, faster and more easily with a high deposition rate on different substrates [ ]. SSPS technique enables the production of more dense and high bonding strength coatings due to the shorter exposure of atmospheric conditions and faster production compared to the conventional plasma spray coating process [ ]. SSPS's density, porosity and adhesion strength of the coating is also higher than the coating prepared by APS [ ]. Compared to the APS technique, it is faster and more efficient in completely melting SSPS powder [ ].

Thermal spray coatings have been widely utilized in various industrial applications against surface damages such as wear, corrosion and oxidation. Therefore, low porosity and good adhesion behavior are desired for the coating. Thermally sprayed MCrAlY bond coats, such as the one used in the present research, are primarily used for serving as an overlay metallic bond coat for thermal barrier coating systems against damages such as high temperature oxidation and hot corrosion. However, few studies are encountered related to their wear performance, particularly those deposited with D gun and SSPS techniques. This work therefore aims to investigate the microstructural characteristics and wear behaviors of CoNiCrAlY based metallic bond coats onto nickel based superalloy substrate Inconel 718 using the D gun and SSPS coating techniques. To analyze the high temperature wear behavior of the coatings, wear tests were applied at different temperatures and different loads. Before and after high temperature wear tests microstructural characteristics and mechanical properties of CoNiCrAlY coatings were examined. SEM, EDS, hardness and 3D topography of the produced and worn samples were comparatively evaluated. As a result of the study, it has been understood that the high temperature wear performances of the coating vary depending on the technique used in the production of coatings and their microstructural characteristics.

2. Materials and Methods

Inconel 718 nickel based superalloy disc samples having 25.4 mm diameter and 3 mm height were used as the substrate material. Before the coating process, surface cleaning and grit blasting of the substrate samples were fulfilled. Grit blasting was applied under a 75° angle and 2.5 bar pressure conditions when the shotgun and the surface of the distance of the substrate was approximately 10 cm. Different process parameters have been used in the production of CoNiCrAlY metallic bond coatings with 36% and D-gun coating techniques. As for the metallic bond coats, the D-gun (Perun S, Kiev, Ukraine) and the 36% (Kiev S plasma installation, Kiev, Ukraine) techniques were applied. The thickness of metallic coatings with MCrAlY content is approximately 100 μm. Coating parameters of D-gun and 36% coating techniques used in CoNiCrAlY bond coating production are given in Tables and

Table 1. Deposition parameters of CoNiCrAlY sprayed using the D-gun technique.

Combustion Gas	Air flow Velocity	Number of Shots	Spray Time	Spray Distance
C₂H₂ (2 l/min) O₂ (25 l/min) Air (2 l/min)	5-7.5 l/min	300	14 s	110-190 mm

Table 2. Deposition parameters of CoNiCrAlY sprayed using the 36% technique.

Airflow Velocity	Current	Voltage	Spray Distance
7.5 l/min	270 A	380 V	200 mm

CoNiCrAlY coated substrates after wear tests by using D-gun and 36% techniques. In the study, wear tests were performed at different loads (2 N and 5 N) and different temperatures (room temperature (rt), 250 and 500 °C) for each sample. Using the control stylus instrument (Hommelwerke device (Hommelwerke T-1000, Villingen-Schwenningen, Germany), the surface roughness values were obtained by measuring from 5 to 10 different points on each sample according to the standard. Microhardness measurements of materials and coatings were made in Duramin brand test device using 200 g load (HV₀.₂) and 15 s dwell time. Porosity measurements of the coatings were made by defining the matrix and porosity structures in microstructures in the Image J image analysis program (Image J) by taking the average of the measurements on 5 SEM images at 200x magnification.

The sliding wear tests were performed using a Pin on disc wear test device (TriboLab Brand, Lamitest, Turkey) with tungsten carbide (WC) balls of 6 mm diameter (RedHill, Prague, Czech Republic) at three different temperatures: rt, 250 and 500 °C. The hardness value of the hard carbide balls used in the experiments is 49 GPa. The wear tests of the coated samples were performed at 0.10 m/s sliding speed by applying 2 and 5 N loads. After the dry sliding, wear tests were performed under different loads on Pin on disc wear device, volume losses of samples were determined with the help of a 3D profilometer (Nanovea, Korea) by taking the average of 10 microstructural area measurements and multiplying this with the track diameter. Coefficient of friction values were evaluated by the frictional force data acquired from the load cell of the wear test rig.

3. Results and Discussion

Figures shows the 2D, 3D and cross-sectional views of the wear tracks. As shown in the figure, the track widths are not uniform along the wear tracks which necessitated performing numerous cross-sectional area measurements.

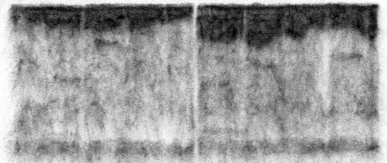

At the end of the dry sliding wear tests, when the SEM wear track photos taken from the sample surfaces after being subjected to etching at at under 2 N load are examined, it was found that the samples produced by both techniques are first exposed to oxidation wear. However, in the samples produced with the D gun technique, it is observed that this occurs more severely in the 86F5 technique, where the fatigue occurring under repeated loads is less effective. In the 86F5 technique, micro cracks that occur due to fatigue perpendicular to the direction of etching caused surface spalling in the future. In experiments carried out at at under 5 N load, delamination type wear mechanism is seen in addition to previous wear mechanisms in the D gun technique. In the 86F5 technique, wear due to fatigue and spalling was detected.

At the SEM wear track photos obtained as a result of the experiments carried out at 2.01 A, at 2 N load (Figure), a more homogeneous oxide layer is observed on the surface of the samples coated with D gun. It is also understood that this oxide layer is damaged by fatigue microcracks. In the 86F5 sample, it is seen that the oxide formation in the wear track region is not homogeneous. The reason for this can be explained by the fact that the sample causes more roughness, as the abrasive ball is starting to break, the high roughness first. While some of these broken roughness are removed from the system, some of them will remain between the abrasive and the substrate and will be crushed and become more compact. This is understood from the SEM photograph (Figure). When the SEM microstructure images are examined (Figures and), it is seen that there are spallings and breaking in parallel with the track of wear. This explains that the sample is not damaged by fatigue, it is dependent on the gaps underneath.

Figure . SEM micrographs after wear test at 2.01 A, under 2 N load, (a) D gun coating in sample (b) 86F5 coating in 2in pin.

Figure . SEM micrographs of the same surface of 86F5 coating technique at 2.01 A, under 2 N load

Figure 5. SEM micrograph of the wear surface of the O coating technique at 200 °C under 2 N load.

When the SEM photographs of the samples at 200 °C and 2 N load are compared, especially the technique produced by O gun has much less volume loss. That is to say, when Figure 5 is examined, it is understood that the abrasive ball wore rather with a small portion of the surface. We can explain this situation as follows: the increased temperature will cause many elements in the material to oxidize much faster. Depending on the nature of this oxidation, the oxide layer will either spalling quickly or adhesip also to the surface.

Figure 6. SEM micrograph after wear test of samples at 200 °C under 2 N load: (a) O gun coating technique, (b) extra gating technique.

In this, we can recognise that the oxide layer becomes compact under load and does not spall. As a result, the wear resistance of the material increased. However, the sample produced by the SEM technique under 2 N loads conditions did not show a similar situation and it can be shown in Figure 6. When the SEM photo is examined, two different wear areas attract attention. The region with a darker tone close to the center of the wear track and two adjacent regions with a lighter tone constitute the wear area.

In Figures and, when the linear and point EDS analyses from different regions of the wear surface are examined after the wear test under 200 °C and 2 N load is examined, it is understood that the ratio is low in the other region where the dark region is rich in Ni, Cr and Al. the peaks here are thought to increase due to the compounds formed by the combination of elements and oxygen in the coating powder. Here, however, when the point analysis given in the other tab of the same figure is analyzed, it can be seen that this decrease in the white region of 117 where spectrum 117 and 118 have more oxygen. The presence of tungsten element, which is not present in the substrate, is remarkable in point analysis. With increasing temperature, it is understood that both the formation of darker oxide layers on the abrasive surface and material transfer from the abrasive ball to the opposite surface due to the change in the plastic deformability of the abrasive surface ball, depending on the temperature. However, after the experiments carried out at it and 200 °C, no traces of tungsten were found on the

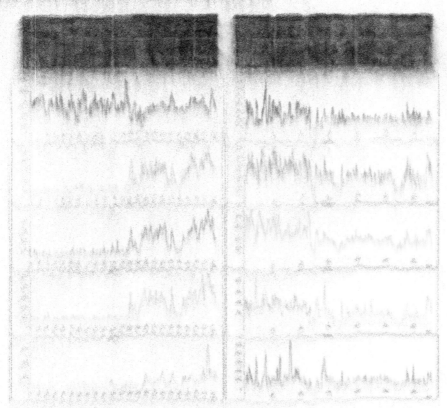

Figure 2. FT-IR linear analysis of cross-tracks at 800 °C under 2 Gd load. (a) IT-gun coating technique; (b) CVD coating technique.

Figure 8. [illegible] (a) D-gun coating technique; (b) the HVOF coating technique.

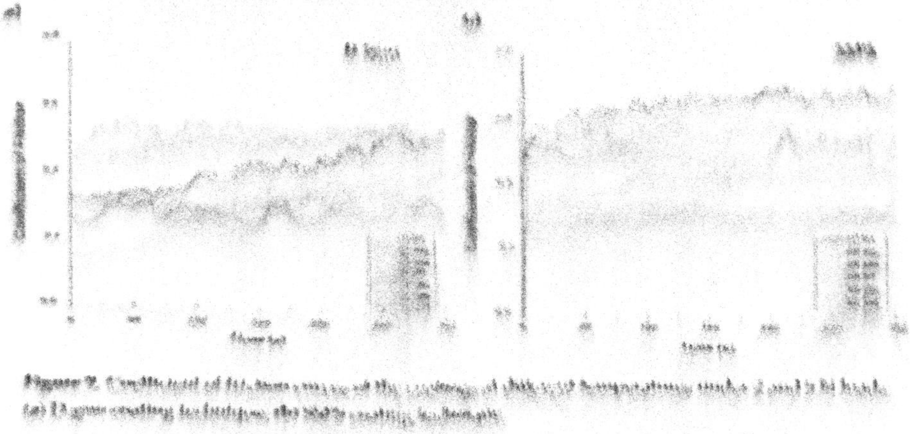

Figure 9. Coefficient of friction curves of the coatings at different temperatures under 2 and 5 N loads. (a) D-gun coating technique; (b) the HVOF coating technique.

A similar situation was observed after the experiments carried out under 5 N load in the friction graphs. However, the friction coefficient values of these samples were at lower levels. The friction coefficient values of the samples coated with the HVOF technique are given in Figure 9b. The lowest friction coefficients were determined at 5 N load and 500 °C. This was followed by 250 °C and rt temperatures. When the friction coefficients were examined under 2 N load, the lowest value was observed in the sample at 500 °C. This was followed by 250 °C and rt values. However, when the samples processed under 2 and 5 N loads are examined (Figure 9), it is noteworthy that the fluctuations in the friction coefficient graphs at 2 N are higher and the graphs are more stable at 5 N loads. It can be attributed that these fluctuations under 2 N load occur as a result of spalling the oxide layer formed faster than the surface.

4. Conclusions

In this study, metallic bond coatings with CoNiCrAlY content were produced on Inconel 718 superalloy substrate material by using D-gun and HVOF coating techniques. The coatings produced were subjected to wear tests at three different temperatures: rt, 250 and 500 °C and different loads 2 and 5 N to understand the wear mechanisms. The salient conclusions arising from this work are as follows:

1. CoNiCrAlY metallic powders were successfully deposited on the Inconel 718 superalloy substrates using D-gun and HVOF coating techniques.
2. The high temperature wear behavior of the coatings has changed depending on the processes used in the coating production and the microstructural properties of the coatings after production

3. Depending on the increasing loading rates and temperature, wear losses were likewise increased. However, this increase was not linear.

4. For D-gun and SHS coatings, increasing load resulted in lower coefficient of friction values. Increasing temperature resulted in lower COF value for SHS coatings; however, those produced with D-gun did not follow the same trend.

5. It has been understood that at 250 °C and at surface fatigue wear by using D-gun technique is comparatively more severe than SHS technique.

6. It has been observed that tribological layers and superficial changes occur in the microstructures of the coatings due to temperature and time by both thermal spray coating techniques.

7. When high temperature wear behaviour of CoNiCrAlY coatings are evaluated, it is seen that D-gun coatings show superior properties compared to SHS coatings.

8. Due to the increased surface hardness and microstructural dense structure with high temperature effect, the wear resistance of the coatings increases.

Author Contributions: A.Ç.K. and D.Ö. designed the experiments; A.Ç.K. and D.Ö. performed the experiments; A.Ç.K., D.Ö. and M.Ö. analyzed the data; A.Ç.K., D.Ö., M.Ö., and M.K. wrote, reviewed and edited the paper. All authors have read and agreed to the published version of the manuscript.

Funding: This research received no external funding.

Acknowledgments: The authors would like to acknowledge Vitrya Ltd. for the production of detonation gun (D-gun) and supersonic plasma spraying (SHS) CoNiCrAlY samples.

Conflicts of Interest: The authors declare no conflict of interest.

References

1. Fauchais, P.; Vardelle, A. Thermal sprayed coatings used against corrosion and corrosive wear. In Advanced Plasma Spray Applications; Jazi, H., Ed.; InTech: Rijeka, Croatia, 2012; Volume 10, p. 344p.

2. Oksa, M.; Turunen, E.; Suhonen, T.; Varis, T.; Hannula, S.P. Optimization and characterization of high velocity oxy fuel sprayed coatings: techniques, materials, and applications. Coatings **2011**, 1, 17-52.

3. Karaoglanli, A.C. Effects of plastic deformation on isothermal oxidation behavior of CoNiCrAlY coatings. Sci. Adv. Mater. **2015**, 7, 171-177.

4. Matthews, S.; James, B. Review of thermal spray coating applications in the steel industry: Part 1 hardware in steel making to the continuous annealing process. J. Therm. Spray Technol. **2010**, 19, 1267-1276.

5. Hardwicke, C.U.; Lau, Y.C. Advances in thermal spray coatings for gas turbines and energy generation: A review. J. Therm. Spray Technol. **2013**, 22, 564-576.

6. Khan, M.A.; Sundarrajan, S.; Duraiselvam, M.; Natarajan, S.; Kumar, A.S. Sliding wear behaviour of plasma sprayed coatings on nickel based superalloy. Surf. Eng. **2017**, 33, 35-41.

7. Huang, C.B.; Du, L.Z.; Zhang, W.G. Microstructure, mechanical and tribological characteristics of plasma detonation gun and HVOF sprayed NiCrAlY + Al₂O₃/TiO₂ coatings. Surf. Eng. **2011**, 27, 762-769.

8. Mehta, J.; Mittal, V.K.; Gupta, P. Role of thermal spray coatings on wear, erosion and corrosion behaviors: A review. J. Appl. Sci. Eng. **2017**, 20, 445-452.

9. Karaoglanli, A.C.; Ersoyl, F.; Ince, A.; Lampke, T. A comparative study of oxidation kinetics and thermal cyclic performance of thermal barrier coatings (TBCs). Surf. Coat. Technol. **2019**, 371, 47-62.

10. Fauchais, P.L.; Heberlein, J.V.; Boulos, M.I. Thermal Spray Fundamentals. From Powder to Part; Springer: Berlin/Heidelberg, Germany, 2014.

11. Winnicki, M.; Baszczuk, A.; Rutkowska-Gorczyca, M.; Malachowska, A.; Ambroziak, A. Corrosion resistance of tin coatings deposited by cold spraying. Surf. Eng. **2016**, 32, 691-700.

12. Bai, Y.; Ding, C.; Li, H.; Han, Z.; Ding, B.; Wang, T.; et al. Isothermal oxidation behavior of supersonic atmospheric plasma sprayed thermal barrier coating system. J. Therm. Spray Technol. **2013**, 22, 1201-1209.

13. Partes, K.; Zambrano, J.; Lampa, M.; Bohm, M.; Amaya, V. Tribology and high temperature friction wear behavior of MCrAlY laser cladding coatings on stainless steel. Wear **2019**, 432, 202-212.

14. Kamal, S.; Jayaganthan, R.; Prakash, S. Hot corrosion behaviour of D-gun sprayed NiCrAlY coatings on superalloys at 900 °C in molten salt environment. Surf. Eng. **2010**, 26, 453-462.

15. Karaoglanli, A.C. Microstructure characteristics of detonation gun sprayed CoNiCrAlY coatings. *J. Aeronaut. Space Technol.* **2016**, *9*, 47–51.

16. Ozgurluk, Y.; Doleker, K.M.; Ozkan, D.; Ahlatci, H.; Karaoglanli, A.C. Cyclic hot corrosion failure behaviors of EB-PVD TBC systems in the presence of sulfate and vanadate molten salts. *Coatings* **2019**, *9*, 166.

17. Kumar, A.; Patnaik, P.C.; Chen, K. Damage assessment and fracture resistance of functionally graded advanced thermal barrier coating systems: Experimental and analytical modeling approach. *Coatings* **2020**, *10*, 474.

18. Karaoglanli, A.C.; Isik, A. Isothermal oxidation behavior and kinetics of thermal barrier coatings produced by cold gas dynamic spray technique. *Surf. Coat. Technol.* **2017**, *318*, 72–81.

19. Bacos, M.P.; Dorvaux, J.M.; Lavigne, O.; Mevrel, R.; Poulain, M.; Rio, C.; Chateau-Cornu, C.; Renollet, Y. Improvement of the isothermal oxidation resistance of CoNiCrAlY coating sprayed by High Velocity Oxygen fuel. *Surf. Coat. Technol.* **2010**, *205*, 1731–1728.

20. Mohammadi, M.; Kobayashi, A.; Javadpour, S.; Jahromi, S.A.J. Evaluation of hot corrosion behaviors of Al2O3-YSZ composite TBC on gradient MCrAlY coatings in the presence of Na2SO4-NaVO3 salt. *Vacuum* **2019**, *167*, 547–553.

21. Bacos, M.P.; Dorvaux, J.M.; Lavigne, O.; Mevrel, R.; Poulain, M.; Rio, C.; Chateau-Cornu, C.; Renollet, Y. Improvement of the oxidation resistance of CoNiCrAlY bond coats sprayed by high velocity oxygen fuel onto nickel superalloy substrate. *Coatings* **2018**, *1*, 1–16.

22. Bai, Y.; Han, Z.H.; Li, H.Q.; Xu, C.; Xu, Y.L.; Ding, C.H.; Yang, J.F. Structure–property differences between supersonic and conventional atmospheric plasma sprayed zirconia thermal barrier coatings. *Surf. Coat. Technol.* **2011**, *205*, 3833–3839.

23. Daroonparvar, M.R.; Kabgani, M.R.; Alizadeh, M.; Peolat, D.; Hadavi, S.M.M.; Vaezi, M.R. Effect of high vacuum heat treatment on microstructure and cyclic oxidation resistance of HVOF-CoNiCrAlY coatings. *Vacuum* **2015**, *115*, 22–33.

24. Kun, H.L.; Cao, M.Q.; Wang, C.L.; Jiang, Z.H.; Cui, X.J. Tribological behaviour of a salt lubricated FeS/WC-12Ni thermal spray coating. *Surf. Eng.* **2019**, *35*, 702–710.

25. Singh, L.; Chawla, V.; Grewal, J. A review on detonation gun sprayed coatings. *J. Miner. Mater. Charact. Eng.* **2012**, *11*, 243.

26. Rani, A.; Bala, N.; Gupta, C. Accelerated hot corrosion studies of D-gun sprayed Cr2O3-50% Al2O3 coating on boiler steel and Fe-based superalloy. *Oxid. Met.* **2017**, *88*, 621–640.

27. Mehta, J.; Goyal, D.; Sidhu, S.S.; Gupta, K. Analysis of wear behavior and surface properties of detonation gun sprayed composite coating of Cr2O3 and Al2O3 on boiler steel. *Proc. Inst. Mech. Eng. Part J J. Mater. Des. Appl.* **2019**, *233*, 2433–2443.

28. Manoj, P.S.; Goyal, D.; Sidhu, S.S.; Kaur, S. Wear between ring and traveler: A pin-on-disc mapping of various detonation gun sprayed coatings. *Mater. Today Proc.* **2017**, *4*, 369–378.

29. Mao, Q.X.; Guo, J.M.; Huang, Z.Y.; Wang, F.; Ding, H.; Wu, Y.C. Comparison of W-Fe composite coatings fabricated by atmospheric plasma spraying and supersonic atmospheric plasma spraying. *Fusion Eng. Des.* **2016**, *105*, 77–85.

30. Bai, Y.; Zhao, L.; Wang, Y.; Chen, D.; Li, B.Q.; Han, Z.H. Fragmentation of in-flight particles and its influence on the microstructure and mechanical property of YSZ coating deposited by supersonic atmospheric plasma spraying. *J. Alloys Compd.* **2015**, *632*, 794–799.

31. Wei, Q.; Yin, Z.; Li, H. Oxidation control in plasma spraying NiCoCrAlY coating. *Appl. Surf. Sci.* **2012**, *258*, 5094–5099.

32. Bai, Y.; Han, Z.H.; Luo, H.Q.; Xu, C.; Xu, Y.L.; Wang, C.; Ding, C.H.; Yang, J.F. High performance nanostructured ZrO2 based thermal barrier coatings deposited by high efficiency supersonic plasma spraying. *Appl. Surf. Sci.* **2011**, *257*, 8210–8216.

33. Li, X.; Zhai, H.; Li, W.; Cui, S.; Ning, W.; Qiu, X. Dry sliding wear behaviors of Fe-based amorphous metallic coating synthesized by D-gun spray. *J. Non-Cryst. Solids* **2020**, *537*, 120016.

34. Zhou, X.; Xu, Z.; Mu, R.; He, L.; Huang, G.; Cao, X. Thermal barrier coatings with a double-layer bond coat on Ni3Al based single-crystal superalloy. *J. Alloys Compd.* **2014**, *591*, 41–51.

35. Saladi, S.; Menghani, J.V.; Prakash, S. Characterization and evaluation of cyclic hot corrosion resistance of detonation gun sprayed Ni-5Al coatings on Inconel-718. *J. Therm. Spray Technol.* **2015**, *24*, 774–788.

36. Liu, L.; Li, G.L.; Wang, H.D.; Kang, J.J.; Xu, Z.L.; Wang, H.J. Structure and wear behavior of NiCr–Cr$_3$C$_2$ coatings sprayed by supersonic plasma spraying and high velocity oxy-fuel technologies. *Appl. Surf. Sci.* **2015**, *356*, 383–390. [CrossRef]

37. Geetha, M.; Sathish, S.; Chava, K.; Joshi, S.V. Detonation gun sprayed Al$_2$O$_3$–13TiO$_2$ coatings for biomedical applications. *Surf. Eng.* **2014**, *30*, 229–236. [CrossRef]

Publisher's Note: MDPI stays neutral with regard to jurisdictional claims in published maps and institutional affiliations.

Article

Interaction of Strontium Zirconate Plasma Sprayed Coating with Natural Silicate (CMAS) Dust—Origin of Luminescent Phases

Pavel Ctibor

Institute of Plasma Physics, ASCR, Za Slovankou 3, 182 00 Prague 8, Czech Republic; ctibor@ipp.cas.cz

Received: 25 June 2020; Accepted: 25 July 2020; Published: 28 July 2020

Abstract: Strontium zirconate (SrZrO3) commercial powder was plasma sprayed using a high-feedrate water-stabilized plasma system (WSP) torch. Coatings with a thickness of about 1 mm were produced. Now, we are concentrating on a topic never addressed for pure SrZrO3 coatings: how the coatings interact with natural dust, known as calcium-magnesium-aluminum-silicate (CMAS). We selected various regimes of thermal treatment where SrZrO3 coatings were exposed to CMAS, and studied chemical changes, phase changes and the microstructure evolution of the influenced coatings. Microhardness of the exposed coatings was monitored as well. The results would help to understand, how the excellent refractory material SrZrO3 interacts with natural silicates. We kept in mind that pure SrZrO3 is not optimal for a thermal barrier application because of high-temperature phase transformations, but to study the CMAS-induced phenomena in more complex compositions, for example La2Zr2O7-SrZrO3, is difficult and interpretations have not been completed currently. The value of the actual research is in the separation of the phenomena typical just for SrZrO3. A potential for newly developed phases to serve as a sacrificial components of various barrier-coating systems is discussed. Several physical aspects of the newly developed components are discussed as well, namely the luminescence. Here the dust-based phases shifted down the temperature at which luminescence can occur in pure SrZrO3 ceramics. The entire thickness of influenced layers was relatively high, around 300 μm. The amorphous component, predominant after short-term CMAS exposure, was subsequently crystallized to various phases, namely SrSiO3 and monoclinic as well as tetragonal zirconia.

Keywords: plasma spraying; SrZrO3; TBC; CMAS; luminescence

---

1. Introduction

To improve their efficiency and design, turbine engines use ceramic-coated components. These coatings, known as Thermal Barrier Coatings (TBC), are designed for use at high temperatures [1–4]. TBCs serve as a protection for the base metal and super-alloy components by preventing them from experiencing high-temperature degradation [5]. They also increase the efficiency and lifetime of the components, besides providing creep resistance, thermal shock resistance, strain tolerance, higher temperature stability with respect to the substrate material and protection against hot corrosion [1–4]. Reducing the temperature of the metal is one objective of the top ceramic TBC. A state-of-the-art TBC is yttria-stabilized zirconia (YSZ) composed of ZrO2 with 6%–8% Y2O3 [1–5]. The microscopic structure of TBC is always very inhomogeneous [6].

Atmospheric plasma spray (APS) is used for depositing ceramic TBC [6]. So called "splats" are created by the plasma spray as flattened particles. Due to its quick solidification, the sprayed powder produces a coating on a clean surface of a substrate. An incomplete bonding between splats caused by the relaxation of residual stresses when the splat is being cooled, or by trapped gases, and also lack of adhesion, are typical APS–TBC drawbacks [6,7]. The structure of the porous TBC, which contains cracks, pores, crack/coating interfaces, pore/coating interfaces and layer interfaces, affects the effective thermal conductivity [...].

In the case of sprayed TBC, the microstructural defects consist of three types of pores: interlamellar pores—that result from the build-up of micro splats; microcracks—that result from the stress relief after coating deposition; and globular pores—that are due to a lack of complete filling. These three types of pores fall into different ranges of size distribution. It has been shown that the thermal conductivity is strongly dependent on the pore morphology and porosity [...]. Optimum porosity level in TBC is considered to be about 15% total porosity as a compromise between positive function of porosity to minimize thermal conductivity and negative function of worsening the coating integrity and mechanical properties. Some 20% to 25% of the total porosity is formed by cracks [...].

Among the investigated ceramic TBC candidates, $SrZrO_3$ with perovskite structure has a high melting point, low thermal conductivity as well as the possibility of extensive substitution of ions at the A or/and B site, making it a promising TBC candidate material [...]. Application of pure $SrZrO_3$ for the TBC seems to be limited because of its high-temperature phase transformations [...]. $SrZrO_3$ exhibits a pseudo-tetragonal structure at 730 °C and a tetragonal structure at temperatures higher than 840 °C. The pseudo-tetragonal structure couples a lattice mismatch between its two axes, so that coating delaminates easily [...]. Delamination at the boundary bond coat/top coat is the most frequent case [...]. Elsewhere [...] the transformation sequence of heating is described as follows: orthorhombic (Pnma, 730 °C) →pseudo-tetragonal (Imma, c/a < 1, 840 °C →tetragonal phase (I4mcm, c/a > 1) →I74/4 →cubic (Pm3m).

When the gas turbine operates in a severe environment, such as the desert or the vicinity of a volcanic eruption, siliceous mineral debris matters (dust, sand and ash) in air are ingested by the turbine and deposited on the hot TBC surfaces as molten calcium–magnesium–alumino–silicate (CMAS) [...]. Immediately when CMAS melting takes place, it infiltrates into the TBC material via open porosities in APS-deposited TBC and undergoes a series of chemical reactions with the TBC forming various [...]. Upon cooling, CMAS solidifies and develops a high stress level because the pores were blocked. In conventional TBC, YSZ partially dissolves in the CMAS, causing disruptive phase transformation (from tetragonal ZrO₂ to monoclinic ZrO₂) accompanied with a significant volume increase (up to 5%) [...]. The size of CMAS particles could be from a nanometer range up to approximately half a millimeter. Kakuda et al. [...] investigated the effect of amorphous CMAS infiltration on the thermal properties and heat transport of plasma sprayed (APS) coatings and observed a rise in both volumetric heat capacity and thermal conductivity of the coating upon infiltration. Concerning the mechanical attack of the dust on TBC, cavitation is mentioned [...], but the chemical attack is considered as more serious.

A paper dealing with an interaction of CMAS and the $La_2Zr_2O_7$-$SrZrO_3$ composite TBC coating [...] expressed a challenge that the interaction behavior of $SrZrO_3$ in contact with CMAS melt at high temperatures requires further investigation in the future. This challenge to elaborate such experiments is now accepted by a co-author of papers dealing with multifunctional $SrZrO_3$ coating [...], and this is in a focus of the actual paper. Keeping in mind that pure $SrZrO_3$ is not optimal for a thermal barrier application because of high temperature phase transformations but to study it directly in a composite with other refractories, for example $La_2Zr_2O_7$-$SrZrO_3$, is difficult [...], the decision was to study it as a single-component coating material. This is the main novelty of the current paper.

2. Materials and Methods

2.1. Sample Preparation

Plasma spray grade strontium zirconate powder supplied by Cerac Incorporated (Milwaukee, WI, USA) was used as the feedstock. The powder size was 71–150 µm. Plasma spraying was done by the water-stabilized plasma system (WSP) torch [...] at 150 kW power (500 A, 300 V). The feeding distance from the plasma exit nozzle to the point of the powder feeding in the plasma stream) was 80 mm and spray distance (from the plasma exit nozzle to the substrate) was 350 mm. Compressed air was used as the feeding gas and the substrates were preheated to 460 °C. This high temperature was selected with the purpose to minimize the cooling rate for impacting splats. Preheating was done by plasma torch passes with the powder feeding switched off. After each pass of the torch, manipulated by a robotic arm, the temperature rose to 350 °C and was pushed down to 170 °C by a compressed air flux before the next pass started [ ].

Reactivity of the SrZrO₃ coating with calcium—magnesium—aluminum-silicate (CMAS) powder was tested. The CMAS powder was Ultrafine Test Dust "Arizona desert sand" produced by Powder Technology (Arden Hills, MN, USA). Its chemical composition provided by the producer is SiO₂ (50%, semi-quantitative content), Na(AlSi₃O₈) albite (33), CaMg(Si₂O₆) diopside (16), CaCO₃ (2). The size of CMAS particles was in single micrometers. The dust powder with a concentration of 30 mg·cm⁻² [ ] was mixed with ethanol and the resulting slurry was applied on the coating surface by a brush. Then, this sample was dried in air at room temperature for 2 h and subsequently annealed in air (laboratory furnace Clasic, Řevnice, Czech Republic) using dwell times of 1, 4, 8 and 10 h, respectively, at 1250 °C. Heating ramp was 8 °C·min⁻¹ and cooling ramp 5 °C·min⁻¹. At this temperature (and during this time) the CMAS melt interacts with the coating, i.e. it both infiltrates into the coating and reacts with it. To better understand the phase constituents of the reaction products, the CMAS powder was mixed with the SrZrO₃ feedstock powder with a weight ratio of 1:1 [ ] by mechanical blending, followed by heat treatment with 10 h dwell time under the same conditions as the TBC specimens.

2.2. Characterization

2.2.1. Phase Composition

Samples of the feedstock powder and sprayed coatings were analyzed by the X-ray diffraction technique. Diffraction patterns were collected with the PANalytical X'Pert PRO diffractometer (Malvern PANalytical, Almelo, The Netherlands) equipped with a conventional X-ray tube (Cu-Kα radiation, 40 kV, 30 mA) and a linear position sensitive detector PIXcel with an anti-scatter shield. A programmable divergence slit set to a fixed value of 0.5°, Soller slit of 0.04 rad and mask of 15 mm were used in the primary beam. A programmable anti-scatter slit set to fixed value of 0.5°, Soller slit of 0.04 rad and Ni beta-filter were used in the diffracted beam. Data were collected in the range of 10°–120° 2θ with the step of 0.013° and 300 s/step producing a scan of about 2 h 18 min.

Qualitative analysis was performed with the HighScorePlus software package (Malvern PANalytical, Almelo, The Netherlands, version 4.9.0) and the PDF-4+ database. Diffrac-Plus Topas software package (Bruker AXS, Karlsruhe, Germany, version 4.2) was used for estimating the Degree of Crystallinity (DoC). Structural models of all identified phases were taken from the PDF-4+ database.

2.2.2. Microstructure

Scanning electron microscopy (SEM) observation was done using the Phenom Pro microscope (Thermo Fisher Sci., Eindhoven, The Netherlands) equipped by the CeB₆ thermionic cathode and working in backscattered electron (BSE) mode. The images were collected at 10 kV electron beam tension. Energy Dispersive X-ray (EDX) analysis, which is a part of the SEM, was used to determine the elemental composition of a sample. Each element emits characteristic X-rays as an interaction between the sample and a focused electron beam. Consequently, the EDX spectrum is evaluated, and based on a unique set of peaks for each element, the composition of the sample is determined. The X-ray signal used for EDX-measurements comes from an area that is at least 1 µm in diameter and around 1.5 µm depth. The element EDX maps were collected at 15 kV electron beam tension.

Polished cross sections of the coatings were prepared for microscopic observation and for microhardness measurement. Light micrographs as a base for image analysis of porosity were taken at 250× magnification via CCD camera EOS 500D (Canon, Tokyo, Japan) attached on the microscope

Neophot 32 (Zeiss, Oberkochen, Germany) and processed with the software Lucia (4.62, Laboratory Imaging, Praha, Czech Republic). For a more complex description of pores, additional criteria besides the porosity percentage (area fraction of voids, i.e., pores and cracks, in the TBC material) were introduced. "Number of Voids per unit area" (N.V.) of the cross section in combination with the porosity percentage could distinguish between porosity composed from a large number of fine voids or from a low number of coarse voids. "Equivalent Diameter" (E.D.) of voids represents their size distribution. Circularity could have values between 1 (i.e., a circle representing a globular pore) and 0 (i.e., a line representing a flat pore or a crack). All parameters were calculated for 3 images of each sample.

Selection of samples for microstructure study was done carefully to represent central parts of the planar TBC coating far enough from the edges. Polished cross-sections were prepared from as-deposited samples. Cutting was done using a diamond blade, subsequently the sections were mounted in a resin, and polishing was carried out using the Tegramin-25 automatic system (Struers, Denmark).

2.2.3. Microhardness

Vickers microhardness was measured on polished TBC sections by optical microscope Neophot 2 (Zeiss, Oberkochen, Germany) equipped with a Hanemann head and Vickers indenter using 1 N load. The mean value of microhardness was calculated as an average from 20 indentations.

3. Results and Discussion

3.1. Microstructure and Porosity

After 1 h a CMAS residuum clearly covers the coating, Figure 1a. Some fine globular particles, however, developed deeper in the coating. The rod-shaped particles and globular particles have developed after 4 h in the interaction layer (Figure 1b), which looks, however, dense and not porous as in the literature [19]. Since the porosity in the coating was discontinuous and irregular, the infiltration was, expectably, inhomogeneous. After 4 h, Figure 1b, the fine globular particles are developed within the entire thickness of the residual CMAS and are visible also on the surface. After 8 h, Figure 1c, they disappear again. The cracks' character on the surface after 4 h and also 8 h correspond to the glassy character of the residual CMAS. After 10 h, Figure 1d, a significant whisker-like crystallization appears, whereas the matrix between the elongated faceted particles looks again glassy. Moreover, some fine globular particles appear again, and porosity is now opened to the surface (like in as-sprayed SrZrO$_3$).

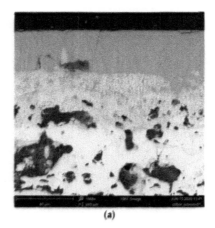

(a)

Figure 1. *Cont.*

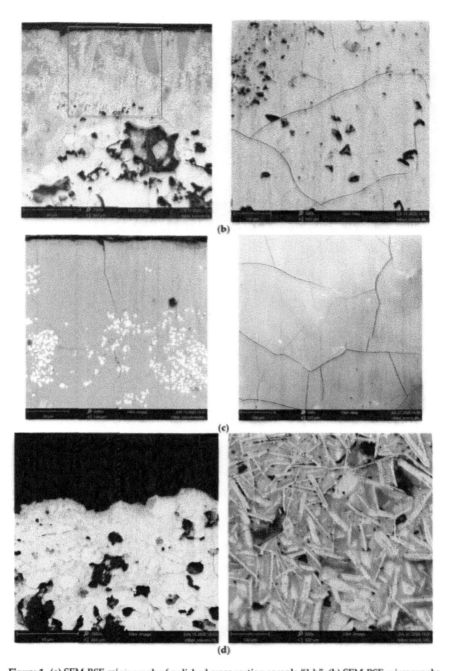

Figure 1. (**a**) SEM-BSE micrograph of polished cross section sample "1 h"; (**b**) SEM-BSE micrographs of polished sample "4 h": cross section (left) and surface; (**c**) SEM-BSE micrographs of polished sample "8 h": cross section (left) and surface; (**d**) SEM-BSE micrographs of polished– sample "10 h": cross section (left) and surface.

The thickness of the influenced layer increased from 222 μm after 1 h CMAS attack to 333 μm after 8 h. Cai et al. [ ] reported only 11 μm after 1 h and 102 μm after 12 h for $La_2Zr_2O_7$-$SrZrO_3$ composite coating, although the annealing schedule was very similar to our case.

Berker et al. [ ] reported 30 μm influenced depth after 4 h at 1300 °C for Yb-doped $SrZrO_3$ coating. In these comparisons the initial growth of the influenced layer in our $SrZrO_3$ coatings looks rather large. This was, first of all, because of the high porosity of the as-sprayed coating and due to this fact by easy proliferation of CMAS into the deeper layers of the coating. In contrast, after CMAS attack the coating surface became rather smooth and dense. Sometimes the published experiments were done with a lower concentration of CMAS per unit area of the coating, e.g., 10 mg·cm^{-2} [ ]. In such a case, any CMAS residuum is formed on the top of the coating and—just in the beginning—the whole amount of CMAS is consumed for the interaction. Which approach is more realistic, from the application standpoint, is doubtful.

Evolution of porosity parameters. Table , indicates a general trend to the coarsening of porosity (pores coagulation) becoming more globular. Porosity area fraction increased and number of voids per mm^2 decreased (i.e., fewer but larger pores), equivalent diameter increased and circularity as well. However, those general trends are affected with certain oscillations—i.e., highest porosity and largest pores after 4 h. Porosity of the $SrZrO_3$ as-sprayed coating was rather high, 23.8%, and after 1 h at 1250 °C it shifted upwards, 26.6%. After 4 h dwell time was it even higher, 32.1%. After 8 h dwell time approached again approximately the as-sprayed level, 25.1%. After 10 h was it even higher, 27.7%. Such oscillations could also be viewed as a sacrificial layer development and "ingation". Repeatedly, a contiguous layer is formed on the surface, sealing the open porosity, but the total porosity is not influenced. The character of CMAS is too aggressive to serve as a simple liquid sintering aid for the base coating. Furthermore, in case of TBC application of $SrZrO_3$, CMAS not only decreases the strain tolerance [ ] of the coating but also left the surface opened for the possible next CMAS attack even after 10 h. Observation of microstructures indicates a "transitive" character of the sample after 4 h. Some CMAS remains always on the $SrZrO_3$ coating surface after CMAS attack at 1250 °C, resulting in the difficulty to identify all the reaction products (hidden below) by XRD.

Coagulation of pores manifested itself by the increase of E-D. (as-sprayed–8.94 μm; 1 h–9.36 μm; 10 h–9.53 μm) and decrease of no. of pores per square millimeter (as-sprayed–5771; 1 h–4341; 10 h–4957). Circularity of pores correspondingly increased, indicating round shape of pores, physically favored after long-term annealing (as-sprayed–0.511; 1 h–0.695; 10 h–0.760). Table .

Table 1. Image analysis results.

Sample	Porosity (%)	N.V. per mm²	E-D. (μm)	Circularity	Thick. (μm)
$SrZrO_3$ coating	23.8	5771	8.94	0.511	0
1h	26.6	4341	9.36	0.695	222
4h	32.1	5410	9.75	0.674	148
8h	25.1	5137	8.63	0.607	333
10h	27.7	4957	9.53	0.760	263

Figure shows that some globular particles disperse in the CMAS melt after 4 h, whereas earlier they were present only in the depth of about 50 μm. Moreover, distinct columnar-like areas with different grey levels developed in the CMAS melt, see in larger details in Figure a. Figure b shows that, based on the EDX measurement, darker columns are Al-rich, lighter columns are Sr-rich and the fine globular particles as well as rod-shaped fine particles (both white) are Zr-rich. At the beginning (1 h) a Si-rich amorphous superficial layer based on molten CMAS is formed, Figure a, with traces of monoclinic ZrO_2, crystalline $SrSiO_3$ and two forms of SiO_2, i.e. cristobalite and quartz, Table . After 4 h, Al-rich (probably spinel $MgAl_2O_4$) columns are combined with the earlier developed features, but an amorphous content is still predominant. Interestingly, the Al-rich columns are free of the fine cracks present in the neighboring Sr-rich columns, Figure a. After 8 h the globular Zr-rich particles "sunk" deeper down to the "glassy matrix", Figure c. The content of amorphous material decreased as the reaction time increased from 1 to 10 h, see below XRD-based results. The Al-rich and Si-rich columns and globular Zr-rich particles are interpenetrated by residual CMAS melt, Figure d. $SrZrO_3$ seems to decompose to SrO and ZrO_2. Sr is depleted in the interaction zone, dissolving into the glass while ZrO_2 precipitated. After 10 h the surface looks recrystallized, Figure d. It contains white globular Zr-rich particles, but the main feature is whisker-like crystals that correspond roughly to $SrSiO_3$ phase, Figure . The resting "matrix" is most probably amorphous, since according to EDX it contains besides Si, Sr and Zr also between 1% and 2% of each: Al, Mg, Na and Ca.

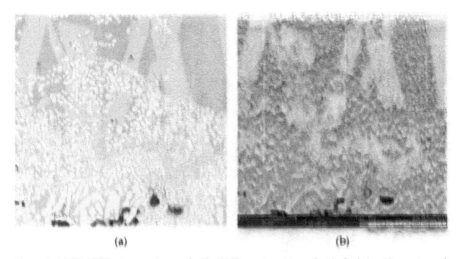

| (a) | (b) |

Figure 2. (a) SEM-BSE micrograph, sample 4 h; (b) Element map, sample 4 h. Scale bar 30 µm. Area of Figure indicated on Figure b by red color.

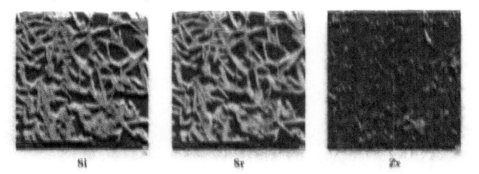

| Si | Sr | Zr |

Figure 3. Element maps corresponding to Figure d-surface. Scale bar 100 µm.

Table 2. XRD phases—semi-quantitative content (%).

CMAS Powder	SrZrO₃ Powder	Sintered Mixed Powders
SiO_2 (50) $Na(AlSi_3O_8)$ albite (32) $CaMg(Si_2O_6)$ diopside (16) $CaCO_3$ (2)	$SrZrO_3$ orthorhombic * impurities under 0.5%	ZrO_2 monoclinic ZrO_2 tetragonal ** $Na_4Ca_4(Si_6O_{18})$ combeite
SrZrO₃ coating $SrZrO_3$ orthorhombic (87) ZrO_2 tetragonal (13)	**Coating+CMAS after 1 h** ZrO_2 monoclinic (2) $SrSiO_3$ (1) SiO_2 cristobalite (2) SiO_2 quartz (3), AMORPH. 92	**Coating+CMAS after 4 h** ZrO_2 monoclinic (12) $SrSiO_3$ (20) ZrO_2 tetragonal ** (4) AMORPH. 64
Coating+CMAS after 8 h ZrO_2 monoclinic (28) $SrSiO_3$ (16) ZrO_2 tetragonal ** (2) AMORPH. 54	**Coating+CMAS after 10 h** ZrO_2 monoclinic (21) $SrSiO_3$ (42) ZrO_2 tetragonal ** (1) AMORPH. 36	

* Producer information. ** Most probably Ca, Na, Al or Si -stabilized (on Zr atom position).

3.2. Phase Composition

X-ray diffraction (XRD) results are summarized in Table 2. ZrO_2 in both—monoclinic "baddeleyite" $P2_1/c$ and tetragonal $P4_2/nmc$—forms has been found in the irradiated volume. After 1 h, Figure 4, the surface is practically totally amorphous with only few percent of crystalline phases—$SrSiO_3$, SiO_2 and ZrO_2 monoclinic. This material is CMAS-based glass. Because of its composition, CMAS behaves as a glass, i.e., the heating/cooling sequence in the furnace is although too fast for its crystallization. After 4 h annealing, Figure 5, $SrSiO_3$ (20%), ZrO_2 monoclinic (12%) and ZrO_2 tetragonal (4%) were detected. ZrO_2 monoclinic started to be the main component after 8 h (content 28%), Figure 6. $SrSiO_3$ content dropped (16%) and ZrO_2 tetragonal did as well (2%). After 10 h, Figure 7, $SrSiO_3$ was again the most important constituent (42%), whereas ZrO_2 monoclinic content dropped (21%) and tetragonal did as well. Always, the rest of the material was amorphous, with the content progressively decreasing with the annealing time (the intensity of peaks increased with time), but being until 8 h higher than 50 percent. XRD results deal only with surface of the samples. Amorphization of the originally crystalline coating is, however, the main aspect of the interaction with CMAS.

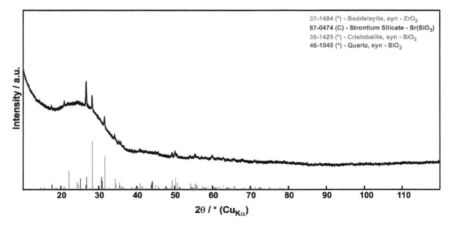

Figure 4. XRD patterns of the sample "1 h".

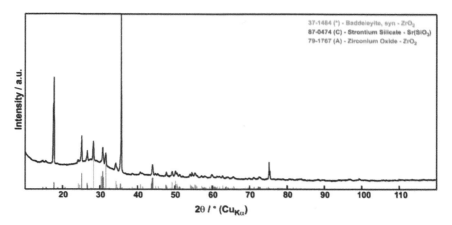

Figure 5. XRD patterns of the sample "4 h".

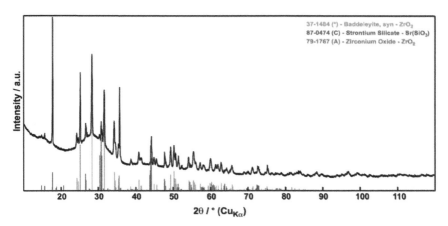

Figure 6. XRD patterns of the sample "8 h".

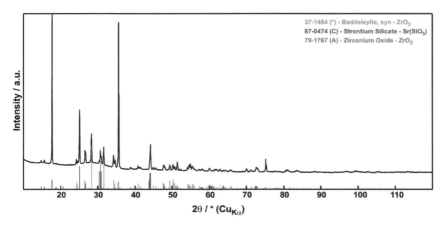

Figure 7. XRD patterns of the sample "10 h".

Based on reported [ ] thermal analysis results, the temperature of the orthorhombic-to-tetragonal phase change has a value of 818 °C for SrZrO₃. A local minimum of weight gain [ ] was recorded by us for the same temperature. Concerning the main phase changes the predominant phenomenon is an inverse run of the reaction described in literature [ ] on samples left at 1073 °C for one hour.

$$SrSiO_3 + ZrO_2 = SrZrO_3 + SiO_2 \tag{1}$$

In our case the process proceeds as:

$$SrZrO_3 + SiO_2 = SrSiO_3 + ZrO_2 \tag{2}$$

ZrO₂ tetragonal (a "frozen" high-temperature phase) from the TBC coating transformed to ZrO₂ monoclinic under 1170 °C due to slow cooling in the furnace.

We suggest that the content (13 percent) of tetragonal ZrO₂ from the as-sprayed coating was converted at the presence of CMAS to monoclinic ZrO₂, whereas the new tetragonal ZrO₂ was transformed from SrZrO₃ by its decomposition via chemical reaction (Equation (2)). When SrZrO₃ will be decomposed to 50 molar percent of SrO and 50 molar percent of ZrO₂, the 50 molar percent of SrO could react with SiO₂ completely to SrSiO₃ [ ].

To identify the reaction products between the CMAS and the SrZrO₃ coating, a mixture of the CMAS powder as the solvent and the SrZrO₃ feedstock powder as the solute (weight ratio: 1:1) was homogeneously mechanically blended and then heat-treated at 1250 °C for 10 h. Besides monoclinic and tetragonal ZrO₂, a Na₄Ca₄(Si₆O₁₈) combeite phase appeared. SrZrO₃ in the La₂Zr₂O₇-SrZrO₃ composite coating [ ] reacted much less intensively with CMAS compared to La₂Zr₂O₇. Absence of CMAS-induced through-thickness cracks in our samples could be ascertained mainly to the identical thermal expansion of SrZrO₃ [ ] and SrSiO₃ [ ], 10.9 × 10⁻⁶ K⁻¹.

Concerning the "oscillations" in the character of the influenced layer(s) we conclude that the amorphous materials formed preferably on the surface from CMAS crystallizes preferably "from the bottom", i.e., in interaction with the coating. The crystallization opens new pores (via dimensional shrinkage). New proportions of CMAS melt fits into these new pores and sinks deeper into the coating. This repeated process stops after 10 h where finally not enough residual CMAS on the surface exists.

From this standpoint SrZrO₃ is not advantageous TBC material since the crystallization front seems to move slowly. Better CMAS blocking layers or sacrificial layers would form when the crystallization is as fast as possible. In this view La₂Zr₂O₇ in the system La₂Zr₂O₇-SrZrO₃ [ ] served as a "crystallization promoter" and SrZrO₃ itself is well CMAS-resistant under ultra-short exposure but started to be CMAS-nonresistant after at least 1 h.

The most stable and most desired phase in the TBC structure among the newly developed phases is tetragonal ZrO₂. It stems from SrZrO₃ by its decomposition. However, amorphous material is always present in high amounts, and evidently monoclinic baddeleyite crystallizes preferably from the amorphous phase. Disadvantageous is also the fact that admixtures are preferably incorporated in the lattice of tetragonal ZrO₂. Among them so called silica-substituted zirconia is rather stable [ ]. However, in case of reacting with CMAS, rather Ca, Al or Na atoms would occupy the place of Si, since Si elements form in large quantities the SrSiO₃ phase.

3.3. Mechanical Properties

We could summarize microhardness data from Table . The SrZrO₃ coating was very similar to the as-sprayed samples with values between 5.6 and 6.1 GPa.

Table 3. Microhardness.

Sample	Microhardness (GPa) =Whole Coating	Microhardness (GPa) =Influenced Layer
SrZrO$_3$ coating	5.6 ± 2.6	=
1 h	6.1 ± 1.6	6.5 ± 2.1
4 h	6.0 ± 1.7	5.9 ± 1.2
8 h	5.6 ± 1.8	5.6 ± 1.6
10 h	6.8 ± 1.9	5.5 ± 0.9
Sint. mix. powders	5.5 *	=

* Different character of sample, non-comparable statistics.

Effect of sintering was negligible in the base material since the annealing temperature was markedly below the sintering temperature of SrZrO$_3$. The influenced superficial layers, visibly changed by interaction with CMAS, were similarly hard but the duration of annealing led to progressively decreased microhardness (GPa): (1 h=6.5; 4 h=5.9; 8 h=5.6; 10 h=5.5). The mixture of powders sintered in a crucible exhibited a very similar value to the coatings: 5.5 GPa. It contained globular (ZrO$_2$-rich) particles and glassy matrix (CMAS-rich) that was in fact a "liquid-phase sintering" agent. In this arrangement, i.e., individual particles of SrZrO$_3$ in contact with the CMAS melt, the interaction process is faster. Among the components the particles were harder, 6.0 GPa than the matrix, 5.0 GPa. SrZrO$_3$ bulk ceramic microhardness was reported to increase after 100 h at 1450 °C to 5.5 GPa compared to 4.5 GPa for the as-sintered sample [ ].

Combining microhardness with thickness and porosity evaluations we see: after 4 h the influenced layer is thinner and weaker than after 1 h. After 8 h the influenced layer is even less hard but thick and less porous—with the lowest porosity and smallest pore size. The influenced layer is again thinner and maintained its hardness but the coating itself is harder due to pore sealing.

3.4. Optical Properties

The scattering coefficient of SrZrO$_3$ is reported to be higher than that of YSZ, which is beneficial for the TBC application because most of the incident radiation will be reflected back to the hot gas stream instead of being absorbed by the coating or penetrating the coating leading to the increase of temperature on the base superalloy [ ].

In plasma-sprayed TBCs, the scattering is mainly due to the refractive index mismatch between the ceramic coating material and the interior of TBC pores and cracks. This was proved by the decrease of scattering/reflectance (or increase of transmittance) through infiltrating TBC with epoxy or CMAS, whose refractive index is close to the coating material [ ]. The decrease of the scattering coefficient with the increase of the wavelength is due to the decrease of the relative size of the scattering centers (internal pores and cracks) compared with the wavelength [ ].

The brown-green color of the CMAS "glaze" is subsequently, with increasing annealing time, turned towards the yellow color typical for SrZrO$_3$ powder and as-sprayed coatings. That is because the residual CMAS is consumed for the reaction, as described above. The yellow reflection as a response on a deep-violet illumination is called luminescence. The sintered mixed powder sample was more luminescent than the coating surfaces, Figure . The longer the dwell time, the lower CMAS amount directly at the surface and the highest the luminescence of the "coating itself". The highest luminescence is seen for the sintered mixture of powders. Here, CMAS transformed into a "brown-green glaze", surrounding fine yellow particles of the initial SrZrO$_3$, serving partly as a "liquid-phase sintering" agent, and by this way decreasing the sintering temperature. The appearance, Figure , is more or less like a two-component composite with "intact" particles embedded in a fully remelted matrix. In fact, the particles are not intact—Sr from SrZrO$_3$ is transferred to the matrix and the fine white globular particles should be ZrO$_2$ (based on XRD and EDX).

Figure 8. From the left: Coatings after CMAS interaction for 1, 4, 8 and 10 h and the cross-sectioned bottom of a crucible with sintered mixture of powders, respectively. Samples illuminated by the 312 nm lamp (i.e., 3.97 eV).

Combeite, a component detected by XRD in the sintered mixed powders and having composition $Na_6Ca_3(Si_6O_{18})$, was reported to exhibit luminescence centered at about 615 nm [34]. $SrZrO_3$ plasma sprayed coating was luminescent only after annealing in air at 1350 °C for 2 h [22]. $SrZrO_3$ is good radiation energy absorber for energies above 3.8 eV [35]. Presence of $SrSiO_3$ (in coatings) and combeite (in mixed powders) shifted the necessary annealing temperature for obtaining luminescent behavior down to 1250 °C. $SrSiO_3$ with band gap energy 4.60 eV (higher than $SrZrO_3$ with value this between 3.37 and 4.53 eV [35]) is itself less efficient luminescence material than $SrZrO_3$ but could be formed with a much lower thermal load.

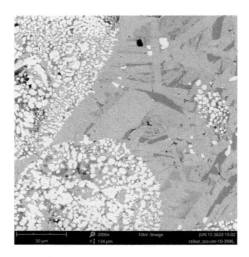

Figure 9. SEM-BSE of the sintered mixture of powders, polished cross section.

Similarly to the coatings, Figure 2, the sintered mixture of powders, Figure 9, contained globular Zr-rich particles with sizes under 10 μm. They originated evidently from $SrZrO_3$, since the big "ball" in the left-bottom quadrant of Figure 9 is a particle of the spray feedstock powder (with diameter about 80 μm). The dark grey and pale grey "matrix" is evidently CMAS-based and similarly to coatings could be divided into a crack-free Si-rich darker component and cracked Sr-rich lighter component. Let us see that the Sr-rich component much more frequently surrounds the spray feedstock big "balls" that is coincident with the assumption of the Sr-depletion. Here, contrary to the coatings, Al concentration in such a matrix was always low, under 3 atomic percent. $MgAl_2O_4$ spinel seems to be absent in the sintered mixture of powders.

In general, to tailor the spraying of a TBC to the "optimum porosity" of about 15% (or having it even higher as in the present case) and in the same way make the TBC well resistant to the penetration of molten CMAS, is a problem. A way is to close the superficial porosity as much as possible. Thin barrier layer formed by e.g., laser remelting [36,37] of few superficial micrometers of as-produced TBC would be helpful. However, this additional step makes the production of TBCs even more expensive. Our strontium zirconate, initially even more porous, is on the beginning of interactions with CMAS rather resistant, due to the glassy character of CMAS, but after disappearing the residual CMAS from the surface is the coating surface again porous. However, the dangerous through-thickness cracks were not induced by CMAS within the microstructure of the coating.

Luminescence could be, in principle, used in the diagnostics of the TBC at room temperature. Let us imagine the $SrZrO_3$-covered functional parts of a turbine. The turbine was in service subjected to CMAS attack. After cooling down at the maintenance interruption of the service, change (i.e., the increase) in luminescence would clearly signalize the reaction of the TBC with CMAS. Such a check would be fast and inexpensive. If the turbine was in service, but evidently not subjected to CMAS attack, the luminescence would help at diagnostics of the maximum service temperature—since pure $SrZrO_3$ started to be luminescent after heat exposure at 1350 °C [22]. Of course, in case of more complex TBCs, like $La_2Zr_2O_7$-$SrZrO_3$, these aspects would be less clear, and this is one interesting avenue for future research to explore.

4. Conclusions

Strontium zirconate $SrZrO_3$ was sprayed by a high feed-rate water-stabilized plasma torch, WSP, with a spray rate over 10 kg per hour to form a thick film. The as-sprayed coatings exhibited a lamellar microstructure and a relatively high porosity of over 23%. This thick film, considered as a thermal barrier coating (TBC), was now studied in interaction with natural silicate dust, so called CMAS, at 1250 °C. The crystalline as-sprayed coating was amorphized, whereas the resting crystalline proportion transformed to different phases than $SrZrO_3$, namely monoclinic ZrO_2 and $SrSiO_3$. The proportion of these predominant phases varied with time of annealing (i.e., CMAS attack), whereas the general trend to crystallization of the amorphous content with longer dwell time was shown by XRD. The whole thickness of the influenced layer was as large as up to 333 µm. This is a typical thickness of the whole TBC coating in many industrial applications. SEM and EDX observation of the cross sections showed, also, an Al-rich component. The cracks' formation selectively in the Sr-rich component and absence in the Al-rich component were observed as one of the results of CMAS attack, whereas the most dangerous through-thickness cracks were absent. A sintered mixture of powders (CMAS plus $SrZrO_3$ spray feedstock) demonstrated the appearance of the most "exotic" phase-$Na_4Ca_4(Si_6O_{18})$ combeite. This component is luminescent, as was shown in our work, whereas contribution of $SrSiO_3$ to the luminescence of the sintered mixture is also highly probable. Due to $SrSiO_3$ presence, the coatings after interaction with CMAS are also partly luminescent. We suggest using the luminescence as a fast and cheap diagnostic technique of CMAS presence/absence in the structure of a potential $SrZrO_3$-based TBC.

Author Contributions: Conceptualization, P.C.; methodology, P.C.; writing—original draft preparation, P.C.; writing—review and editing, P.C.; XRD and SEM analyses were arranged externally as barter services or paid services; other processing and analyses, P.C. All authors and collaborators have read and agreed to the published version of the manuscript.

Funding: This research received no external funding.

Acknowledgments: The author would like to thank to XRD (Petr Bezdička) and SEM (Petr Veselý) operators.

Conflicts of Interest: The author declares no conflict of interest.

References

1. Padture, N.P.; Gell, M.; Jordan, E.H. Thermal Barrier Coatings for Gas-Turbine Engine Applications. *Science* 2002, 296, 280–298. [CrossRef]
2. Evans, A.G.; Mumm, D.R.; Hutchinson, J.W.; Meier, G.H.; Pettit, F.S. Mechanisms Controlling, Durability of Thermal Barrier Coatings. *Prog. Mater. Sci.* 2001, 46, 505–532. [CrossRef]
3. Levi, C.G. Emerging Materials and Processes for Thermal Barrier Systems. *Curr. Opin. Solid State Mater. Sci.* 2003, 8, 77–99. [CrossRef]
4. Clarke, D.R.; Levi, C.G. Materials Design for the Next Generation Thermal Barrier Coatings. *Annu. Rev. Mater. Sci.* 2003, 33, 383–397. [CrossRef]
5. Evans, A.G.; Clarke, D.R.; Levi, C.G. The Influence of Oxides on the Performance of Advanced Gas Turbines. *J. Eur. Ceram. Soc.* 2008, 28, 1405–1418. [CrossRef]
6. Vassen, R.; Ophelia-Jarligo, M.; Steinke, T.; Emil-Mack, D.; Stöver, D. Overview on Advanced Thermal Barrier Coatings. *Surf. Coat. Technol.* 2010, 5, 938–949. [CrossRef]
7. Clarke, D.R.; Philpot, S.R. Thermal Barrier Coating Materials. *Mater. Today* 2005, 8, 22–29. [CrossRef]
8. Kulkarni, A.; Wang, Z.; Nakamura, T.; Sampath, S.; Goland, A.; Herman, H.; Allen, J.; Ilavsky, J.; Long, G.; Frahm, J.; et al. Comprehensive Microstructural Characterization and Predictive Property Modeling of Plasma-sprayed Zirconia Coatings. *Acta Mater.* 2003, 51, 2457–2475. [CrossRef]
9. Wang, Z.; Kulkarni, A.; Deshpande, S.; Nakamura, T.; Herman, H. Effects of Pores and Interfaces on Effective Properties of Plasma Sprayed Zirconia Coatings. *Acta Mater.* 2003, 51, 5319–5334. [CrossRef]
10. Cao, X.Q.; Vassen, R.; Jungen, W.; Schwartz, S.; Tietz, F.; Stöver, D. Thermal Stability of Lanthanum Zirconate Plasma-sprayed Coating. *J. Am. Ceram. Soc.* 2001, 84, 2086–2090. [CrossRef]
11. Venkatesh, G.; Blessto, B.; Santhosh Kumar Rao, C.; Subramanian, R.; John Berchmans, L. Novel Perovskite Coating of Strontium Zirconate in Inconel Substrate. *IOP Conf. Ser. Mater. Sci. Eng.* 2018, 314, 012010. [CrossRef]
12. Carlsson, L. High-temperature Phase Transitions in SrZrO$_3$. *Acta Crystallogr.* 1967, 23, 901–905. [CrossRef]
13. Li, W.; Zhao, H.; Zhong, X.; Wang, L.; Tao, S. Air Plasma-Sprayed Yttria and Yttria-Stabilized Zirconia Thermal Barrier Coatings Subjected to Calcium-Magnesium-Alumino-Silicate (CMAS). *J. Thermal Spray Technol.* 2014, 23, 975–983. [CrossRef]
14. Berker Iyi, C.; Mecartney, M.; Mumm, D.R. On the CMAS Problem in Thermal Barrier Coatings: Benchmarking Thermochemical Resistance of Oxides Alternative to YSZ Through a Microscopic Standpoint. *Uluslararasi Fen Arastirmalarinda Yenilikei Yaklasimlar Dergisi* 2019, 3, 20–40.
15. Kramer, S.; Yang, J.; Levi, C.G.; Johnson, C.A. Thermochemical Interaction of Thermal Barrier Coatings with Molten CaO-MgO-Al$_2$O$_3$-SiO$_2$ (CMAS) Deposits. *J. Am. Ceram. Soc.* 2006, 89, 3167–3175. [CrossRef]
16. Jing, W.; Hong-bo, G.; Yu-zhi, G.; Sheng-kai, G. Microstructure and Thermo-Physical Properties of Yttria Stabilized Zirconia Coatings with CMAS Deposits. *J. Eur. Ceram. Soc.* 2011, 31, 1881–1888.
17. Kakuda, T.R.; Levi, C.G.; Bennett, T.D. The Thermal Behavior of CMAS-infiltrated Thermal Barrier Coatings. *Surf. Coat. Technol.* 2015, 272, 350–356. [CrossRef]
18. Clarke, D.R.; Oechsner, M.; Padture, N.P. Thermal-barrier Coatings for More Efficient Gas-turbine Engines. *MRS Bull.* 2012, 37, 891–898. [CrossRef]
19. Cai, L.; Ma, W.; Ma, B.; Guo, F.; Chen, W.; Dong, H.; Shuang, Y. Air Plasma-Sprayed La$_2$Zr$_2$O$_7$-SrZrO$_3$ Composite Thermal Barrier Coating Subjected to CaO-MgO-Al$_2$O$_3$-SiO$_2$ (CMAS). *J. Thermal Spray Technol.* 2017, 26, 1076–1083. [CrossRef]
20. Ctibor, P.; Nevrla, B.; Cizek, J.; Lukac, F. Strontium Zirconate TBC Sprayed by a High Feed-Rate Water-Stabilized Plasma Torch. *J. Thermal Spray Technol.* 2017, 26, 1804–1809. [CrossRef]
21. Ctibor, P.; Sedlacek, J.; Janata, M. Dielectric Strontium Zirconate Sprayed by a Plasma Torch. *Prog. Colol Colorants Coat.* 2017, 10, 225–230.
22. Ctibor, P. After-glow Luminescence of SrZrO$_3$ Prepared by Plasma Spraying. *Boletin Sociedad Espanola Ceramica Y Vidrio* 2018, 57, 190–194. [CrossRef]
23. Hrabovsky, M. Water-stabilized Plasma Generators. *Pure Appl. Chem.* 1998, 70, 1157–1162. [CrossRef]

24. Mikulla, C.; Naraparaju, R.; Schulz, U.; Toma, F.-L.; Barbosa, M.; Leyens, C. Investigation of CMAS Resistance of Sacrificial Suspension Sprayed Alumina Topcoats on EB-PVD 7YSZ Layers. In Proceedings of the International Thermal Spray Conference and Exposition (ITSC 2019), Yokohama, Japan, 26–29 May 2019; pp. 79–85.

25. Hasegawa, S.; Sugimoto, T.; Hashimoto, T. Investigation of Structural Phase Transition Behavior of SrZrO$_3$ by Thermal Analyses and High-temperature X-ray Diffraction. *Solid State Ionics* **2010**, *181*, 1091–1097. [CrossRef]

26. Mikhailov, M.M.; Verevkin, A.S. Photostability of Reflecting Coatings Based on the ZrO$_2$ Powders Doped with SrSiO$_3$. *J. Spacecr. Rocket.* **2005**, *42*, 716–722. [CrossRef]

27. Kagomiya, I.; Suzuki, I.; Ohsato, H. Microwave Dielectric Properties of (Ca$_{1-x}$Sr$_x$)SiO$_3$ Ring Silicate Solid Solutions. *Jpn. J. Appl. Phys.* **2009**, *48*, 09KE02. [CrossRef]

28. Thieme, C.; Russel, C. Thermal Expansion Behavior of SrSiO$_3$ and Sr$_2$SiO$_4$ Determined by High-temperature X-ray Diffraction and Dilatometry. *J. Mater. Sci.* **2015**, *50*, 5533–5539. [CrossRef]

29. Ctibor, P.; Pala, Z.; Nevrlá, B.; Neufuss, K. Plasma-sprayed Fine-grained Zirconium Silicate and Its Dielectric Properties. *J. Mater. Eng. Perform.* **2017**, *26*, 2388–2393. [CrossRef]

30. Liu, Y.; Bai, Y.; Li, E.; Qi, Y.; Liu, C.; Dong, H.; Jia, R.; Ma, W. Preparation and Characterization of SrZrO3–La2Ce2O7 Composite Ceramics as a Thermal Barrier Coating Material. *Mater. Chem. Phys.* **2020**, *247*, 122904. [CrossRef]

31. Wang, L.; Zhang, P.; Habibi, M.H.; Eldridge, J.I.; Guo, S.M. Infrared Radiative Properties of Plasma-sprayed Strontium Zirconate. *Mater. Lett.* **2014**, *137*, 5–8. [CrossRef]

32. Limarga, A.M.; Clarke, D.R. Characterization of Electron Beam Physical Vapor-deposited Thermal Barrier Coatings Using Diffuse Optical Reflectance. *Int. J. Appl. Ceram. Technol.* **2009**, *6*, 400–409. [CrossRef]

33. Makino, T.; Kunitomo, T.; Sakai, I.; Kinoshita, H. Thermal Radiation Properties of Ceramic Materials. *Heat Transf. Jpn. Res.* **1984**, *13*, 33–50.

34. Baranowska, A.; Lesniak, M.; Kochanowicz, M.; Zmojda, J.; Miluski, P.; Dorosz, D. Crystallization Kinetics and Structural Properties of the 45S5 Bioactive Glass and Glass-Ceramic Fiber Doped with Eu^{3+}. *Materials* **2020**, *13*, 1281. [CrossRef]

35. Shawahni, A.M.; Abu-Jafar, M.S.; Jaradat, R.T.; Ouahrani, T.; Khenata, R.; Mousa, A.A.; Ilaiwi, K.F. Structural, Elastic, Electronic and Optical Properties of SrTMO$_3$ (TM = Rh, Zr) Compounds: Insights from FP-LAPW Study. *Materials* **2018**, *11*, 2057. [CrossRef] [PubMed]

36. Múnez, C.J.; Gómez-García, J.; Sevillano, F.; Poza, P.; Utrilla, M.V. Improving Thermal Barrier Coatings by Laser Remelting. *J. Nanosci. Nanotechnol.* **2011**, *11*, 1–6. [CrossRef] [PubMed]

37. Ctibor, P.; Kraus, L.; Tuominen, J.; Vuoristo, P.; Chráska, P. Improvement of Mechanical Properties of Alumina and Zirconia Plasma Sprayed Coatings Induced by Laser Post-treatment. *Ceram. Silikáty* **2007**, *51*, 181–189.

Article

Experimental and Modeling Studies of Bond Coat Species Effect on Microstructure Evolution in EB-PVD Thermal Barrier Coatings in Cyclic Thermal Environments

Zhe Lu [1], Guanlin Lyu [2], Abhilash Gulhane [3], Hyeon-Myeong Park [2], Jun Seong Kim [2], Yeon-Gil Jung [2,*] and Jing Zhang [3]

[1] School of Materials and Metallurgy Engineering, University of Science and Technology Liaoning, No. 185 High-Tech District, An Shan 114051, China; lz19870522@126.com

[2] School of Materials Science and Engineering, Changwon National University Changwon, Gyeongnam 51140, Korea; lyuguanlin@naver.com (G.L.); cd99106@naver.com (H.-M.P.); 20137083@changwon.ac.kr (J.S.K.)

[3] Department of Mechanical and Energy Engineering, Indiana University-Purdue University Indianapolis, Indianapolis, IN 46202-5132, USA; aagulhan@iu.edu (A.G.); jz29@iupui.edu (J.Z.)

* Correspondence: jungyg@changwon.ac.kr; Tel.: +82-55-213-3712; Fax: +82-55-262-6486

Received: 26 July 2019; Accepted: 11 September 2019; Published: 28 September 2019

Abstract: In this work, the effects of bond coat species on the thermal barrier coating (TBC) microstructure are investigated under thermal cyclic conditions. The TBC samples are prepared by electron beam-physical vapor deposition with two species of bond coats prepared by either air-plasma spray (APS) or high-velocity oxygen fuel (HVOF) methods. The TBC samples are evaluated in a variety of thermal cyclic conditions, including flame thermal fatigue (FTF), cyclic furnace thermal fatigue (CFTF), and thermal shock (TS) tests. In FTF test, the interface microstructures of TBC samples show a sound condition without any delamination or cracking. In CFTF and TS tests, the TBCs with the HVOF bond coat demonstrate better thermal durability than that by APS. In parallel with the experiments, a finite element (FE) model is developed. Using a transient thermal analysis, the high-temperature creep-fatigue behavior of the TBC samples is simulated similar to the conditions used in CFTF test. The FE simulation predicts a lower equivalent stress at the interface between the top coat and bond coat in bond coat prepared using HVOF compared with APS, suggesting a longer cyclic life of the coating with the HVOF bond coat, which is consistent with the experimental observation.

Keywords: thermal barrier coating; bond coat species; electron beam-physical vapor deposition; cyclic thermal exposure; thermal durability

1. Introduction

Thermal barrier coatings (TBCs) are insulating overlayers deposited on superalloy substrates, which are usually employed in high-temperature components of gas turbines. TBCs reduce the surface temperature of the metallic component substrate, improving the thermal durability and increasing the fuel efficiency in gas turbines [1–6]. The TBC is usually comprised of four different layers: (1) a ceramic top coat, (2) a metallic bond coat, (3) a Ni- and/or Co-based superalloy substrate, and (4) a thin thermally grown oxide (TGO) layer. The TGO layer acts as a protective layer to retard the thermal and oxidation diffusion. However, the TGO layer may increase the internal stress in TBC systems, which causes potential cracking at the interface between the bond and top coats, eventually leading to spallation or delamination of the top coat [7–10]. The bond coat in a TBC system is to ensure the structural integrity and to protect the superalloy substrate from oxidation. Moreover, the metallic bond coat can reduce the coefficient of thermal expansion (CTE) mismatch between the superalloy substrate and the ceramic top coat, and enhance adhesion with the top coat [11–15]. The bond coat can be deposited by a variety of thermal spraying processes, such as vacuum plasma spray, high-velocity oxygen fuel (HVOF), and air-plasma spray (APS). Although MCrAlY (M = Ni and/or Co) feedstock has been used for a bond coat for several decades, the failure of the TBC system is often resulted from the thermomechanical mismatch between the bond and top coats. The durability and stability of TBC systems can be improved by reducing the CTE mismatch between the top and bond coats, decreasing the excessive TGO layers, and eliminating the resultant residual stresses. For example, TGO layer growth may be modified through powder oxidation which forms a duplex oxide scale with an outer layer and an inner Al_2O_3 layer composed of $NiAl_2O_4$, Cr_2O_3, and other spinel structures [16].

In the present study, a new combined experimental and modeling study of the effect of bond coat species on the microstructure evolution of electron beam-physical vapor deposition processed (EB-PVD) yttria stabilized zirconia (YSZ) TBCs is conducted. Three types of thermal exposure tests, i.e., flame thermal fatigue (FTF), cyclic furnace thermal fatigue (CFTF), and thermal shock (TS), are employed in order to understand the TBCs' thermomechanical properties in thermal cyclic environments. A finite element (FE) model is developed to simulate the distribution of stresses in different bond coats and thermal exposure environments. The relationship between coating failure behavior and the bond coat is investigated, based on the microstructure evaluation in the thermal cyclic tests.

2. Experimental Procedure

2.1. Coating Materials and Sample Preparation

In this study, Ni-based superalloy (GTD–111, with the nominal composition of Ni–14Cr–9.5Co–4.9Ti–3.8W–3Al–2.8Ta–1.5Mo–0.1C–0.03Zr, in wt.%) is used as the substrate. The diameter and thickness of the test specimen are 25.4 and 5 mm, respectively. The surface of the substrate is blasted using an alumina powder, cleaned before coating processes, and then the coatings are deposited within 2 h. AMDRY 962 (Nominal composition of Ni–22Cr–10Al–1.0Y in wt.% and particle size of 56–106 µm; Sulzer Metco Holding AG, Winterthur, Switzerland) and AMDRY 9951 (Nominal composition of Co–32Ni–21Cr–8Al–0.5Y in wt.% and particle size of 5–37 µm; Sulzer Metco Holding AG) are used as the feedstock powders to fabricated the bond coats by APS and HVOF process, respectively. The top coat is formed by the EB-PVD process on the bond coats using 204C-NS (particle size of 45–140 µm, Oerlikon Metco AG, Pfäffikon, Switzerland). The thicknesses of the bond and top coats are designed as 300 ± 20 and 600 ± 50 µm, respectively. In the spray process of TBCs, the parameters recommended by the Chrome-Alloying Co. Ltd (London, UK) are employed.

2.2. Characterizations

To obtain the cross-sectional microstructure and mechanical properties of the TBCs, the specimens are cold-mounted with an epoxy resin and then polished using SiC papers and finally polished with 3 and 1 µm diamond pastes in sequence. The cross-sectional microstructures of TBC samples are observed using a scanning electron microscope (SEM; Model JSM–5610, JEOL, Tokyo, Japan). The hardness of the coatings is determined using a microindentor (HM-114, Mitutoyo Corp., Kanagawa, Japan) with a Vickers tip for a load of 3 N [17]. More than 10 indentation points are measured for achieving statistical results. The sizes of hardness impression are measured using the SEM and all experiments are performed at a room temperature. The adhesive strength of the TBC samples is determined following the American society for testing and materials (ASTM) standard (ASTM C-633-01) [18].

2.3. Cyclic Furnace Thermal Fatigue, Flame Thermal Fatigue, and Thermal Shock Tests

CFTF test are performed for all samples in a specially designed programmable furnace until 1429 cycles. The surface of the sample is about 1100 °C and the backside of the sample is air-cooled to keep the temperature difference of 150 °C. The dwell time is 60 min. Then the samples are cooled in a static air environment for 10 min. FTF tests are also performed for 1429 cycles using liquefied petroleum gas as the heating source. The top surface of sample is heated with flame of about 1100 °C for 5 min. Then the samples are cooled in a static air environment for 25 min. The criterion of failure in FTF test is defined as over 25% spalling of top coat. The TBC samples are cycled to the failure criterion for observing indication of failure. For TS tests, the TBC samples are heated in a muffle furnace till 1100 °C for 60 min, then the samples are directly quenched in water for 5 min. The water temperature is kept at 20–35 °C during the test. For failure criteria, over 50% of the spalled region in top coat is used [19–22]. In TS tests, more than five specimens are tested to achieve statistical results.

3. Model Details

3.1. Finite Element Model

Due to symmetry, a two-dimensional (2D) axisymmetric FE model of TBCs is developed to simulate the coating behavior in CFTF test conditions, and correlate the predictions with the experimental observations. The model consists of an YSZ coat (top), NiCrCoAlY bond coat (middle), and Inconel 718 substrate (bottom). Because the TGO layer is very thin, it is not included in the model. The dimensions of the TBCs are consistent with those described in Section 2.1. The computation is conducted using FE software ANSYS Workbench (ANSYS 19) with PLANE182 axisymmetric element type.

3.2. Properties of Materials Used in the FE Model

To evaluate the thermal cyclic effect on the TBCs, the fatigue-creep behavior of the bond coat is focused on as a potential contributor leading to TBCs failure. The creep of the bond coat leads to TBC system failure and spalling due to differential stresses in the coating layers during thermal cycling. This means that life prediction of the TBC system must take into account of the fatigue-creep of the bond coat.

In this FE model, a secondary steady-state creep equation is incorporated to account for high-temperature creep, using Norton power-law creep ($\epsilon = A\sigma^n$). The temperature-dependent creep constants "A" and "n" for YSZ, Inconel 718, and NiCoCrAlY bond coat made using HVOF and APS [23,24] are noted in Table 1. The materials properties of YSZ [25], bond coat [25], and substrate Inconel 718 [26] as listed in Table 2.

Table 1. Temperature-dependent creep constants used in the FE model [23,24].

Material	Temperature (°C)	A	n
YSZ	750	2.00×10^{-22}	4.5
	850	2.00×10^{-20}	4.32
	950	3.00×10^{-18}	4.15
	1050	3.77×10^{-16}	3.98
	1150	4.80×10^{-14}	3.8
NiCrCoAlY (HVOF)	750	1.25×10^{-14}	4.5
	850	1.40×10^{-11}	3.8
	950	2.30×10^{-22}	3.1
	1050	9.50×10^{-8}	2.55
NiCrCoAlY (APS)	750	6.00×10^{-20}	7.9
Inconel 718	10	4.85×10^{-36}	1.0
	1200	2.25×10^{-9}	3.0

Table 2. Temperature-dependent material properties used in the FE model [25,26].

Material	Temperature, T (°C)	Young's Modulus, E (GPa)	Coefficient of Thermal Expansion, α (10^{-6}/°C)	Poisson's Ratio, ν	Thermal Conductivity, k (W/(m·°C))	Specific Heat, C (J/(kg·°C))
	25	53	7.2	0.25	1.5	500
YSZ	400	52	9.4	0.25	1.2	576
	800	46	16	0.25	1.2	637
	25	225	14	0.3	4.3	501
NiCoCrAlY	400	186	24	0.3	6.4	592
	800	147	47	0.3	10.2	781
	25	205	11.8	0.321	14.7	480
	400	175.5	14.1	0.339	18.3	493.9
Inconel 718	500	168.5	14.4	0.344	19.6	514.8
	650	142	15.1	0.361	22	556.2
	750	130.5	16.2	0.381	23.2	594.35

3.3. Boundary Conditions

A transient thermomechanical analysis is conducted with the same cycle timings and boundary conditions as CFTF test described in Section 2.3. In transient thermal analysis, a single cycle of total 4200 s, with 3600 s of constant heating at 1100 °C, is followed by 600 s of cooling at ambient thermal conditions of 25 °C. The convection coefficient between samples and the environment is assumed as 25 W/(m²·°C). Because the TBC samples are rested on a sample holder, the bottom surface is assumed to be perfectly insulated.

4. Results and Discussion

4.1. The Microstructure Analysis

The cross-sectional microstructures of the TBC samples are shown in Figure 1, where Figure 1(a–1,b–1) are the microstructures of the bond coats fabricated by APS and HVOF, respectively. The top layers of all the samples are prepared by the same method using the EB-PVD method. The top coat of all the coating systems show a columnar structure with small gaps between the columns. The gaps develop from the interface between the top and bond coats to the coating surface. The fine inter columnar pores are mostly aligned to the heat flow direction. These pores help reducing the thermal conductivity of TBC systems. The interface of the TBC samples (Figure 1(a–2,b–2)) shows no cracks and a relatively flat shape. A thin TGO layer about 1–2 μm is found at the interface of each samples without thermal tests. The heat treatment for deposition of the top coat is the main reason for the formation of the thin TGO layer. The dense TGO layer can prevent oxygen diffusing into the bond coat. The bond coat prepared by APS shows several intrinsic defects, such as unmelted particles, oxides, and pores. The microstructures of bond coats that prepared by HVOF are denser and don't have oxide formation and interlayer cracks.

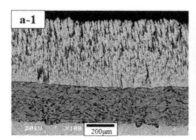

Figure 1. *Cont.*

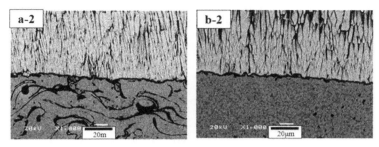

Figure 1. Cross-sectional microstructures of as-prepared TBCs: APS bond coat TBC system (the overall (**a–1**) and the interface (**a–2**) microstructures), and HVOF bond coat TBC system (the overall (**b–1**) and the interface (**b–2**) microstructures).

4.2. Service Life of TBC Systems

The cross-sectional microstructures of TBCs with different bond coats after FTF tests are shown in Figure 2. During cyclic thermal exposure tests, the ceramic top coat appear starting sintering phenomenon. The microstructures of the top coats are more compact and the porosity is reduced due to the densification during the sintering process.

After FTF tests, the interface microstructures are very similar to each other, compared with the as-prepared samples. There is no cracking or delamination in the interface microstructures of each TBC system, as shown in Figure 2(a–2,b–2). The relatively short heating time (5 min) and continuous high-temperature time of the interface (only 2 min) result in that the TGO layer is not fully developed after 1429 cycles. The total heating time is only 119 h. The thickness of the TGO layer is in the range of 2–3 μm without substantial increase.

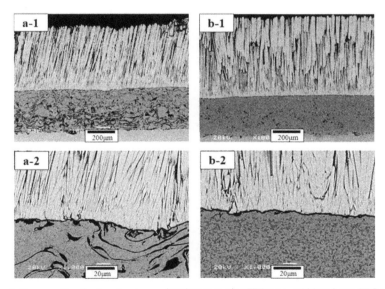

Figure 2. Cross-sectional microstructures of TBC system after FTF tests: APS bond coat TBC system (the overall (**a–1**) and the interface (**a–2**) microstructures) and HVOF bond coat TBC system (the overall (**b–1**) and the interface (**b–2**) microstructures).

Figure 3 shows the cross-sectional microstructures of each TBCs system after CFTF tests. The APS and HVOF bond coats (Figure 3(a–1,b–1)) are delaminated at the interface between the TGO layer and the bond coat in the range of 100–380 and 210–390 cycles, respectively. The APS bond coat shows more degree of oxidation in the interbond coat after CFTF test compared with APS bond coat without any test. The oxidation of the bond coat leads to a change in the sign of stresses due to the smaller CTEs of the TGO layer. It is assumed that small cracks will be created at the peak tips [27]. After CFTF test, the HVOF bond coat shows a different oxidation behavior compared with APS bond coat. No internal oxides are found, but element segregation occurs.

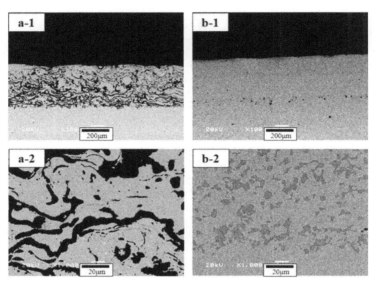

Figure 3. Cross-sectional microstructures of TBCs after CFTF tests: TBC with APS bond coat (the overall (**a–1**) and the interface (**a–2**) microstructures) and TBC with HVOF bond coat (the overall (**b–1**) and the interface (**b–2**) microstructures).

The service lives of the all the TBC systems are summarized in Figure 4. The safe zone of the TBC systems with the HVOF bond coat is twice that with the APS bond coat, although they can reach the same ultimate lifetime. After CFTF tests, the HVOF bond coat TBCs (Figure 3(b–2)) show a diffusion zone near the interface, indicating that these elements are involved in the late reaction to form the TGO consisting of mixed oxide clusters [28]. The increase of the thickness of the TGO layer leads to TBC system failure. In addition, the TBCs with the APS bond coat show a different oxidation behavior. The outer APS bond coat near the interface of the top and bond coats shows a diffusion zone similar to the HVOF bond coat, while the inter-APS bond coat has more oxidation. The lifetime of the TBCs indicates that the TBC systems with the HVOF bond coat show a better thermal durability than those with the APS bond coat.

Figure 5 shows the cross-sectional microstructures of the TBCs after TS tests. It shows a typical mode of delamination at the interface between the bond coat and the TGO layer. During the thermal shock process, a large temperature difference is developed between the substrate and the top coat, which causes thermal or residual stresses at the interface between the TGO layer and the bond coat. When the TGO layer reaches a certain thickness in cyclic thermal fatigue, the TBC will be cracked or delaminated at the interface between the TGO layer and the bond coat, owing to the relatively low adhesive strength of the TGO layer and bond coat in the EB-PVD TBC system. In addition, the mismatch in the CTEs between the ceramics layer, TGO layer, and the bond coat leads to delamination and failure. In TS test, the lifetime of TBCs with the HVOF bond coat is obviously longer than those with the APS bond coat. The TBCs with the HVOF bond coat are delaminated in the range of 345–372 cycles, whereas the TBCs with the APS bond coats are delaminated in the range of 44–80 cycles, showing an aluminum depletion region in the HVOF bond coats similar to that after CFTF test. The results of thermal durability for the TBCs with different bond coats are summarized in Table 3 as a function of thermal exposure species.

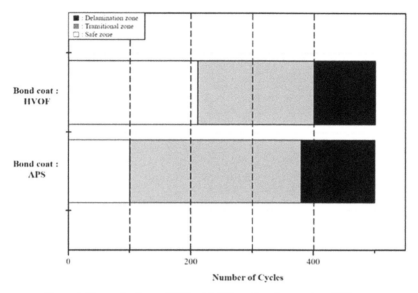

Figure 4. The service lives of TBCs with different bond coats after CFTF tests.

Figure 5. Surface micrographs and cross-sectional microstructures of TBCs after TS tests: TBC with APS bond coat (the surface micrographs (**a–1**), cross-sectional (**a–2**) and magnified interface (**a–3**) microstructures) and TBC with HVOF bond coat (the surface micrographs (**a–1**), cross-sectional (**a–2**) and magnified interface (**a–3**) microstructures).

Table 3. Thermal durability of TBCs with bond coat species in various thermal exposure tests.

Specimen Species	TBC with APS Bond Coat	TBC with HVOF Bond Coat
Cyclic furnace thermal fatigue (CFTF)	100–380 cycles	210–390 cycles
Flame thermal fatigue (FTF)	1429 cycles	1429 cycles
Thermal shock (TS)	44–80 cycles	345–372 cycles

4.3. Mechanical Properties

The hardness values of top coats before and after cyclic thermal exposure, which were measured using a Vickers indentation method, are shown in Figure 6.

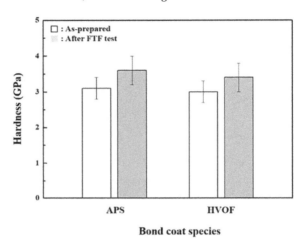

Figure 6. Hardness values of top coats before and after cyclic thermal exposure. Indentation for hardness was conducted on the sectional planes with a load of 3 N. Open and filled marks indicate the hardness values of top coats before and after FTF tests, respectively.

The indentation tests are conducted on the samples' sectional planes. For the as-prepared samples, the hardness values of top coats, APS and HVOF bond coats, are determined to be 3.1 ± 0.3 (mean $\pm$ standard deviation) and 3.0 ± 0.3 GPa, respectively. After FTF tests, the hardness values of top coats are increased to 3.6 ± 0.4 and 3.4 ± 0.3, 3.3 ± 0.3 GPa for the APS and HVOF bond coats, respectively. The increase in the hardness values after FTF tests is due to the reduction of gaps between the adjacent columns, which is consistent with the microstructure evolution (Figure 2a,b). The microstructure evolution of the EB-PVD top coat is more advanced in CFTF and TS tests. The microstructure is densified owing to resintering in CFTF and TS tests, resulting in the disappearance of space between the columns and showing the delamination of the top coat at the interface between the TGO layer and the bond coat.

Adhesive strength is an important mechanical property for TBC systems, with a direct connection to interface stability. Therefore, the adhesive strength values of samples are measured before and after FTF test, which are shown in Figure 7. For the as-prepared samples with APS and HVOF bond coats, the adhesive strength values are determined to be 66.8 ± 5.4 and 76.9 ± 1.2 MPa, respectively. After FTF tests, the adhesive strength values of the samples with APS and HVOF bond coats are determined to be 35.7 ± 13.1 and 70.1 ± 8.9 MPa, respectively. The adhesive strength values of the samples with APS bond coats show a significant decrease, due to the TGO growth and internal APS bond coat oxidation behavior during FTF tests. The TBCs with HVOF bond coats show no obvious change after FTF test by virtue of the HVOF bond having a better oxidation resistance than APS bonds.

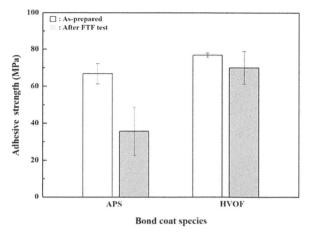

Figure 7. Adhesive strength values of TBCs before and after FTF tests.

The surface photographs and cross-sectional microstructures of the as-prepared samples after measuring the adhesive strength are shown in Figure 8. All of the as-prepared samples are completely delaminated near the interface between the jig fixture and the epoxy adhesive, indicating that the adhesive strength of the EB-PVD is sufficiently high.

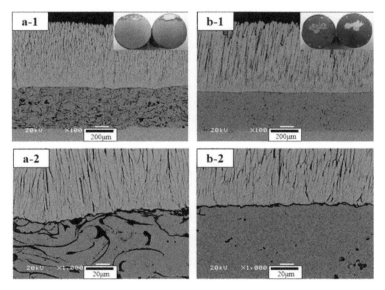

Figure 8. Surface and cross-sectional microstructures after measuring adhesive strength for as-prepared TBCs: TBC with APS bond coat (the entire (**a–1**) and magnified (**a–2**) microstructures) and TBC with HVOF bond coat (the entire (**b–1**) and magnified (**b–2**) microstructures). Surface morphologies of each sample are inserted in each figure.

The surface and cross-sectional microstructures after measuring the adhesive strength values for the TBCs after FTF tests for 1429 cycles are shown in Figure 9.

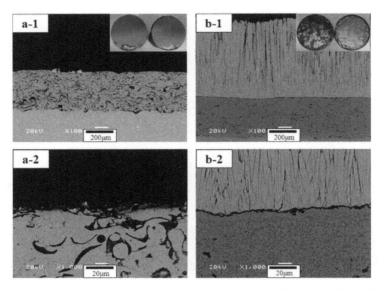

Figure 9. Surface and cross-sectional microstructures after measuring adhesive strength for TBCs after 1429 cycles in FTF tests: TBC with APS bond coat (the entire (**a–1**) and magnified (**a–2**) microstructures) and TBC with HVOF bond coat (the entire (**b–1**) and magnified (**b–2**) microstructures). Surface morphologies of each sample are inserted in each figure.

The fracture microstructure of the samples with APS bond coat is entirely different from the samples with HVOF bond coat. Adhesive failure, such as cracking, fragmentation, and spallation, in the samples with APS bond coat is initiated near the interface between the TGO layer and the bond coat with a complete delamination. The samples with the HVOF bond coats are completely delaminated near the interface between the jig fixture and the epoxy adhesive, indicating that the interface stability of the sample with HVOF bond coat is better than that with APS bond coat. Therefore, the samples with the HVOF bond coats will provide a superior TBC performance in cyclic thermal exposure environments.

4.4. Simulated Temperature Evolution

Under cyclic thermal conditions, the temperature response of TBCs increases in a transient manner initially and reaches a steady-state temperature after approximately 700 s. The temperature falls rapidly during the cooling phase. The temperature evolution is shown in Figure 10.

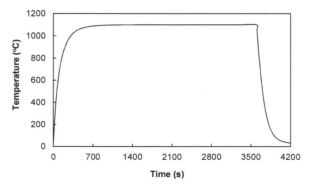

Figure 10. Temperature evolution in the coating.

The temperature distribution of TBCs is shown in Figure 11, during the transient heating and cooling phases. Figure 11a,b shows the results of the two bond coats. Because the thermal conductivity of TBCs is similar in both APS and HVOF, the temperature distribution is similar in both cases.

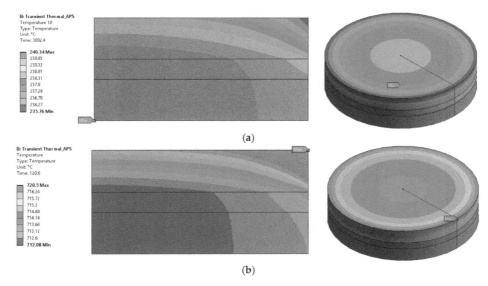

(a)

(b)

Figure 11. Temperature distribution in the coatings (**a**) during the heating cycle, and (**b**) during the cooling cycle.

4.5. Simulated Stress and Creep Strain Evolutions

Figure 12 shows a comparison of the equivalent von Mises stress of TBCs in both cases at the end of the heating cycle, i.e., at 3600 s. In both cases, the maximum stresses are observed at the interface between the bond coat and substrate. For the APS deposited bond coat (Figure 12a), the maximum stress is about 83 MPa, and the stress difference within the bond coat is large. In comparison, the maximum stress in the HVOF deposited bond coat (Figure 12b) is only about 40 MPa, so the stress variation within the coat is less than the APS case.

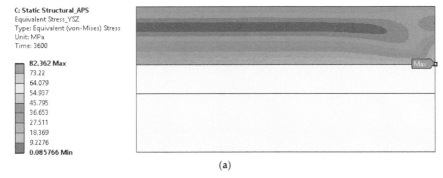

(a)

Figure 12. *Cont.*

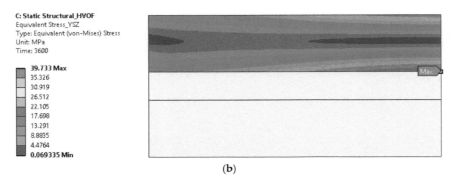

C: Static Structural_HVOF
Equivalent Stress_YSZ
Type: Equivalent (von-Mises) Stress
Unit: MPa
Time: 3600

39.733 Max
35.326
30.919
26.512
22.105
17.698
13.291
8.8835
4.4764
0.069335 Min

(**b**)

Figure 12. Temperature distribution in the coatings (**a**) during the heating cycle and (**b**) during the cooling cycle.

A comparison of equivalent stress evolution in the YSZ layer in response to temperature in both cases is plotted in Figure 13. The results are extracted from the extreme node at the interface of YSZ and bond coat, indicated by "Max" in Figure 12.

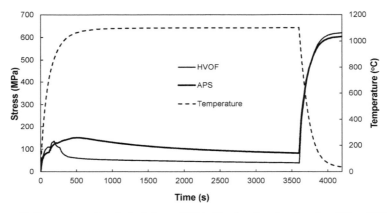

Figure 13. Comparison of equivalent stress of TBC with a bond coat made using APS and HVOF.

In the case of a bond coat made using the HVOF process, the equivalent stress increases with a corresponding increasing temperature until 750 °C. The creep constants are defined to actuate at 750 °C, and thus a stress relaxation is observed once the temperature is beyond 750 °C. The relaxation in the case of TBCs made using APS is not as steep—it relaxes gradually until the end of the heating cycle. In addition, creep strain in the YSZ layer is plotted on the same location (Figure 14). It is evident that in the case of bond coat prepared using HVOF, the induced creep strain is significantly lower than with APS, suggesting that the HVOF bond coat has a better cyclic life.

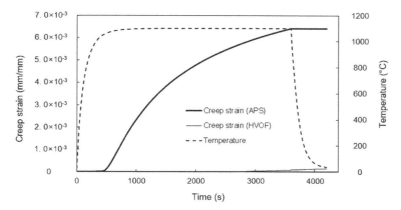

Figure 14. Comparison of creep strain of TBC with a bond coat made using APS and HVOF.

5. Conclusions

The effects of bond coat species on the thermal durability of EB-PVD TBC samples are investigated through cyclic thermal exposure tests. The major conclusions are summarized below.

- After FTF tests, the TBC samples show a sound condition without cracking or delamination, independent of bond coat species. The interface microstructures show a thin TGO layer of 1–2 μm in thickness. The TGO layer is not fully developed in FTF tests, owing to the relatively short thermal exposure time.
- After FTF tests for 1429 cycles, the hardness values of top coats are slightly increased. The adhesive strength values are reduced, with a higher value for the TBCs with the HVOF bond coat than the APS ones.
- In CFTF tests, the TBCs with the APS and HVOF bond coats are delaminated in the range of 100–380 and 210–390 cycles, respectively.
- In TS tests, the TBCs with the bond coats prepared using the APS and HVOF processes are fully delaminated after 44–80 and 345–372 cycles, respectively, suggesting that HVOF bond coat is more effective in improving thermal durability than APS.
- The FE model simulation predicts a lower equivalent stress at the interface of the top coat and bond coat interface in TBCs prepared using the HVOF process compared with APS, suggesting a longer cyclic life of the coating with the HVOF bond coat, which is consistent with the experimental observations.

Author Contributions: Conceptualization, Z.L., Y.-G.J. and J.Z.; methodology, Z.L., Y.-G.J. and J.Z.; software, J.Z. and A.G.; validation, Z.L., H.-M.P., J.S.K. and G.L.; investigation, Z.L., J.S.K. and G.L.; resources, Z.L. and Y.-G.J.; writing—original draft preparation, Z.L. and G.L.; writing—review and editing, Y.-G.J., G.L. and J.Z.; supervision, Y.-G.J. and J.Z.; project administration, Y.-G.J.; funding acquisition, Z.L. and Y.-G.J.

Funding: This work was supported by the "Human Resources Program in Energy Technology" of the Korea Institute of Energy Technology Evaluation and Planning (KETEP), with financial support from the Ministry of Trade, Industry and Energy, Korea (No. 20194030202450), by the National Nature Science Foundation of China (Nos. 51702145), Youth Foundation and Innovation Group Project from the University of Science and Technology Liaoning (2016QN03 & 2017TD01).

Acknowledgments: The authors wish to acknowledge Jing Zhang for providing the FE analysis in the present study.

Conflicts of Interest: The authors declare no conflict of interest.

References

1. DeMasi-Marcin, J.T.; Gupta, D.K. Protective coatings in the gas turbine engine. *Surf. Coat. Technol.* **1994**, *68*, 1–9. [CrossRef]

2. Stecura, S. *NASA Technical Memorandum*; NASA Lewis Research Center: Cleveland, OH, USA, 1985.

3. Strangman, T.E. Thermal barrier coatings for turbine airfoils. *Thin Solid Films* **1985**, *127*, 93–106. [CrossRef]

4. Meier, S.M.; Gupta, D.K.; Sheffler, K.D. Ceramic thermal barrier coatings for commercial gas turbine engines. *JOM* **1991**, *43*, 50–53. [CrossRef]

5. Łatka, L. Thermal barrier coatings manufactured by suspension plasma spraying—A review. *Adv. Mater. Sci.* **2018**, *18*, 95–117. [CrossRef]

6. Sokołowski, P.; Nylen, P.; Musalek, R.; Łatka, L.; Kozerski, S.; Dietrich, D.; Lampke, T.; Pawłowski, L. The microstructural studies of suspension plasma sprayed zirconia coatings with the use of high-energy plasma torches. *Surf. Coat. Technol.* **2017**, *318*, 250–261. [CrossRef]

7. Shillington, E.; Clarke, D. Spalling failure of a thermal barrier coating associated with aluminum depletion in the bond-coat. *Acta Mater.* **1999**, *47*, 1297–1305. [CrossRef]

8. Rabiei, A. Failure mechanisms associated with the thermally grown oxide in plasma-sprayed thermal barrier coatings. *Acta Mater.* **2000**, *48*, 3963–3976. [CrossRef]

9. Cheng, Z.; Yang, J.; Shao, F.; Zhong, X.; Zhao, H.; Zhuang, Y.; Ni, J.; Tao, S. Thermal stability of YSZ coatings deposited by plasma spray–physical vapor deposition. *Coatings* **2019**, *9*, 464. [CrossRef]

10. Miller, R.A.; Lowell, C.E. Failure mechanisms of thermal barrier coatings exposed to elevated temperatures. *Thin Solid Films* **1982**, *95*, 265–273. [CrossRef]

11. Evans, A.; Mumm, D.; Hutchinson, J.; Meier, G.; Pettit, F. Mechanisms controlling the durability of thermal barrier coatings. *Prog. Mater. Sci.* **2001**, *46*, 505–553. [CrossRef]

12. Vaßen, R.; Jarligo, M.O.; Steinke, T.; Mack, D.E.; Stöver, D. Overview on advanced thermal barrier coatings. *Surf. Coat. Technol.* **2010**, *205*, 938–942. [CrossRef]

13. Vassen, R.; Stuke, A.; Stöver, D. Recent developments in the field of thermal barrier coatings. *J. Therm. Spray Technol.* **2009**, *18*, 181–186. [CrossRef]

14. Sidhu, T.S.; Prakash, S.; Agrawal, R.D. Investigations on role of HVOF sprayed Co and Ni based coatings to combat hot corrosion. *Corros. Eng. Sci. Technol.* **2008**, *43*, 335–342. [CrossRef]

15. Jung, S.-H.; Jeon, S.-H.; Lee, J.-H.; Jung, Y.-G.; Kim, I.-S.; Choi, B.-G. Effects of composition, structure design, and coating thickness of thermal barrier coatings on thermal barrier performance. *J. Korean Ceram. Soc.* **2016**, *53*, 689–699. [CrossRef]

16. Young Seok, S.; Jung, S.I.; Kwon, J.Y.; Lee, J.H.; Jung, J.G.; Paik, U.Y. Fracture behavior of plasma-sprayed thermal barrier coatings with different bond coats upon cyclic thermal exposure. *Mater. Sci. Forum* **2009**, *620*, 343–346.

17. Lawn, B. *Fracture of Brittle Solids*; Cambridge University Press: Cambridge, UK, 1993.

18. *ASTM Standards C633 Standard Test Method for Adhesion or Cohesion Strength of Thermal Spray Coatings*; American Society of Testing and Materials: Philadelphia, PA, USA, 2001.

19. Tsantrizes, P.G.; Kim, G.G.; Brezinski, T.A. Thermal barrier coatings. In Proceedings of the AGARD Smp Meeting, Aalborg, Denmark, 15–16 October 1997.

20. Knight, R.; Zhangxiong, D.; Kim, E.H.; Smith, R.W.; Sahoo, P.; Bucci, D. Influence of bond coat surface characteristics on the performance of Tbc systems. In Proceedings of the 15th International Thermal Spray Conference, ASM Thermal Spray Society, Nice, France, 25–29 May 1998.

21. Chwa, S.O.; Ohmori, A. Microstructures of ZrO_2–8wt.%Y_2O_3 coatings prepared by a plasma laser hybrid spraying technique. *Surf. Coat. Technol.* **2002**, *153*, 304–312. [CrossRef]

22. Ma, X.; Takemoto, M. Quantitative acoustic emission analysis of plasma sprayed thermal barrier coatings subjected to thermal shock tests. *Mater. Sci. Eng. A* **2001**, *308*, 101–110. [CrossRef]

23. Bednarz, P. *Finite Element Simulation of Stress Evolution in Thermal Barrier Coating Systems*; Forschungszentrum, Zentralbibliothek: Julich, Germany, 2006.

24. Chen, H.; Hyde, T.H.; Voisey, K.T.; McCartney, D.G. Application of small punch creep testing to a thermally sprayed CoNiCrAlY bond coat. *Mater. Sci. Eng. A* **2013**, *585*, 205–213. [CrossRef]

25. Zhu, D.; Miller, R.A. Determination of creep behavior of thermal barrier coatings under laser imposed high thermal and stress gradient conditions. *J. Mater. Res.* **1999**, *14*, 146–161. [CrossRef]

26. Wang, L.; Zhong, X.H.; Zhao, Y.X.; Tao, S.Y.; Zhang, W.; Wang, Y.; Sun, X.G. Design and optimization of coating structure for the thermal barrier coatings fabricated by atmospheric plasma spraying via finite element method. *J. Asian Ceram. Soc.* **2014**, *2*, 102–116. [CrossRef]

27. Chang, G.C.; Phucharoen, W.; Miller, R.A. Behavior of thermal barrier coatings for advanced gas turbine blades. *Surf. Coat. Technol.* **1987**, *30*, 13–28. [CrossRef]

28. Cui, Q.; Seo, S.-M.; Yoo, Y.-S.; Lu, Z.; Myoung, S.-W.; Jung, Y.-G.; Paik, U. Thermal durability of thermal barrier coatings with bond coat composition in cyclic thermal exposure. *Surf. Coat. Technol.* **2015**, *284*, 69–74. [CrossRef]

Article

Thermal Stability of YSZ Coatings Deposited by Plasma Spray–Physical Vapor Deposition

Zefei Cheng [1,2], Jiasheng Yang [1,2,*], Fang Shao [1,2], Xinghua Zhong [1,2], Huayu Zhao [1,2], Yin Zhuang [1,2], Jinxing Ni [1,2] and Shunyan Tao [1,2,*]

1   The Key Laboratory of Inorganic Coating Materials CAS, Shanghai Institute of Ceramics, Chinese Academy of Science, Shanghai 201899, China
2   Center of Materials Science and Optoelectronics Engineering, University of Chinese Academy of Sciences, Beijing 100049, China
*   Correspondence: jiashengyang@mail.sic.ac.cn (J.Y.); sytao@mail.sic.ac.cn (S.T.); Tel.: +86-21-6990-6321 (S.T.)

Received: 18 April 2019; Accepted: 22 July 2019; Published: 24 July 2019

Abstract: The plasma spray–physical vapor deposition (PS–PVD) process has received considerable attention due to its non-line of sight deposition ability, high deposition rates, and cost efficiency. Compared with electron beam–physical vapor deposition (EB–PVD), PS–PVD can also prepare thermal barrier coatings (TBCs) with columnar microstructures. In this paper, yttria-stabilized zirconia (YSZ) coatings were fabricated by PS–PVD. Results showed that the as-deposited coating presented a typical columnar structure and was mainly composed of metastable tetragonal (t′-ZrO$_2$) phase. With thermal exposure, the initial t′ phase of YSZ evolved gradually into monoclinic (m-ZrO$_2$) phase. Significant increase in hardness (H) and the Young's modulus (E) of the coating was attributed to the sintering effect of the coating during the thermal exposure, dependent on exposure temperature and time. However, the values of H and E decreased in the coatings thermally treated at 1300–1500 °C for 24 h, which is mainly affected by the formation of m-ZrO$_2$ phase.

Keywords: plasma spray–physical vapor deposition; thermal stability; thermal barrier coatings

1. Introduction

In recent years, to improve the service temperature of the hot section of an aircraft engine, besides cooling gas film, thermal barrier coatings (TBCs) consisting of an oxidation-resistant metallic bond coat and a thermally insulating ceramic topcoat of yttria-stabilized zirconia (YSZ) have been applied due to their low thermal conductivity and high thermal expansion coefficient [1–4]. At present, air plasma spraying (APS) and electron beam–physical vapor deposition (EB-PVD) are the two main technologies that are used for TBC deposition [5]. However, both of the above technologies exhibit limitations. YSZ coatings prepared by the APS process have a typical layered microstructure with a large number of interfaces, micro-cracks and pores, which contribute to low thermal conductivity and poor thermal shock resistance [6]. Different from the APS case, TBCs with super strain tolerance and improved spallation lifetime with high thermal conductivity can be obtained through the EB–PVD process. This is because of the columnar microstructure with an inter-columnar gap that is perpendicular to the top-coat/bond-coat interface [7,8].

To meet the increasing temperature demands of engines, coatings with better thermal insulation and high strain tolerance are preferred. Recently, many efforts have been devoted to investigating plasma spray–physical vapor deposition (PS–PVD) TBCs with various microstructures, including dense coatings, PVD-like columnar coatings, nano-sized solid clusters columnar coatings (quasi-PVD) and mixed microstructure coatings [9–13]. As we know, PS–PVD combines the advantages of APS (high deposition rate and cost efficiency) and EB–PVD (the ability to produce columnar structured coatings). TBCs with the initially favorable columnar microstructure can be prepared by PS–PVD, which combines the high thermal insulating property of the APS coatings and the high strain tolerance of the EB–PVD coatings [9–11]. Therefore, many existing results show that the PS–PVD process has the promising potential to fabricate durable YSZ coatings.

It is noted that YSZ TBCs must be exposed to high temperature during harsh service and their thermal stability is a key factor for evaluating the performance of the coatings. As a consequence, the ceramic top-coat may be exposed to high temperatures for a long time, which has great influence on the phase composition, microstructure and mechanical properties. It has been reported that thermal insulation ability and strain tolerance of the as-sprayed TBCs dramatically decreased upon annealing at high temperature because of the micro-cracks and pores healing during the sintering process [14–16]. The initial metastable tetragonal (t'-ZrO_2) phase is the main phase of the as-sprayed TBCs, which is believed to be a direct consequence of both the slow diffusion rate of Y^{3+} ions and a small driving force [17]. The t'-ZrO_2 phase could toughen the ceramic by re-orienting its *c*-axis in crystal cells and absorbing fracture energy to increase the resistance to cracking [18]. The t'-ZrO_2 phase is not the equilibrium phase, and transforms to equilibrium tetragonal (t-ZrO_2) and cubic (c-ZrO_2) phase at high temperature. Upon further cooling, the newly precipitated t-ZrO_2 will transform to monoclinic (m-ZrO_2) phase. Moreover, the T/M phase transformation will cause cracking due to the huge volume change (approximately 5%) caused by the large density difference between T and M phases [19]. For these reasons, it is necessary to qualitatively analyze the phase and microstructural stability at high temperature and their relation to mechanical properties. However, research on the relationship between phase degradation and properties in PS–PVD YSZ TBCs at high temperature is rarely reported. Therefore, in the current work, with the aim of studying the durability of the PS–PVD coatings, the effect of exposure time and temperature on the high-temperature stability of PS–PVD YSZ coatings will be evaluated. Thermal stability is investigated through the evolution of phase composition, microstructure, and mechanical properties under various temperatures and times. This basic research might provide some useful insight for beneficial adjustments and further improvements to the performance of PS–PVD YSZ TBCs.

2. Materials and Methods

2.1. Preparation and Heat Treatment of PS–PVD Coating

The as-deposited YSZ coatings with a thickness of about 310 μm were fabricated on polished graphite substrates (50 mm in length, 10 mm in width, and 10 mm in thickness) using a PS–PVD system (Oerlikon Metco, Wohlen, Switzerland) using an O3CP-type plasma gun with a 60CD powder feeder. An agglomerated ZrO_2–(6–8 wt.%) Y_2O_3 powder (YSZ, Metco 6700) was used as feedstock; the particle size range was 5–22 μm. Prior to depositing the TBC, the polished graphite substrates were preheated by plasma flame flow. The detailed spraying parameters are listed in Table 1.

The free-standing samples used for thermal aging treatment were stripped from graphite substrates through the mismatch between the expansion coefficients of the substrate and coating. Free-standing YSZ coatings were isothermally heat-treated in a high-temperature chamber furnace (HTK 20/17, ThermConcept, Bremen, Germany) at 1200–1600 °C for 24 h and at 1550 °C for 20–100 h, respectively. Free-standing YSZ coating samples were put in a furnace and heated at about 10 °C/min to the target temperature, followed by holding for the selected time. Then, the samples were cooled naturally in the furnace to room temperature. All of the free-standing coating samples were placed in vacuum with epoxy, cut to supply the observation of the cross-sections, and finely polished by routine metallographic methods.

Table 1. Spray parameters for YSZ coatings by PS–PVD.

Items	Preheating Parameters	Coating Parameters
Plasma gas flow rate (slpm)	Ar: 50, He: 110	Ar: 35, He: 60
Power (kW)	64	130
Current (A)	1400	2600
Feed rate (g/min)	–	5
Spray distance (mm)	800	900
Oxygen flow rate (splm)	–	2
Carrier gas (slpm)	Ar: 6	Ar: 8

2.2. Coating Characterization

X-ray diffraction (XRD) and Raman spectroscopy (RS) were used to characterize the phase composition of the as-deposited and isothermally heated coating samples. XRD measurements were performed on the X-ray diffractometer (D/Max 2550 V, Rigaku, Tokyo, Japan) operating in the reflection mode with Cu-Kα radiation (40 kV, 100 mA), using a step scan mode with the step of 0.02° (2θ) and 1 s per step. A Raman microscope system (Invia, Renishaw, Glouchestershire, UK) was used to record Raman spectra at the room temperature with a 532 nm laser excitation. Microstructures and grain size of the heat-treated samples together with the as-deposited coating samples were characterized by a scanning electron microscope (SEM, MIRA3 LM, TESCAN, Brno, Czech Republic) in backscattered electron image mode. A rectangular intercept method on secondary electron images which recorded the fracture surfaces of the coatings was used for measuring the grain size of the coatings. The average grain size, D, was then given by:

$$D = \sqrt{\frac{4A}{\pi(n_i + \frac{n_o}{2})}} \tag{1}$$

where A is the rectangle area, n_i and n_o are the grain numbers in the rectangle and on the rectangular boundary, respectively [20]. The number and magnification of the as-sprayed coating micrographs employed for grain size measurements were 10 and 100,000 times, those of the coatings which were heat-treated in air were 10 and 10,000 times. Hardness (H) and Young's Modulus (E) of all coatings were measured on the cross-section before and after thermal treatment through a G-200 nanoindenter (Agilent Technologies, Oak Ridge, TN, USA) equipped with a Berkovich indenter. Specific test schemes are listed in the literature [21].

3. Results and Discussion

3.1. Microstructure

The microstructure of the as-deposited PS–PVD coatings with the fracture surface and polished cross-section are shown in Figure 1. The PS–PVD coatings exhibited a distinctive microstructure with relatively independent columns perpendicular to the coating surface. Additionally, a lot of nanoparticles (2 μm on average size) were observed, which were an accumulation of unmelted and partially melted feedstock powder particles at long spray distance due to the plasma jet's heating capability [22]. The columnar structure can provide a high strain tolerance due to the gaps between the columns, which is similar to the EB–PVD coatings [23].

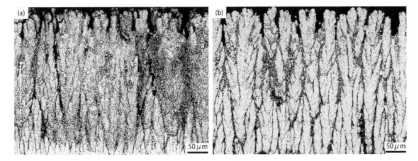

Figure 1. SEM micrographs of the as-sprayed PS–PVD TBCs: (**a**) fracture surface; (**b**) polished cross-section.

Figures 2 and 3 are the SEM diagrams of grain growth of PS–PVD columnar coatings, which were heat-treated in air at 1200–1600 °C for 24 h and at 1550 °C for 20–100 h, respectively. An apparent increasing trend in grain size can be observed with increasing heat-treatment temperature and time from Figures 2 and 3. It can be seen that the grain size of as-deposited columnar coating is very fine, and is about 100 nm. After 1500 °C/24 h or 1550 °C/20 h, the grains grew obviously, and a clear crystal boundary was formed between the grains. Figure 2 shows that the grain growth rate improves significantly with increasing heat-treatment temperature. The grain growth was fast at high temperature, while it was slow at low temperature, indicating that the effect of temperature on grain growth rate was very obvious. Figure 3 shows the grain growth was quick during the initial stage and slower after 20 h. It can be deduced that the temperature dominated the grain growth of YSZ columnar coatings, rather than heating duration.

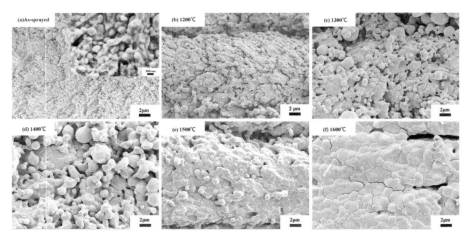

Figure 2. SEM micrographs of fracture surface of PS–PVD TBCs as a function of temperature: (**a**) as-sprayed; (**b**) 1200 °C; (**c**) 1300 °C; (**d**) 1400 °C; (**e**) 1500 °C; (**f**) 1600 °C.

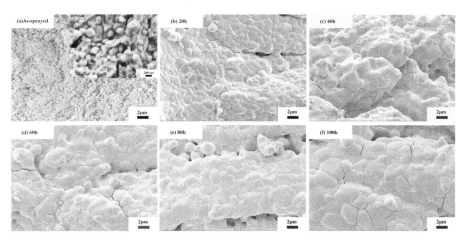

Figure 3. SEM micrographs of fracture surface of PS–PVD TBCs as a function of time: (**a**) as-sprayed; (**b**) 20 h; (**c**) 40 h; (**d**) 60 h; (**e**) 80 h; (**f**) 100 h.

For a more intuitive description of grain change, grain size measured by image analysis is plotted in Figure 4. The average grain size increased up to 0.94 ± 0.3 µm after 1600 °C/24 h heat-treatment, which was about 9.4 times larger than that of the as-deposited coatings. After 1550 °C/100 h heat-treatment, the average grain size grew up to 1.41 ± 0.16 µm, which was about 14 times larger than that of the as-deposited coatings. According to thermodynamic conditions, the larger the grain size, the smaller the total grain boundary surface area and the lower the total surface energy. Because grain coarsening can reduce surface energy and bring the material into a more stable state with low free energy, grain growth was a spontaneous change. To realize this change, it is necessary for the atoms to have strong diffusion ability to complete the grain boundary migration when the grains grew. The higher heating temperature is enabling this ability.

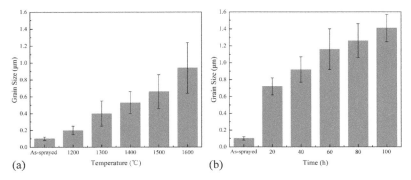

Figure 4. Grain size of the as-sprayed coating and heat-treated coatings: (**a**) samples after heat-treatment for 24 h at different temperatures; (**b**) samples after heat-treatment at 1550 °C for different times.

The polished cross-sections of the PS–PVD coatings after heat treatment at various temperatures for 24 h and at 1550 °C for different times were inspected via SEM to characterize the microstructure evolution process. The micrographs of the PS–PVD coatings are shown in Figures 5 and 6. There were significant differences between the as-deposited coatings and the heat-treated coatings. Large gaps existed between the columnar features in the as-deposited coatings, and those gaps became narrower after heat treatment. Particles at the edge of the columns were in contact with each other, and sintered together during the heat treatment. The nanoparticles between the columns promoted the diffusion between adjacent columns. Compared with the as-deposited YSZ coating, the feather-like structure disappeared, the columns became smooth, the grain size coarsened, and the fine grains of the feather-like structure disappeared because of strong diffusion at high temperature. In addition, micro pores were not observed in the as-deposited columns until these columns underwent high-temperature annealing at 1200–1600 °C with an exposure time from 20 to 100 h. The formation mechanism of micro pores may be the aggregation of vacancies in columns during high-temperature annealing [24]. Vacancy aggregation led to the collapse of the lattice and the formation of pores, which led to the decrease of vacancy concentration in the crystal. To maintain the equilibrium concentration of vacancies in the crystal, new vacancies will be generated. Vacancy proliferation and vacancy aggregation promoted each other. The formation of vacancy clusters made the atoms near the grain boundary diffuse.

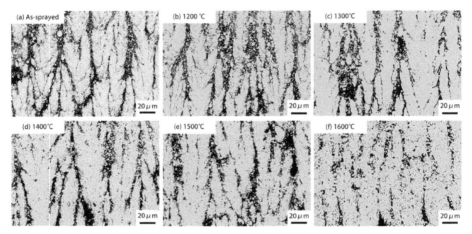

Figure 5. SEM micrographs of polished cross-sections of PS–PVD coatings as a function of temperature: (**a**) as-sprayed; (**b**) 1200 °C; (**c**) 1300 °C; (**d**) 1400 °C; (**e**) 1500 °C; and (**f**) 1600 °C.

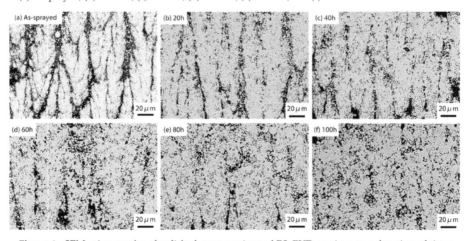

Figure 6. SEM micrographs of polished cross-sections of PS–PVD coatings as a function of time: (**a**) as-sprayed; (**b**) 20 h; (**c**) 40 h; (**d**) 60 h; (**e**) 80 h; and (**f**) 100 h.

3.2. Phase Transformation

To further understand the thermally induced morphological and composition evolution of the PS–PVD YSZ coatings, Raman spectroscopy (RS) was used to detect the phase compositions. Five bands at 147, 267, 322, 463 and 642 cm^{-1} correspond to the Raman-active modes of tetragonal phase, while the peaks at 178, 189, 221, 308, 334, 346, 382, 476, 503, 539, 559, 615 and 637 cm^{-1} are the characteristic bands of monoclinic phase [25,26]. Figures 7–9 show the XRD patterns and Raman spectra of the coatings. The results indicate that the main phase of the as-deposited coatings was t-ZrO$_2$, which indicates that the coating was mainly formed by vapor mixture of zirconia and yttrium oxide. Figure 8 shows that t-ZrO$_2$ of the as-sprayed coating is the non-transformable metastable phase (t'-ZrO$_2$). A small quantity of m-ZrO$_2$ also existed in the as-deposited YSZ coatings. As the feedstock powder is an agglomeration of monoclinic zirconia and cubic yttria (not pre-alloyed yttria-stabilized zirconia), it is inferred that there were some unmelted or unevaporated feedstock powder particles directly incorporated and solidified in the coating [22]. The results show that t-ZrO$_2$ and m-ZrO$_2$ coexisted in the YSZ coatings after high-temperature exposure. This indicates that temperature played the most important role in the extent of the phase transformation. At 1550 °C, the phase transformation from t-ZrO$_2$ to m-ZrO$_2$ occurred over a short period of time, indicating that the temperature was a stronger promoter of phase transformation than time.

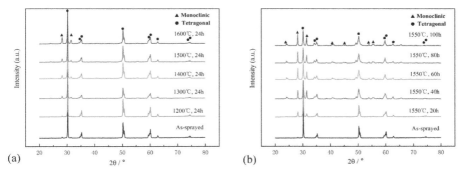

Figure 7. XRD patterns of the as-sprayed coating and heat-treated coatings: (**a**) samples after heat-treatment for 24 h at different temperatures; (**b**) samples after heat-treatment at 1550 °C for different times.

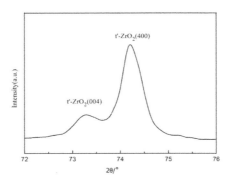

Figure 8. XRD patterns of the as-sprayed coating with 2θ between 72° and 76°.

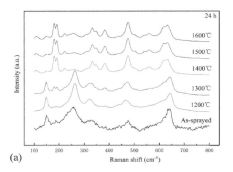
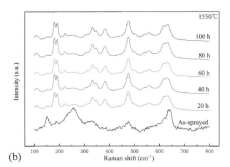

Figure 9. Raman spectra of the as-sprayed coating and heat-treated coatings: (**a**) samples after heat-treatment for 24 h at different temperatures; (**b**) samples after heat-treatment at 1550 °C for different times.

3.3. Mechanical Properties

After high-temperature heat treatment, the microstructure, including grain size, cracks and pores, of the YSZ coatings changed significantly, and the mechanical properties of the YSZ coatings also changed accordingly. Hardness (*H*) and Young's Modulus (*E*) are very important mechanical properties for YSZ coatings under long-term service conditions at high temperature. Previous studies in TBCs have reported that the Young's modulus measured on the cross-section was 1.3 times higher than that on the plan-section [27]. Because PS–PVD coatings have a typical columnar microstructure, the mechanical properties measured on the surface and cross-section are not the same, so the nanoindentation method under identical conditions was used to measure the variation of *H* and *E* on the polished cross-section of the coating.

As shown in Figure 10a, the average *H* and *E* values of the coating before thermal exposure were 6.7 ± 1.6 GPa and 95.5 ± 13.7 GPa, respectively. In the process of variable temperature and constant time (24 h) heat treatment, *H* increased obviously up to 1300 °C, and then decreased with further temperature enhancement. The highest *H* value of the coatings was 15.6 ± 1.0 GPa, after heat treatment in air at 1300 °C for 24h, which was increased by 133% compared to the as-deposited coating. In addition, there was then a continuous decrease of *H* value until 1500 °C; after that, a constant average *H* value can be observed with further increase of the heat treatment temperature. Concerning *E* results, the *E* value of the YSZ coating increased significantly to a maximum of 203.8 ± 22.7 GPa, about 113% higher than that of the as-deposited coating, and then the *E* value gradually decreased to a constant value. Figure 10b shows the measured *H* and *E* values as a function of exposure time for PS–PVD coatings before and after heat treatment at 1550 °C. The *H* and *E* values increased first and then remained stable. The *H* and *E* values of the coating after being heat-treated at 1550 °C for 60 h reached maximum values of 11.1 ± 1.7 GPa and 188.4 ± 19.3 GPa, respectively, representing increases by approximately 66% and 97%, respectively, compared to the as-deposited coating. Similar trends of the *H* and *E* values of coatings have been reported previously; in particular, Zhao et al. found that in axial suspension plasma spraying (ASPS) YSZ TBCs, the mechanical properties firstly increased significantly with sintering, and then decreased with prolonged thermal aging time, which was caused by a t-ZrO_2 → m-ZrO_2 phase transformation after thermal exposure at 1550 °C for 60 h [21]. Sintering can increase the *H* and *E* values due to thermal exposure, which has been reported for APS, ASPS and EB–PVD coatings [27–29]. For example, Zhao et al. showed that the *H* and *E* values of ASPS TBCs increased by about 50% and 44% on the cross-section after 1300 °C/24 h exposure in air [21]. An early study on a plasma-sprayed TBC also reported that the *E* value of the ceramic coating increased after exposure, which was attributed to the healing of pores and grain growth and the improvement in bonding and coherence across the splat boundary during exposure at high temperature as a result of the sintering effect [30]. In the present study, the microstructure evolution of PS–PVD TBCs after heat treatment from 1200 to 1600 °C for 24 h and at 1550 °C for 20–100 h is similar to the above-mentioned studies.

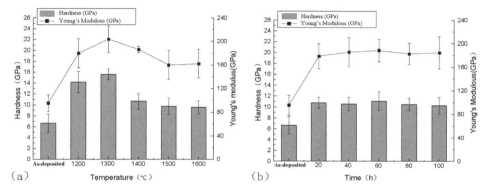

Figure 10. Hardness and Young's modulus of the as-sprayed coating and the heat-treated coatings: (**a**) samples after heat-treatment for 24 h at different temperatures; (**b**) samples after heat-treatment at 1550 °C for different times.

Figures 2, 3, 5 and 6 schematically show that grain growth and the closer contact between single columns after thermal exposure lead to a stiffer structure, and thus should create a higher hardness and Young's modulus, resulting from the sintering effect of PS–PVD TBCs during thermal exposure. The sintering effect during the first 20 or 24 h was much more important, especially at 1300 °C, than the later stage of heat treatment, producing a sharp increase in the mechanical properties. The theoretical equation between porosity and Young's modulus (*E*) in porous material can be given as follows:

$$E = E_0 \exp\left[-\left(bp + cp^2\right)\right] \tag{2}$$

where p, E and E_0 are the porosity, and the Young's modulus of porous material and dense material, respectively. The terms b and c are empirical values depending on pore morphology [31]. The above formula illustrates that the Young's modulus of porous material decreases with increasing porosity. Therefore, the E value of the YSZ coating after heat treatment at 1300 °C/24 h reached the highest point due to its having the lowest porosity. Previous literature has reported that the phase transformation from t-ZrO_2 to m-ZrO_2 will cause cracking due to the huge volume change (approximately 5%) [19]. In combination with Figures 5, 7 and 9, lots of pores and cracks formed between the grain boundaries with increasing exposure temperature for 24 h caused by the formation and accumulation of m-ZrO_2 phase. Thus, it is reasonable to conclude that the initial increase in the measured hardness and Young's modulus were attributable to a stiffer structure induced by sintering after thermal exposure, and the mechanical properties decreased obviously due to the m-ZrO_2 phase formation accompanied by volume expansion and micro cracks formation.

4. Conclusions

The microstructure, phase transformation and mechanical properties of PS–PVD YSZ TBCs have been examined before and after exposure at 1200–1600 °C for 24 h and at 1550 °C for 20–100 h in air. PS–PVD TBCs showed a typical columnar structure with porosity between the individual columns before thermal exposure. Conclusions are summarized as follows:

- After thermal exposure, the columnar structure degraded and micro pores were generated in the columns, resulting in a close contact of columns as a result of sintering effect.

- After high-temperature exposure for a long time, the initial t-ZrO_2 phase of PS–PVD YSZ TBCs evolved gradually into m-ZrO_2 and cracks form between the grain boundaries with increasing exposure temperature caused by the formation and accumulation of m-ZrO_2 phase.

- The significant improvement of hardness and Young's modulus of the coatings were attributed to a stiffer structure caused by the sintering effect during the thermal exposure at 1200–1300 °C for 24 h and 1550 °C for 20–100 h. For coatings exposed at different temperatures for 24 h, the hardness and Young's modulus decreased in the range of 1300–1500 °C, which is caused by the generation of micro cracks accompanied with the formation of m-ZrO_2 phase.

Author Contributions: Conceptualization, Z.C. and S.T.; Data Curation, Z.C., X.Z., H.Z., Y.Z. and J.N.; Formal Analysis, Z.C. and F.S.; Writing—Original Draft Preparation, Z.C.; Writing—Review & Editing, J.Y. and S.T.

Funding: This research was funded by Fundamental Research of Aero-engine and Combustion Gas Turbine Major Special Project (No. 2017-VI-0010-0082), National Natural Science Foundation of China (NSFC) (No. 51701235), Science and Technology Innovation of Shanghai (No. 18511108702) and Natural Science Foundation of Shanghai (No. 17ZR1412200).

Conflicts of Interest: The authors declare no conflict of interest.

References

1. Padture, N.P.; Gell, M.; Jordan, E.H. Thermal barrier coatings for gas-turbine engine applications. *Science* **2002**, *296*, 280–284. [CrossRef] [PubMed]
2. Ganvir, A.; Markocsan, N.; Joshi, S. Influence of isothermal heat treatment on porosity and crystallite size in axial suspension plasma sprayed thermal barrier coatings for gas turbine applications. *Coatings* **2017**, *7*, 4. [CrossRef]
3. Parks, W.P.; Hoffman, E.E.; Lee, W.Y.; Wright, I.G. Thermal barrier coatings issues in advanced land-based gas turbines. *J. Therm. Spray Technol.* **1997**, *6*, 187–192. [CrossRef]
4. Smialek, J.L.; Miller, R.A. Revisiting the birth of 7YSZ thermal barrier coatings: Stephan Stecura [†]. *Coatings* **2018**, *8*, 225. [CrossRef]
5. Montavon, G. Recent developments in thermal spraying for improved coating characteristics and new applications/process controls and spray processes. *High Temp. Mater. Process.* **2004**, *8*, 45–93. [CrossRef]
6. Hass, D.D.; Slifka, A.J.; Wadley, H.N.G. Low thermal conductivity vapor deposited zirconia microstructures. *Acta Mater.* **2001**, *49*, 973–983. [CrossRef]
7. Peichl, A.; Beck, T.; Vohringer, O. Behaviour of an EB–PVD thermal barrier coating system under thermal-mechanical fatigue loading. *Surf. Coat. Technol.* **2003**, *162*, 113–118. [CrossRef]
8. Schulz, U.; Menzebach, M.; Leyens, C.; Yang, Y.Q. Influence of substrate material on oxidation behavior and cyclic lifetime of EB–PVD TBC systems. *Surf. Coat. Technol.* **2001**, *146*, 117–123. [CrossRef]
9. Rezanka, S.; Mauer, G.; Vaßen, R. Improved thermal cycling durability of thermal barrier coatings manufactured by PS–PVD. *J. Therm. Spray Technol.* **2013**, *23*, 182–189. [CrossRef]
10. Mauer, G.; Hospach, A.; Vaßen, R. Process development and coating characteristics of plasma spray-PVD. *Surf. Coat. Technol.* **2013**, *220*, 219–224. [CrossRef]
11. Mauer, G.; Vaßen, R. Plasma spray–PVD: Plasma characteristics and impact on coating properties. *J. Phys. Conf. Ser.* **2012**, *406*, 012005. [CrossRef]
12. Hospach, A.; Mauer, G.; Vaßen, R.; Stöver, D. Characteristics of ceramic coatings made by thin film low pressure plasma spraying (LPPS–TF). *J. Therm. Spray Technol.* **2012**, *21*, 435–440. [CrossRef]
13. Hospach, A.; Mauer, G.; Vaßen, R.; Stöver, D. Columnar-structured thermal barrier coatings (TBCs) by thin film low-pressure plasma spraying (LPPS–TF). *J. Therm. Spray Technol.* **2010**, *20*, 116–120. [CrossRef]
14. Paul, S.; Cipitria, A.; Tsipas, S.A.; Clyne, T.W. Sintering characteristics of plasma sprayed zirconia coatings containing different stabilisers. *Surf. Coat. Technol.* **2009**, *203*, 1069–1074. [CrossRef]
15. Choi, S.R.; Zhu, D.M.; Miller, R.A. Effect of sintering on mechanical properties of plasma-sprayed zirconia-based thermal barrier coatings. *J. Am. Ceram. Soc.* **2005**, *88*, 2859–2867. [CrossRef]
16. Zhu, D.M.; Miller, R.A. Sintering and creep behavior of plasma-sprayed zirconia- and hafnia-based thermal barrier coatings. *Surf. Coat. Technol.* **1998**, *108*, 114–120. [CrossRef]

17. Clarke, D.R.; Levi, C.G. Materials design for the next generation thermal barrier coatings. *Annu. Rev. Mater. Res.* **2003**, *33*, 383–417. [CrossRef]

18. Ren, X.; Pan, W. Mechanical properties of high-temperature-degraded yttria-stabilized zirconia. *Acta Mater.* **2014**, *69*, 397–406. [CrossRef]

19. Chevalier, J.; Gremillard, L.; Virkar, A.V.; Clarke, D.R. The tetragonal-monoclinic transformation in zirconia: Lessons learned and future trends. *J. Am. Ceram. Soc.* **2009**, *92*, 1901–1920. [CrossRef]

20. Luo, J.; Adak, S.; Stevens, R. Microstructure evolution and grain growth in the sintering of 3Y-TZP ceramics. *J. Mater. Sci.* **1998**, *33*, 5301–5309. [CrossRef]

21. Zhao, Y.; Wang, L.; Yang, J.; Li, D.; Zhong, X.; Zhao, H.; Shao, F.; Tao, S. Thermal aging behavior of axial suspension plasma-sprayed yttria-stabilized zirconia (YSZ) thermal barrier coatings. *J. Therm. Spray Technol.* **2015**, *24*, 338–347. [CrossRef]

22. He, W.; Mauer, G.; Gindrat, M.; Wäger, R.; Vaßen, R. Investigations on the nature of ceramic deposits in plasma spray–physical vapor deposition. *J. Therm. Spray Technol.* **2016**, *26*, 83–92. [CrossRef]

23. Kulkarni, A.; Goland, A.; Herman, H.; Allen, A.J.; Dobbins, T.; DeCarlo, F.; Ilavsky, J.; Long, G.G.; Fang, S.; Lawton, P. Advanced neutron and X-ray techniques for insights into the microstructure of EB–PVD thermal barrier coatings. *Mater. Sci. Eng. A* **2006**, *426*, 43–52. [CrossRef]

24. Dalach, P.; Ellis, D.E.; van de Walle, A. First-principles thermodynamic modeling of atomic ordering in yttria-stabilized zirconia. *Phys. Rev. B* **2010**, *82*, 144117. [CrossRef]

25. Huang, W.; Yang, J.; Wang, C.; Zou, B.; Meng, X.; Wang, Y.; Cao, X.; Wang, Z. Effects of Zr/Ce molar ratio and water content on thermal stability and structure of ZrO_2–CeO_2 mixed oxides prepared via sol–gel process. *Mater. Res. Bull* **2012**, *47*, 2349–2356. [CrossRef]

26. Stefanic, G.; Music, S.; Popovic, S.; Sekulic, A. FT-IR and laser Raman spectroscopic investigation of the formation and stability of low temperature t-ZrO_2. *J. Mol. Struct.* **1997**, *408*, 391–394. [CrossRef]

27. Guo, S. Young's moduli of zirconia top-coat and thermally grown oxide in a plasma-sprayed thermal barrier coating system. *Scripta Mater.* **2004**, *50*, 1401–1406. [CrossRef]

28. Guo, S.Q.; Kagawa, Y. Effect of thermal exposure on hardness and Young's modulus of EB–PVD yttria-partially-stabilized zirconia thermal barrier coatings. *Ceram. Int.* **2006**, *32*, 263–270. [CrossRef]

29. Zotov, N.; Bartsch, M.; Eggeler, G. Thermal barrier coating systems—Analysis of nanoindentation curves. *Surf. Coat. Technol.* **2009**, *203*, 2064–2072. [CrossRef]

30. Thompson, J.A.; Clyne, T.W. The effect of heat treatment on the stiffness of zirconia top coats in plasma-sprayed TBCs. *Acta Mater.* **2001**, *49*, 1565–1575. [CrossRef]

31. Jang, B.K.; Matsubara, H. Influence of porosity on hardness and Young's modulus of nanoporous EB–PVD TBCs by nanoindentation. *Mater. Lett.* **2005**, *59*, 3462–3466. [CrossRef]

Article

High Temperature Anti-Friction Behaviors of a-Si:H Films and Counterface Material Selection

Qunfeng Zeng [1,2,*] and Liguo Qin [1]

[1] Key Laboratory of Education Ministry for Modern Design and Rotor-Bearing System,
    Xi'an Jiaotong University, Xi'an 710049, China
[2] College of Materials Science and Engineering, Yangtze Normal University, Chongqing 408100, China
*   Correspondence: qzeng@xjtu.edu.cn

Received: 21 June 2019; Accepted: 13 July 2019; Published: 18 July 2019

Abstract: In the present paper, the influence of self-mated friction materials on the tribological properties of hydrogenated amorphous silicon films (a-Si:H films) is studied systemically at high temperature. The results are obtained by comparing the tribological properties of a-Si:H films under different friction pair materials and temperatures. The a-Si:H films exhibit super-low friction of 0.07 at a temperature of 600 °C, and ceramic materials are appropriate for anti-friction behaviors of a-Si:H films at high temperature. The results of tribotests and observations of the fundamental friction mechanism show that super-low friction of a-Si:H films and ceramic materials of the friction system are involved in high temperature oxidation; this also applies to the tribochemical reactions of a-Si:H films, steel and iron silicate in open air at elevated temperature in the friction process.

Keywords: hydrogenated amorphous silicon films; high temperature oxidation; super-low friction

1. Introduction

With the rapid development of military, aerospace and industrial robots, equipment have been run under harsh operating conditions such as high temperature. It is well known that the tribological problem is one of the scientific challenges of engineering applications in friction systems under high temperature conditions [1]. Moreover, high temperature evokes tribological properties of machinery parts that are complicated due to the tribological chemistry reaction at high temperature and friction heating [2–4]. Diamond-like carbon (DLC) films have been the subject of intensive studies in recent years and exhibit a number of attractive tribological properties such as super-low friction and DLC films being considered excellent candidate materials for tribological applications below 300 °C [5–7]. In open air, DLC films are confined to the environmental temperature above 300 °C where oxidation occurs. In a previous work, a superlubricity system relating to DLC films at high temperature was proposed. Moreover, the lubricious composite oxides are generated from the interlayer of hydrogenated amorphous silicon films (a-Si:H films) at the interface due to tribochemistry reactions in the friction process [8]. Therefore, it was concluded that a-Si:H films are beneficial to produce lubricious oxides and achieve high temperature super-low friction. It would be expected to resolve high friction problems of high temperature tribology in industrial applications [9,10]. The a-Si:H films were deposited on a steel substrate and the tribological properties of a-Si:H films were investigated under high temperature. The a-Si:H films exhibit super-low friction under high temperature [11].

The tribological properties of materials depends on many factors such as temperature, applied load, sliding velocity, and properties of matting materials. Due to the complexity of friction phenomena in composite oxides, the friction mechanisms are not fully understood. Therefore, it is necessary to build an anti-friction system and probe high temperature anti-friction behaviors of a-Si:H films and clarify high temperature anti-friction and oxidation mechanisms of the a-Si:H film-related friction systems to extend the wide tribological applications of a-Si:H films under high temperature. The aim of the present work is to investigate the influence of friction-matted materials for high temperature antifriction behavior of a-Si:H films and select appropriate friction-pair materials for a-Si:H films in open air from 200 to 600 °C. High temperature super-low friction and the super-low friction mechanism of a-Si:H films are expected to achieve and clarify the potential engineering applications at high temperature.

2. Experimental Details

2.1. Preparation of a-Si:H Films

The a-Si:H films were deposited on high speed tool steel (HSS) flats in a plasma-enhanced chemical vapor deposition (PECVD) system, with a mix gas of Ar and SiH_4. Ar gas is introduced into a chamber to clean the ambient air for 5 min. Then, SiH_4 gas is used to deposit hydrogenated amorphous silicon films for 2 h. After deposition of films, Ar gas is introduced into the chamber again to clear the reaction gas of SiH_4. The deposition pressure is about 80 Pa. The thickness of the a-Si:H films is 1 μm. The deposition details of hydrogenated amorphous silicon films are given in our previous paper [11].

2.2. Characterization of a-Si:H Films

Raman spectroscopy (HR800, Horbia Jobin Yvon, Villeneuve d'Ascq, France) with 633 nm and a resolution of 1 cm^{-1} was employed to estimate the microstructure of a-Si:H films. All Raman spectra were measured at room temperature to avoid heating the sample. As expected, the measurement of Fourier Transform Infrared Spectrometry (FTIR, Nicolet iS50, Thermo Fisher Scientific, Madison, WI, USA) was also performed to analyze the microstructure of a-Si:H films.

2.3. High Temperature Tribotests of a-Si:H Films

Tribotests of a-Si:H films were carried out by a high-temperature tribometer (Universal Tribometer, Rtec Instruments, San Jose, CA, USA) to investigate the friction and wear behaviors of a-Si:H films and influence of the friction-pair materials of a steel ball, ZrO_2 ball, Si_3Ni_4 ball and DLC films-coated steel ball on the tribological properties of a-Si:H films at the temperatures of 200, 400 and 600 °C in ambient air. The a-Si:H films-coated disc was slid against the ball at a speed of 0.05 m/s and applied load of 5 N. The friction pairs were cleaned by the ultrasound device in acetone and then blown by dry air before tests and measurements. The microstructure of the worn surface of ball and flat was investigated by Raman spectroscopy within the wear scar zone. Surface morphology of the worn surface of the ball and flat was observed by optical microscopy after tribotests.

3. Results and Discussion

3.1. Raman Spectra and FTIR of a-Si:H Films

Figure 1 shows Raman spectrum of a-Si:H films on a flat. The films exhibit a strong Raman peak at 480 cm^{-1}, showing amorphous silicon, and a weak peak at 220 cm^{-1}, showing hydrogenated amorphous silicon. The band at 2000 cm^{-1} is assigned to the stretching vibration of Si–H bond and the peak at 630 cm^{-1} is assigned to the bending vibration of Si–H bond in FTIR. It also indicates there is hydrogen in amorphous silicon films. In the FTIR spectrum of a-Si:H films, the strong bands at 630, 2018 and 2178 cm^{-1} are the typical and characteristic peaks of a-Si:H films [12]. The band at 630 cm^{-1} belongs to the Si–H bond. It is also found that the absorption peaks of SiH and SiH_2 are observed occurring to peaks at 2018 and 2178 cm^{-1}. According to FTIR measurements, the obtained a-Si:H films contain lots of hydrogen. There are asymmetric Si–O–Si stretching vibrations at 1040 cm^{-1} and a Si–O–Si bending mode at 890 cm^{-1} in FTIR spectrum.

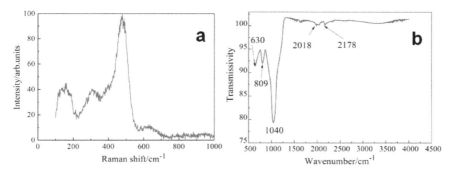

Figure 1. (**a**) Raman and (**b**) FTIR spectrum of a-Si:H films.

3.2. Tribological Properties of Steel Ball/a-Si:H Films under Different Temperatures

Figure 2 shows CoF of steel ball/a-Si:H films under different testing temperatures. At 200 °C, initial CoF is 0.4 and fluctuates subsequently to 0.47. At 400 °C, initial CoF is 0.26 and average CoF is 0.36. However, there is a big difference in the CoF curve between 400 and 600 °C. At 600 °C, initial CoF is 0.35 and then drops down to around 0.1 and average CoF is 0.09. It is found that a-Si:H films exhibit excellent high temperature anti-friction behavior at 600 °C.

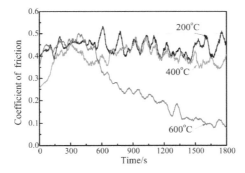

Figure 2. CoF of steel ball/a-Si:H films under different temperatures.

The topography of the worn surfaces was investigated by a non-contact profilometer (CX40M, Sunny Instruments Co., Ltd., Ningbo, China). Figure 3 shows surface topography of the worn surface of ball and flat at 600 °C. The wear scar width on flat is about 824.0 μm and the wear track width of ball is 1436.2 μm at 600 °C. There are lots of black materials on wear scar on disc and wear debris with circle scar on ball. It seems that there are chemical reactions due to environmental high temperature and friction heating and oxidation products on wear scar during sliding.

The a-Si:H films exhibit super-low friction at 600 °C. The structure and component of the worn surface of the friction pair are indispensable to be measured at 600 °C. Figure 4 shows SEM (S-3000N, Hitachi, Tokyo, Japan) image and Raman spectrum of steel ball/a-Si:H films friction pair at 600 °C. Figure 4a shows SEM image of the worn surface of disc. There are some small and circle particles in the wear scar on disc. Figure 4b shows Energy Dispersive X-ray Spectroscopy (EDS, S-3000N, Hitachi) of the worn surface of disc. There are Si, O and Fe elements in the wear scar, which indicates that there are tribological chemistry reactions and maybe SiO_2 and iron oxides after tribotests. Figure 4c shows a typical peak of Fe_3O_4. The band at 665.2 cm^{-1} is the typical peak of Fe_3O_4 about A_{1g} model. The peak at 537.1 cm^{-1} is the typical peak of Fe_3O_4 for the $T_{2g}(2)$ model and the peak at 291.0 cm^{-1} is the typical peak of Fe_3O_4 about the E_g model. The peak of 1320.2 cm^{-1} is the characteristic peak of α-Fe$_2$O$_3$. Figure 4d shows Raman spectrum of a-Si:H films. The peak at 660.3 cm^{-1} is the main peak of Fe$_3$O$_4$. The band of 660.3 cm^{-1} is the typical peaks of α-Fe$_2$O$_3$, and there are bands at 223.7 cm^{-1} of α-Fe$_2$O$_3$, 290.2 cm^{-1} of α-Fe$_2$O$_3$, 409.7 cm^{-1} of α-Fe$_2$O$_3$ and 611.4 cm^{-1} of α-Fe$_2$O$_3$ [13]. These measurements show these oxides include α-Fe$_2$O$_3$ and Fe$_3$O$_4$ except for a-Si:H films on the worn surface of ball and flat. The peak at 940 cm^{-1} is actually the typical peak of Si–O–Si bond stretching. According to Raman measurements and tribotest results, there are iron oxides of α-Fe$_2$O$_3$ and Fe$_3$O$_4$ on ball and the composite oxides of α-Fe$_2$O$_3$ and SiO$_2$ with few Fe$_3$O$_4$ on flat. Therefore, the friction pair is iron oxides of α-Fe$_2$O$_3$ and Fe$_3$O$_4$ and self-generated composite oxides of α-Fe$_2$O$_3$ and SiO$_2$ on the flat through high temperature oxidation reaction, which results in high temperature super-low friction at the temperature of 600 °C.

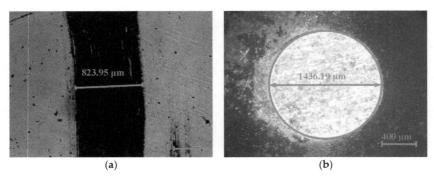

(a)   (b)

Figure 3. Images of wear scar of steel ball/a-Si:H films at 600 °C: (**a**) disc; (**b**) ball.

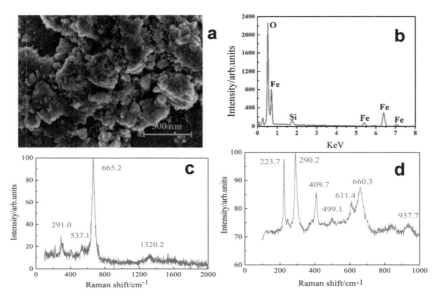

Figure 4. SEM images and EDS of wear scar of disc and Raman spectrum of steel ball/a-Si:H films: (**a**) SEM images and (**b**) EDS spectroscopy of wear scar disc at 600 °C. (**c**) Raman spectrum of wear scar on ball. (**d**) Raman spectrum of wear scar on disc.

3.3. Tribological Properties of DLC Films on Steel Ball/a-Si:H Films under Different Temperatures

Figure 5 shows CoF of DLC films on steel ball/a-Si:H films under different tribotest temperatures. At 200 °C, initial CoF is 0.1 and fluctuates to 0.38 until the end of tribotest. At 400 °C, initial CoF is 0.49 and then fluctuates to the maximum value of 0.56 and finally CoF decreases to below 0.1 after 1000 s. The average CoF is 0.08. At 600 °C, initial CoF is 0.36 and then goes down slowly to below 0.1 and average CoF is about 0.07. The antifriction behaviors of DLC films/a-Si:H films are different these of steel ball/a-Si:H films, especially in high temperature. At 400 °C, CoF of steel ball/a-Si:H films is low at the initial stage and fluctuates on a stable stage, however, CoF of DLC films/ a-Si:H films is high at the initial stage and then decreases slightly to low CoF after the maximum value. At 600 °C, CoF of steel ball/a-Si:H films reaches the maximum value and decreases slightly to low CoF at a stable stage, however, CoF of DLC films/a-Si:H films decreases to low CoF with the increase of sliding time.

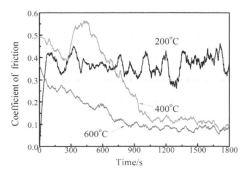

Figure 5. CoF of DLC films on steel ball/a-Si:H films under different temperatures.

Figure 6 shows the surface topography of the worn surface of ball and flat at 600 °C. The wear track width of flat is about 795.4 μm and the wear track width of ball is 1456.1 μm at 600 °C. There are also lots of black materials on the wear scar on the flat, however, there is not only wear debris in the wear scar but also few deep plough grooves in the circle wear scar on ball.

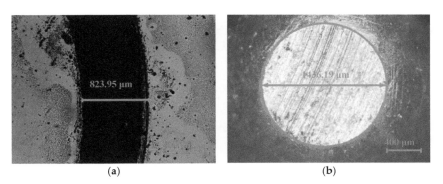

(a) **(b)**

Figure 6. Images of wear scar of DLC films on steel ball/a-Si:H films at 600 °C: (**a**) disc; (**b**) ball.

Figure 7 shows Raman spectra of DLC films/a-Si:H films at 600 °C. For ball, the most representative bands of hematite (α phase) are around 228.6 and 295.2 cm^{-1}. The 507.5 cm^{-1} band is due to SiC lattice vibrations that were recorded in the sample. The region of the Raman spectrum in which spectral features associated with carbon inclusions could be expected. The spectrum contains one strongly resolved band (1324.8 cm^{-1}) band that is probably due to carbon present (graphitic phase) at this point in the sample in the *sp*^{3} configuration. The Si–O–Si modes of silicate chains appear at 668.6 cm^{-1}. It can be seen that transverse (TO) at 1049.6 cm^{-1} Si modes appear weak in the spectra. Figure 7b shows Raman spectrum of the disc. There are bands of 227.9 cm^{-1} of α-Fe$_2$O$_3$ with A$_{1g}$ model, 287.4 cm^{-1} of α-Fe$_2$O$_3$ with E$_g$(3) model. The temperature produced by the friction heating will result in the oxidation of the steel substrate. Hence Raman spectrum shows significantly intense modes at 287.4 and 405.2 cm^{-1} which correspond to α-Fe$_2$O$_3$, but the Raman mode at 1308.2 cm^{-1} is not affected significantly. According to Raman measurements and tribotest results, there are mainly α-Fe$_2$O$_3$ with few SiC and carbon on ball and the oxides of α-Fe$_2$O$_3$ and SiO$_2$ on flat. Therefore, the friction pair exhibits better anti-friction behavior than those for DLC films/a-Si:H films at 600 °C because there are carbon-related materials on the contact surface.

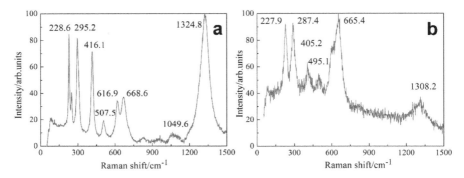

Figure 7. Raman spectrum of wear scar of DLC films/silicon films under different temperatures: (**a**) ball; (**b**) disc.

3.4. Tribological Properties of ZrO$_2$ Ball/a-Si:H Films under Different Temperatures

Figure 8 shows CoF of ZrO$_2$ ball/a-Si:H films under different tribotesting temperatures. At 200 °C, initial CoF is 0.35 and decreases to around 0.2 at the stable stage. At 400 °C, initial CoF is 0.3 and decreases to around 0.2. The average CoF is 0.2. At 600 °C, initial CoF is 0.22 and then goes down slowly to 0.1 and average CoF is about 0.07. It is found that CoF of ZrO$_2$ ball/a-Si:H films is relatively low at the initial stage and CoF is also low at the stage comparing other friction pairs, especially at high temperature.

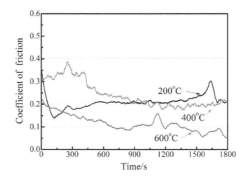

Figure 8. CoF of ZrO$_2$ ball/a-Si:H films under different temperatures.

3.5. Tribological Properties of Si$_3$N$_4$ Ball/a-Si:H Films under Different Temperatures

Figure 9 shows CoF of Si$_3$N$_4$ ball/a-Si:H films under different testing temperatures. At 200 °C, initial CoF is 0.3 and decreases to around 0.33 at the stable stage. At 400 °C, initial CoF is 0.3 and decreases to around 0.2. The average CoF is 0.21. At 600 °C, initial CoF is 0.24 and then decreases slowly to below 0.1 and average CoF is about 0.07. It is found that CoF of Si_3N_4 ball/a-Si:H films is also relatively low at the initial stage and CoF is also low at the stage comparing other friction pairs, especially in high temperature. It means that Si_3N_4 is suitable for using as frictional matted material for a-Si:H films and the friction pair exhibits lower than that of ZrO_2 ball, which is important to get super-low friction and high wear-resistance.

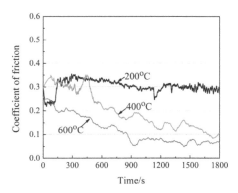

Figure 9. CoF of Si_3Ni_4 ball/a-Si:H films under different temperatures.

Figure 10 shows surface topography of the worn surface on ball and flat under different temperatures. The wear scar width of flat is about 775.7 μm and the wear scar width of ball is 889.5 μm at 600 °C. It is found that the width of Si_3N_4 ball/a-Si:H films is low. There are some black materials on the wear scar on flat and there are wide plough grooves in wear scar of ball; it seems that the ball surface looks smooth and few wear debris, which means that the iron oxides adhered hardly to Si_3N_4 ball and reduce the friction and adhesion.

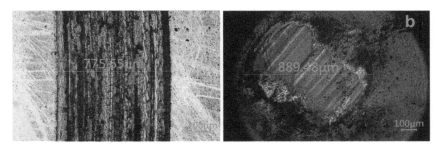

Figure 10. Images of wear scar of Si_3N_4 ball/a-Si:H films at 600 °C: (**a**) a-Si:H; (**b**) ball.

Figure 11 shows Raman spectrum of Si_3N_4 ball/a-Si:H films at 600 °C. Note the low frequency mode at 182.0 cm^{-1} because this is an external vibration model of Si_3N_4. The shifts of the bands at 182, 203, 861.8 and 926.7 cm^{-1} have been observed. These bands are the characteristic bands of Si_3N_4. The bands in the low frequency range at 615.8 and 658.8 cm^{-1} are associated with the overlapping of the symmetrical stretching vibrations and the bending vibrations of Si–O–Si bonds of silicate chains. Figure 11b shows the Raman spectrum of a flat. There are bands of 225.9 cm^{-1} of α-Fe_2O_3 with A_{1g} model, 291.9 cm^{-1} of α-Fe_2O_3 with $E_g(3)$ model. Therefore, the Raman spectrum shows a significantly intense mode at 409.9 cm^{-1} which corresponds to α-Fe_2O_3. According to Raman measurements and tribotest results, there is mainly Si_3N_4 or few α-Fe_2O_3 on ball and the composite oxide of α-Fe_2O_3 and SiO_2 on the flat. The friction pair exhibits better anti-friction behaviors than those for Si_3N_4 ball/a-Si:H films at 600 °C.

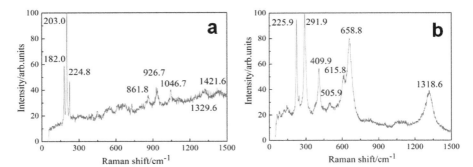

Figure 11. Raman spectrum of wear scar of Si₃N₄/a-Si:H films under different temperatures: (**a**) ball; (**b**) disc.

3.6. High Temperature Anti-Friction Mechanism of a-Si:H Films

Figure 12 shows the CoF of different friction pair materials and a-Si:H films under different tribotest temperatures. At 200 °C, CoF is very high (around 0.5) during high temperature tribotests for steel ball and DLC films on steel ball sliding against a-Si:H films. However, CoF is relatively low (around 0.2) for Si_3N_4 and ZrO_2 balls sliding against a-Si:H films. The reason maybe that the difference in hardness of the friction pair is low. When the temperature increases to 400 °C, DLC films started to be graphitized, even oxidized and the steel was oxidized with oxygen and water vapor under high contact pressure and high temperature conditions, especially for a-Si:H films on the ball contacting with the flat all the time and resulting in high flash temperature during friction and wear tests. There are mainly iron oxides at 400 °C, thus, CoF is low at the initial and stable stage. At 600 °C, there is α-Fe_2O_3 on the contact surface, and CoF is low even in the stable stage. There are iron oxides on the ball before the friction test and there are composite oxides of α-Fe_2O_3 and SiO_2 on flat, therefore, the friction pair is α-Fe_2O_3/α-Fe_2O_3 and SiO_2, which results in high temperature super-low friction [14]. There are self-generated composite oxides of α-Fe_2O_3 and SiO_2 on flat surfaces before the tribotest due to a high temperature oxidation reaction at 600°C. For steel ball, DLC films on ball and Si_3N_4 ball, CoF decreases with an increase in temperatures. For ZrO_2 ball, CoF is almost the same below 600 °C, and then decreases to super-low friction at 600 °C. It is shown that Si_3Ni_4 is suitable for hydrogenated amorphous silicon films according to tribotest results and Raman observations. This is because CoF is higher for ZrO_2 ball (0.21) than for Si_3N_4 ball (0.09) at 400 °C and CoF is the same for ZrO_2 ball (0.07) than for Si_3N_4 ball (0.07) at 600 °C. Moreover, CoF is higher for steel ball (0.36) than and almost same for DLC ball (0.08) for Si_3N_4 ball (0.09) at 400 °C, and CoF is almost same for steel ball (0.09) and DLC ball (0.07) as for Si_3N_4 ball (0.07) at 600 °C. Raman measurements show that oxygen reacts with the steel surface and a-Si:H films during the tribological process and produces complex oxide films, which are composed of α-Fe_2O_3 and SiO_2 on flat. However, not all tribological chemistry reaction products in this tribological process can be employed to improve high temperature anti-friction behaviors. There are different oxidation products due to tribological chemistry on the ball. There are α-Fe_2O_3 and Fe_3O_4, α-Fe_2O_3 and SiC, α-Fe_2O_3 and ZrO_2 and α-Fe_2O_3 and Si_3N_4 on ball for steel ball, DLC films, ZrO_2 and Si_3N_4 ball respectively [15]. The friction pair exhibits high temperature super-low friction when there are hard materials such as Si_3N_4 and soft material such as α-Fe_2O_3, which is important for the achievement of super-low friction of the friction system.

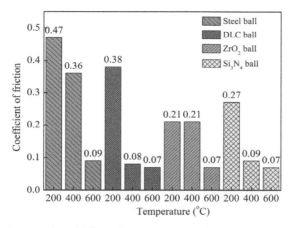

Figure 12. CoF of different friction pair materials and temperatures.

4. Conclusions

The effect of the friction pair materials on the antifriction behaviors of a-Si:H films is investigated under high temperature in open air and super-low friction mechanism of a-Si:H films-related friction system under high temperature is also discussed in the present paper. Conclusions can be summarized as follows.

- CoF of the friction system decreases from 200 to 600 °C independent of the friction pair materials. CoF of the friction system is as low as 0.07 at the stable stage at 600 °C in ambient air. The friction system exhibits excellent high temperature anti-friction behavior.
- The initial CoF is high for steel ball and DLC films on steel ball and low for ceramic ball due to high thermal stability of ceramic materials in ambient air event at 600 °C. The ceramic materials are suitable for tribological applications under high temperature due to the stable and initial low CoF of the friction system.
- Super-low friction of the friction system at the temperature of 600 °C is achieved independent of the friction pair materials. Moreover, Si_3N_4 is appropriate for a-Si:H films at a wide temperature, especially in high temperatures.
- Super-low friction of the a-Si:H films-related friction system is attributed to high temperature oxidation of a-Si:H films and the metal substrate and the tribochemical products including iron oxides and adhered to surface of ball. The tribochemical reaction generated between the contact surface and oxygen during sliding is beneficial to high temperature antifriction behaviors of hydrogenated amorphous silicon films.

Author Contributions: Conceptualization, Q.Z.; methodology, L.Q.; software, Q.Z.; validation, Q.Z.; Formal Analysis, L.Q.; Investigation, Q.Z.; Resources, Q.Z.; Data Curation, Q.Z.; Writing—Original Draft Preparation, Q.Z.; Writing—Review and Editing, Q.Z. Visualization, L.Q.; Supervision, Q.Z.; Project Administration, Q.Z.; Funding Acquisition, Q.Z.

Funding: The present work is funded by the National Natural Science Foundation of China (No. 51675409), Natural Science Basic Research Plan in Shaanxi Province of China (No. 2019JM-274), the Fundamental Research Funds for the Central Universities (No. xjj2017163) and the Open Project Program of Beijing Key Laboratory of Pipeline Critical Technology and Equipment for Deepwater Oil & Gas Development (No. BIPT2018001), and the key project of Shaanxi province Science and Technology Department (No. 2017ZDXM-GY-115).

Conflicts of Interest: The authors declare no conflict of interest. The funders had no role in the design of the study; in the collection, analyses, or interpretation of data; in the writing of the manuscript, or in the decision to publish the results. All authors agree to submit the report for publication.

References

1. Zhu, S.; Cheng, J.; Qiao, Z.; Yang, J. High temperature solid-lubricating materials: A review. *Tribol. Int.* **2019**, *133*, 206–223. [CrossRef]
2. Sliney, H.E. Solid lubricant materials for high temperatures—A review. *Tribol. Int.* **1982**, *15*, 303–315. [CrossRef]
3. Kumar, S.; Panwar, R.S.; Pandey, O. Effect of dual reinforced ceramic particles on high temperature tribological properties of aluminum composites. *Ceram. Int.* **2013**, *39*, 6333–6342. [CrossRef]
4. Li, J.; Xiong, D. Tribological properties of nickel-based self-lubricating composite at elevated temperature and counterface material selection. *Wear* **2008**, *265*, 533–539. [CrossRef]
5. Zeng, Q.; Eryilmaz, O.; Erdemir, A. Analysis of plastic deformation in diamond like carbon films–steel substrate system with tribological tests. *Thin Solid Films* **2011**, *519*, 3203–3212. [CrossRef]
6. Zeng, Q.; Erdemir, A.; Eryilmaz, O. Ultralow friction of ZrO_2 ball sliding against DLC films under various environments. *Appl. Sci.* **2017**, *7*, 938. [CrossRef]
7. Zeng, Q. Thermally induced super-low friction of DLC films in ambient air. *High Temp. Mater. Process.* **2018**, *37*, 725–731. [CrossRef]
8. Eryilmaz, O.; Zeng, Q.; Erdemir, A. Superlubricity of the DLC films-related friction system at elevated temperature. *RSC Adv.* **2015**, *5*, 93147–93154.
9. Zeng, Q.; Cai, S.; Li, S. High-temperature low-friction behaviors of γ-Fe_2O_3@SiO_2 nanocomposite coatings obtained through sol–gel method. *J. Sol-Gel Sci. Technol.* **2018**, *85*, 558–566. [CrossRef]
10. Zeng, Q.; Cai, S. Low-friction behaviors of Ag-doped γ-Fe_2O_3@SiO_2 nanocomposite coatings under a wide range of temperature conditions. *J. Sol-Gel Sci. Technol.* **2019**, *90*, 271–280. [CrossRef]
11. Zeng, Q.; Chen, T. Super-low friction and oxidation analysis of hydrogenated amorphous silicon films under high temperature. *J. Non Cryst. Solids* **2018**, *493*, 73–81. [CrossRef]
12. Lengsfeld, P.; Nickel, N.H.; Fuhs, W. Step-by-step excimer laser induced crystallization of a-Si:H. *Appl. Phys. Lett.* **2000**, *76*, 1680–1682. [CrossRef]
13. Jiang, Y.; Song, N.; Wang, C.; Pinna, N.; Lu, X. A facile synthesis of Fe_3O_4/nitrogen-doped carbon hybrid nanofibers as a robust peroxidase-like catalyst for the sensitive colorimetric detection of ascorbic acid. *J. Mater. Chem. B* **2017**, *5*, 5499–5505. [CrossRef]
14. Erdemir, A. A crystal-chemical approach to lubrication by solid oxides. *Tribol. Lett.* **2000**, *8*, 97–102. [CrossRef]
15. Zeng, Q.; Zhu, J.; Long, Y.; De Barros Bouchet, M.I.; Martin, J.M. Transformation-induced high temperature low friction behaviors of ZrO_2-steel system at temperatures up to 900 °C. *Mater. Res. Express* **2019**, *6*, 0865f5. [CrossRef]

Article

Crack-Growth Behavior in Thermal Barrier Coatings with Cyclic Thermal Exposure

Dowon Song [1], Taeseup Song [1,*], Ungyu Paik [1], Guanlin Lyu [2], Yeon-Gil Jung [2,*], Baig-Gyu Choi [3], In-Soo Kim [3] and Jing Zhang [4]

[1] Department of Energy Engineering, Hanyang University, Seoul 133-791, Korea; songdw@hanyang.ac.kr (D.S.); upaik@hanyang.ac.kr (U.P.)

[2] School of Materials Science and Engineering, Changwon National University, Changwon, Gyeongnam 641-773, Korea; lyuguanlin@naver.com

[3] High Temperature Materials Research Group, Korea Institute of Materials Science, 797 Changwondaero, Changwon, Gyeongnam 641-831, Korea; choibg@kims.re.kr (B.-G.C.); kis@kims.re.kr (I.-S.K.)

[4] Department of Mechanical and Engineering, Indiana University–Purdue University Indianapolis, Indianapolis, IN 46202-5132, USA; jz29@iupui.edu

* Correspondence: tssong@hanyang.ac.kr (T.S.); jungyg@changwon.ac.kr (Y.-G.J.); Tel.: +82-22-220-2333 (T.S.); +82-55-213-3712 (Y.-G.J.); Fax: +82-55-262-6486 (Y.-G.J.)

Received: 3 May 2019; Accepted: 3 June 2019; Published: 4 June 2019

Abstract: Crack-growth behavior in yttria-stabilized zirconia-based thermal barrier coatings (TBCs) is investigated through a cyclic thermal fatigue (CTF) test to understand TBCs' failure mechanisms. Initial cracks were introduced on the coatings' top surface and cross section using the micro-indentation technique. The results show that crack length in the surface-cracked TBCs grew parabolically with the number of cycles in the CTF test. Failure in the surface-cracked TBC was dependent on the initial crack length formed with different loading levels, suggesting the existence of a threshold surface crack length. For the cross section, the horizontal crack length increased in a similar manner as observed in the surface. By contrast, in the vertical direction, the crack did not grow very much with CTF testing. An analytical model is proposed to explain the experimentally-observed crack-growth behavior.

Keywords: thermal barrier coating; cyclic thermal fatigue; crack growth; initial crack length; failure

1. Introduction

Thermal barrier coatings (TBCs) are employed for the accommodation of the turbine-inlet temperature increase as well as protection of the hot components from severe operating conditions in gas turbine and jet engine systems [1–4]. A typical TBC system includes a thermal insulating ceramic top coat, metallic bond coat, and thermally-grown oxide (TGO), which results from oxidation of metallic elements diffused from the bond coat [5]. Yttria-stabilized zirconia (YSZ) with 7–8 wt.% yttria is commonly used for top-coat material because of its excellent thermomechanical properties, such as low thermal conductivity, relatively high coefficient of thermal expansion (CTE), and mechanical properties of fracture toughness and hardness [6,7]. In some cases, however, a bare metal substrate or metallic bond coat of rotational components is directly exposed to a flame when TBCs are delaminated or spalled because of crack propagation and coalescence during operation. This exposure can cause the fracture of rotational components as well as the other parts, which results in fatal problems. Some researchers have shown that the delamination of TBCs occurs just above the interface between the top coat and TGO layer [5,8–10]. Khan et al. [10] evaluated the thermal durability of an air-plasma-sprayed (APS) TBC through a thermal cyclic exposure test, indicating that the 8YSZ-based TBC is delaminated within the top coat around the interface between the top coat and the TGO layer. Accordingly, the investigation of crack propagation and its coalescence is essential for understanding the failure mechanism of TBCs, predicting the lifetime performance of TBCs, and designing reliable TBCs.

During actual operation, the TBC system is placed in severe circumstances [11,12]: (i) thermal stress from hot-gas exposure; (ii) mechanical stress caused by high-speed rotation; (iii) corrosive environment with Calcia–Magnesia–Alumina–Silica; (iv) erosion caused by direct flame and/or particles from outside; and (v) interaction through the diffusion between top and bond coats. Under these conditions, the failure of TBCs, especially plasma-sprayed TBCs, is explained by a complex mechanism with one or more combined phenomena [5,11,13–21]. (i) At the initial operation stage, the TGO layer is grown by oxidation of the bond coat. Further oxidation of the bond coat can be avoided owing to the uniformly grown TGO layer, which functions as a diffusion barrier. During thermal exposure, the TGO thickness increases with the undulating interface. As heating and cooling procedures continue; however, the TGO layer is cracked by interfacial stress resulting from CTE mismatch between the top and bond coats. Cracks can play a role in the oxygen path, so the bond coat suffers from further oxidation. (ii) As oxidation continues, Al is depleted and some other brittle oxides, such as chromia and spinel, can be formed by oxidation of Co, Ni, and Cr components around the TGO layer with volume change, which can cause crack nucleation and further oxidation, finally leading to TBC failure. On the other hand, (iii) high thermal stress, especially compressive stress in a hot area, is imposed on the surface of the coating during engine operation, and the surface area suffers deformation with stress relaxation. Then, a surface crack is initiated because of the tensile stress during cooling, resulting in delamination along the TBC to the bond coat interface.

Donohue et al. [22] suggested converting the energy release rate into toughness within dense vertically-cracked TBCs, indicating the positive impact of the segmented microstructure on long-crack toughness. The fracture toughness of plasma-sprayed TBC was investigated according to the aspects of processing, microstructure, and thermal aging [23]. Recently, there are extensive experimental work and analytical calculations on more complicated TBCs, such as multilayered structure [24–26], solution precursor plasma spray coating [27], and suspension plasma spray coating [28,29]. Their crack initiation and propagation under a thermal cyclic environment were investigated with analysis of mechanical and thermal properties.

In this study, crack-growth behavior just above the TGO layer was observed to understand the failure mechanism of TBCs. An initial crack was formed (i) on the TBC surface to simulate damage due to extrinsic factors (e.g., erosion or foreign object debris (FOD)) and (ii) within the top coat just above the interface between the top and bond coats in the cross section, which simulates the cracking initiation site due to bond coat oxidation and TGO growth in a typical APS coating. The crack growth behavior was investigated and described in detail through cyclic thermal fatigue (CTF) tests. An analytical model was employed to predict the residual stress distribution and fatigue crack-growth behavior. The results and analysis of this study can be helpful for further understanding of the TBC failure mechanism, resulting in the development of reliable TBC systems.

2. Experimental Procedure

2.1. Sample Preparation

In this study, typical 8YSZ TBC systems were prepared using commercial feedstock powders. The Ni-based superalloy (Nimonic 263, ThyssenKrupp VDM, Essen, Germany; nominal composition of Ni–20Cr–20Co–5.9Mo–0.5Al–2.1Ti–0.4Mn–0.3Si–0.06C, in wt.%) was used as a substrate in the shape of a disk and dimensions of 25 mm in diameter and 5 mm in thickness. Sandblasting using Al_2O_3 powder (particle size $\approx$ 420 μm) was performed before the deposition of the bond coat. A bond coat with a thickness of about 300 μm was formed on the substrate by the APS method, using AMDRY 9625 (Sulzer Metco Holding AG, Winterthur, Switzerland, the nominal composition of Ni–22Cr–10Al–1.0Y in wt.% and particle size 45–75 μm). After creating the bond coat, the top coat was deposited by the APS method with a thickness of about 600 μm, using METCO 204 C-NS (Sulzer Metco Holding AG,

Switzerland, $8Y_2O_3$–ZrO_2) and particle size of 45–125 µm. The fabrication parameters employed for the bond and top coats were recommended by the manufacturer; see Table 1.

Table 1. Parameters of air plasma spraying.

Parameter	Gun Type	Current (A)	Primary Gas, Ar (L/min)	Secondary Gas, H_2 (L/min)	Powder Feed Rate (g/min)	Spray Distance (mm)	Gun Speed (mm/s)	Turn Table Speed (mm/s)
Top coat	METCO-3MB	480	23.6	5.6	40	80	4	1300
Bond coat	METCO-3MB	420	28.3	5.6	30	80	4	1300

2.2. Crack Formation and Observation

To create the initial cracks on the surface, the selected TBC samples before crack formation were polished using silicon carbide paper and fine polished with a 1 µm diamond paste. On the other hand, the selected TBC samples for the cross-sectional cracks were sectioned and given a final polish with a 1 µm diamond paste. The initial surface crack was generated in the center of the polished top coat surface, while the cross-sectional crack was generated above the interface of top and bond coats within 100 µm. A micro-indenter (HM-114, Mitutoyo Corp., Kawasaki City, Japan) with a Vickers tip was used for the formation of cracks through the indentation load with loading levels of 30 and 50 N for the surface, but only 30 N of load was employed on the cross section because of the formation of large imprints (>100 µm).

CTF tests were performed for both the surface and cross-sectional-cracked TBCs to impose thermal fatigue conditions and observe the growth behavior of the induced cracks. The TBC samples were held in the furnace with a dwell time of 40 min at a temperature of 1121 °C and then naturally cooled for 20 min in air. The CTF tests were performed up to 640 cycles and the criterion of delamination was defined as about 25% spallation of the top coat. At least five specimens were tested for each crack formation condition, and each specimen had only one imprint to avoid interrelation of stresses and/or cracks between the imprints in different locations. The microstructure was observed by scanning electron microscope (SEM, JEOL Model JSM-5610, Tokyo, Japan) to investigate the crack-growth behavior. The samples after 10, 20, 40, 80, 160, and 320 cycles in the CTF tests were cleaned to observe the microstructure around the induced cracks and to measure the crack length grown after the CTF tests. The crack length was measured from the center of the indentation imprints. The surface crack length was measured regardless of the direction, while vertical and horizontal cracks were measured on the cross section.

3. Modeling of Residual Stress and Crack-Growth Behavior in TBC Samples

In cyclic thermal exposure environments, thermally-induced residual stress forms in the TBC multilayers because of differential coefficients of thermal expansion in each layer [30,31]. In this work, a linear elastic analytical model was employed to understand the residual stress distribution and resultant cracking phenomena, as in [30–33]. In the model, the interface between the substrate and the bond coat was defined as the origin line, where $z = 0$. The distance from layer i to the substrate was defined as h_i [32,34,35]. The thermal residual stress in the substrate and the i_{th} coating layer, which is related to the misfit strain ε_i and bending curvature K, can be expressed as [32,33]:

$$\sigma_s = E_s[\varepsilon_s + K(z + \delta)] \ (-t_s \ \leq \ z \ \leq \ 0) \tag{1}$$

$$\sigma_i = E_i[\varepsilon_i + K(z + \delta)] \ (1 \ \leq \ i \ \leq \ n, \ h_{i-1} \ \leq \ z \ < \ h_i) \tag{2}$$

where E_s and E_i are Young's moduli of the substrate and i_{th} coating layer, respectively. δ is the distance from the bending axis, where the bending strain is zero. ε_i, ε_s, δ, and K can be individually expressed as [33]:

$$\varepsilon_i = \Delta\alpha\Delta T + \sum_{k=1}^{n} \frac{E_k t_k}{E_s t_s}(\alpha_k - \alpha_i)\Delta T \tag{3}$$

$$\varepsilon_s = -\sum_{i=1}^{n} \frac{E_i t_i}{E_s t_s}\Delta\alpha\Delta T \tag{4}$$

$$\delta = \frac{t_s}{2} - \sum_{i=1}^{n} \frac{E_i t_i}{E_s t_s}(2h_{i-1} + t_i) \tag{5}$$

$$K = -\sum_{i=1}^{n} \frac{6E_i t_i \Delta\alpha\Delta T}{E_s t_s^2} \tag{6}$$

where α is the CTE, k is the coating layers range from 1 to n, and t_i is the thickness of the i_{th} layer.

4. Results

4.1. Crack Initiation

The images around the indentation imprints formed by different loading levels on the surface of the TBC are shown in Figure 1. Figure 1A,B is imprints generated by loading levels of 30 and 50 N, respectively, and the white arrows indicate induced cracks. Crack formation initiated from the center of the rhombus through the angular points and edges regardless of direction, and showed larger rhombus-shaped imprints as well as longer crack length in the indentation load of 50 N, compared to 30 N. The as-coated microstructure image and the induced cracks on the cross-sectional area are shown in Figure 2. The typical APS-coated microstructure was observed with some defects like pores and splat boundaries. The red-dotted line designates the interface between the top and bond coats, suggesting the imprint was formed just above the interface. The high-resolution back-scattering emission mode image of the white-dotted box from the normal SEM image of Figure 2B is shown in Figure 2C. The horizontal crack that was parallel to the interface was evidently formed longer than that in the vertical direction.

Figure 3 shows the initial crack lengths before the CTF test with the indented position, loading level, and crack direction. The surface crack length with different loads of 30 and 50 N were 101 ± 17 and 121 ± 30 μm, respectively. On the other hand, the cross-sectional crack lengths induced by 30 N were noticeably different depending on the direction. The vertical crack length was 50 ± 10 μm, while the horizontal crack length was 153 ± 7 μm, which was larger than the 50 N loaded on the surface.

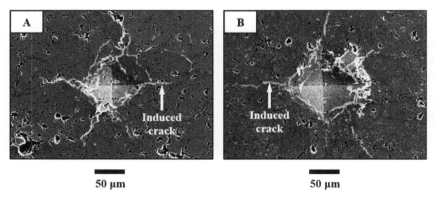

Figure 1. Surface images of Thermal Barrier Coatings (TBCs) with cracks induced by indentation: (**A**) 30 N and (**B**) 50 N.

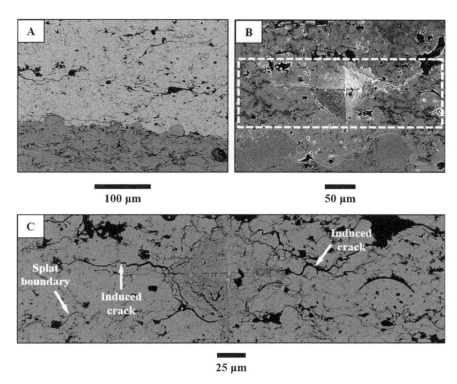

Figure 2. Cross-sectional images of TBCs with cracks induced by an indentation load of 30 N: (**A**) as-prepared image; (**B**) image of crack generation; and (**C**) highly-magnified image of the boxed area.

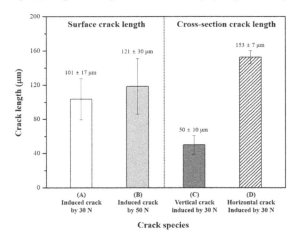

Figure 3. Crack lengths measured on the surface and cross-sectional images before cyclic thermal fatigue (CTF) tests.

4.2. Crack Propagation

Crack coalescence and increase of crack dimension due to the damage accumulation from thermal stress were detected during CTF tests, as shown in Figures 4 and 5, respectively, which were observed after 320 cycles. The crack length formed on the surface was increased through their linkage, and microstructural degradation was observed, including defects such as pores and small cracks. At the same time, the dimension of the surface crack was increased during the CTF tests about 20–100 μm, showing degraded surface microstructure.

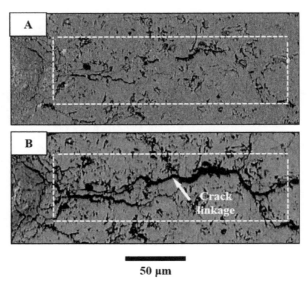

50 μm

Figure 4. Surface crack-growth behavior during CTF tests: (**A**) as-prepared crack and (**B**) crack grown after 320 cycles.

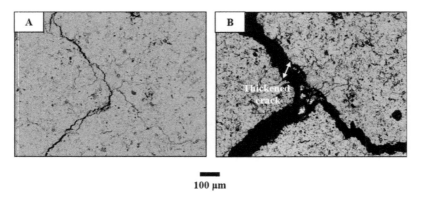

100 μm

Figure 5. Surface crack thickening during CTF tests: (**A**) as-prepared crack and (**B**) thickened crack after 320 cycles.

The crack-growth behavior on the cross section during CTF tests is shown in Figure 6. The cracks formed in the direction vertical to the interface did not grow compared with the horizontal crack, while crack coalescence and thickening were observed in the horizontal crack with an undulating shape.

Overall, the microstructure was degraded after the CTF tests, showing increased defects, such as pores and small cracks.

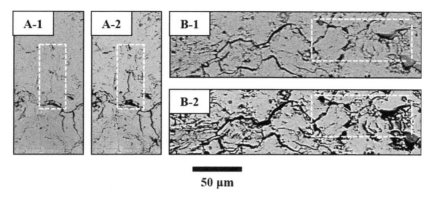

Figure 6. Crack-growth behavior on the cross section during CTF tests: (**A**) vertical crack and (**B**) horizontal crack. Each number indicates crack images: (**1**) before test and (**2**) after 320 cycles.

4.3. Crack Growth to Failure

The crack-growth behavior on the surface is shown in Figures 7 and 8 with cycle during CTF tests. The crack lengths were measured through SEM images after 10, 20, 40, 80, 160, and 320 cycles. The dotted and solid curves are empirical data fits for each crack length grown during CTF tests for the initial cracks formed by 30 and 50 N, respectively. The vertical dotted and solid lines indicate the average failure cycle number in the CTF tests, respectively, indicating that the nominal numbers of cycles to failure for each TBC with cracks formed by 30 and 50 N were 593 and 460 cycles, respectively. The crack-growth behavior showed a similar trend with the number of cycles, independent of initial crack length. The nominal difference of crack length with applied load was changed from 20 μm in the initial stage to 50 μm after 320 cycles between 30 and 50 N, with linear slopes of 0.37 ± 0.16 and 0.41 ± 0.17, respectively. In the failure point, each of the computed crack lengths were about 189–392 and 244–381 μm for 30 and 50 N, respectively.

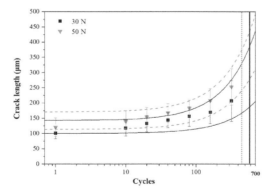

Figure 7. Variation of crack length on the surface during CTF tests. Dotted and solid curves indicate empirical data fits for 30 and 50 N, respectively. Dotted and solid vertical lines are the failure cycles of TBCs with cracks formed by 30 and 50 N, respectively.

On the other hand, comparable crack-growth behavior for the initial cracks formed by 30 N on the cross section is shown in Figure 8, displaying longer crack lengths in the horizontal direction.

The dotted and solid curves are empirical data fits for the horizontal and vertical cracks, respectively, grown during the CTF tests. The dotted vertical line indicates average cycles for TBC failure in CTF tests, with 396 cycles. The nominal difference in the initial lengths between the horizontal and vertical cracks gap was about 100 μm with linear slopes of 0.15 ± 0.08 and 0.52 ± 0.21, respectively, and the gap was increased to about 180 μm after 320 cycles. Each crack length in the failure could be expected to be about 217–419 and 70–141 μm on the cross section for the horizontal and vertical cracks, respectively.

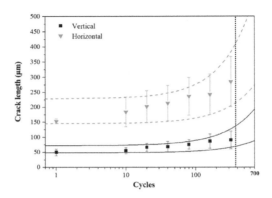

Figure 8. Variation of crack length on the cross section during CTF tests. Dotted and solid curves indicate empirical data fits for the horizontal and vertical cracks, respectively. The dotted vertical line is the failure cycles of TBCs with cracks formed by 30 N.

4.4. Modeling of Residual Stress Distribution and Fatigue Crack-Growth Behavior

The calculated residual stress distribution in the TBC sample is shown in Figure 9. As shown in the figure, in the top coat 8YSZ layer, there was extensive compressive residual stress, with maximum stress on the top coat interface. Similar to the results shown in Figures 7 and 8, the crack lengths in decreasing order were 30 N in the horizontal direction of cross section > 50 N on surface > 30 N on surface > 30 N in the vertical direction of the cross section.

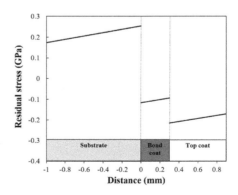

Figure 9. Calculated residual stress distribution in the TBC sample.

5. Discussion

5.1. Crack Initiation Behavior

Typical microstructures of YSZ-based APS-TBCs were observed on both the surface and cross section with some defects, such as pores, splat boundaries, and cracks, as shown in Figures 1 and 2.

The cracks connected with the rhombus-shaped imprints suggest that the induced crack formation was initiated from the angular points as well as the edge of the imprints during the indentation loading procedure. Moreover, the embedded defects, such as pores, can obstruct the formation of the cracks, but cracks beyond the defects were occasionally observed in both cases. However, the cracks on the surface and cross section are induced by different mechanisms, as it can be seen from microstructural images. On the surface, the imprint size and crack length were determined by the loading level regardless of the direction. However, the direction of the crack is a crucial factor in determining the crack length in the cross section. The vertical crack length was less than half of the horizontal crack length, indicating that the vertical crack is more difficult to form than the horizontal crack in cross section. This is because of the intrinsic characteristics of the APS deposition method. During APS deposition, the instantaneously-melted feedstock powder is sprayed onto the substrate from the perpendicular direction of the interface, resulting in horizontal splat boundaries, which are an obstacle to the formation of the vertical cracks. Meanwhile, the horizontal cracks are formed more easily along the horizontal splat boundaries as intergranular cracks. Consequently, three-times-longer crack length and undulating shape were observed in the horizontal direction on the cross section, as shown in Figure 3.

Basically, typical APS-TBCs contain some defects randomly, so a broad deviation of the initial crack length is observed in just one imprint. Moreover, a larger variation is obtained depending on the indented area, even when the same loading is imposed. However, on the cross section the crack lengths are almost identical regardless of the direction. In the case of surface cracks, the indentation load was imposed perpendicularly to the splat boundary surface. By contrast, the indentation load was parallel to the splat boundary surface on the cross section where in-plane tensile stress is included when the feedstock is cooled after splat [36]. This leads to a detachment of coatings through relatively easy crack growth in the horizontal direction during CTF tests.

5.2. Crack-Growth Behavior

In the APS-TBC system, the crack propagation is continued through linkage and coalescence of microcracks and discontinuities due to damage evolution during temperature change [9,37]. The surface crack-growth behavior was found to be similar regardless of the loading level. As shown in Figure 4, the surface cracks were coalesced because of thermal stresses and propagated through existing defects, such as pores, splat boundaries, and small cracks. Macroscopically, the crack thickness was enlarged because of repeating thermal expansion and contraction, resulting in partial spalling on the surface with the lengthened and thickened cracks. On the other hand, the crack-growth behavior on the cross section depended on the direction to the interface, as shown in Figure 6. Vertical cracks were almost never generated and grown up in the perpendicular direction to most of the splat boundaries, showing a slight increase in thickness. However, horizontal cracks grew through the linkage among existing splat boundaries and pores, which have stresses and low bonding energy, observed in the shape of undulations; this can be evidence of intergranular fracture [38]. In this study, the descriptive crack-growth behavior of conventional APS-TBCs was mainly investigated through thermal cycling tests. The crack-growth behavior based on the porosity and mechanical properties will be further studied as a future work.

5.3. Threshold Crack Length for Failure

The crack-growth behavior on the surface with the number of cycles in CTF tests was similar with loading level and direction, showing similar linear slope and calculated crack length ranges of 189–392 and 244–381 μm for 30 and 50 N at the failure point, respectively. On the other hand, the crack-growth behavior on the cross section was considerably different from that on the surface. As explained previously, the formation of vertical cracks was inhibited by the splat boundaries, while horizontal cracks were formed with relative ease. During CTF tests, the nominal difference of crack length starting at about 100 μm increased to about 180 μm after 320 cycles on the cross section, expecting calculated crack lengths of 70–141 and 217–419 μm for the vertical and horizontal cracks at the failure point, respectively. This is because of the originally imposed stresses during coating formation, paving a path along which cracks can grow more easily. Eventually, the threshold crack length can be considered as suggested above in cyclic thermal exposure conditions, especially in typical YSZ-based TBC systems. Thus, the probability of coating failure will be higher and coating reliability is reduced when cracks increase larger than the threshold crack length.

Even when the same load of 30 N was imposed on the surface and cross section, more rapid crack growth was observed in the horizontal crack on the cross section. This can be explained by the following argument. First, the inherent microstructure affects the crack propagation behavior, showing a kind of lamellar structure of splats. The other is thermal stresses during the CTF tests. During the CTF test, the stress is caused by CTE mismatch between the top and bond coats (CTEs of 8YSZ: $10.7 \times 17.5 \times 10^{-6} \text{ K}^{-1}$, bond coat: $17.5 \times 10^{-6} \text{ K}^{-1}$) [7,39]. The surface cracks are positioned above the top coat with a thickness of 600 μm, while the cross-section cracks are located just above the interface between top and bond coats. Greater stresses are imposed on the horizontal crack of the cross section in the repeated heating and cooling, and the cracks on the surface suffer comparatively weak stresses.

5.4. Modeling of Residual Stress Distribution and Fatigue Crack-Growth Behavior

As shown in Figure 9, higher residual tensile stress existed on the surface of the 8YSZ top coat than in the middle of the coating. This stress distribution explains the experimentally-observed crack length sequence in Figures 7 and 8 (i.e., 50 N on surface > 30 N on surface > 30 N in the vertical direction of the cross section). The crack length of 30 N in the horizontal direction of the cross-section case is higher than the above three cases; this is due to the unique splat microstructure formed in the APS process, which is not accounted for in the residual stress model. The residual stress model is isotropic and does not capture the anisotropic feature of TBCs. Tracking the crack-growth behavior within the isotropic dense microstructure shows clear observation rather than the anisotropic porous microstructure, due to the limited contents of defects in dense TBC, such as pores and splat boundaries [22]. TBCs can be reasonably approximated as transversely isotropic materials, where the properties are the same for all directions in the plane, such as along the coating surface, but different from the deposition direction. The horizontal direction in TBCs is the weakest because of splat and void formation during the APS process. This explains why the 30 N in the horizontal direction of the cross-section case has the highest crack-growth length among the four cases.

6. Conclusions

Cyclic thermal exposure tests were conducted for the TBCs with cracks induced by micro-indentation to investigate the crack-growth behavior of YSZ-based APS-TBCs as a function of initial crack position and length. The cracks on the surface grew in a similar trend independent of the loading level, while the cracks formed on the cross section showed a different growth behavior with respect to the direction to the interface between top and bond coats. Crack thickening and coalescence were observed together with crack growth during cyclic thermal exposure. The surface showed threshold crack lengths with ranges of 189–392 and 244–381 μm for the 30 and 50 N loads at the failure point, respectively, and the cross section with cracks formed by 30 N was 70–141 and 217–419 μm for the vertical and horizontal cracks, respectively. Therefore, failure criteria in the TBC systems can be proposed in view of crack length on both the surface and cross section.

Author Contributions: Conceptualization, D.S., T.S., and Y.-G.J.; Methodology, D.S., T.S., G.L., Y.-G.J., and J.Z.; Software, J.Z.; Formal Analysis, D.S., and G.L.; Investigation, D.S., T.S., G.L., Y.-G.J., B.-G.C., I.-S.K., and J.Z.; Writing—Original Draft Preparation, D.S.; Writing—Review and Editing, D.S., T.S., U.P., Y.-G.J., B.-G.C., I.-S.K., and J.Z.; Supervision, T.S., U.P., and Y.-G.J.; Project Administration, T.S., U.P., and Y.-G.J.; Funding Acquisition, T.S., U.P., and Y.-G.J.

Funding: This research was funded by "Human Resources Program in Energy Technology" (No. 20194030202450) and "Power Generation and Electricity Delivery grant" (No. 20181110100310) of the Korea Institute of Energy Technology Evaluation and Planning (KETEP), a granted financial resource from the Ministry of Trade, Industry, and Energy, Korea, and by the Fundamental Research Program of the Korean Institute of Materials Science (KIMS, No. PNK5620).

Conflicts of Interest: The authors declare no conflicts of interest.

References

1. Clarke, D.; Levi, C. Materials design for the next generation thermal barrier coatings. *Annu. Rev. Mater. Res.* **2003**, *33*, 383–417. [CrossRef]
2. Evans, A.G.; Mumm, D.; Hutchinson, J.; Meier, G.; Pettit, F. Mechanisms controlling the durability of thermal barrier coatings. *Prog. Mater. Sci.* **2001**, *46*, 505–553. [CrossRef]
3. Miller, R.A. Current status of thermal barrier coatings—An overview. *Surf. Coat. Technol.* **1987**, *30*, 1–11.
4. Padture, N.P.; Gell, M.; Jordan, E.H. Thermal barrier coatings for gas-turbine engine applications. *Science* **2002**, *296*, 280–284. [CrossRef] [PubMed]
5. Rabiei, A.; Evans, A. Failure mechanisms associated with the thermally grown oxide in plasma-sprayed thermal barrier coatings. *Acta Mater.* **2000**, *48*, 3963–3976. [CrossRef]
6. Beshish, G.; Florey, C.; Worzala, F.; Lenling, W. Fracture toughness of thermal spray ceramic coatings determined by the indentation technique. *JTST* **1993**, *2*, 35–38. [CrossRef]
7. Cao, X.; Vassen, R.; Stoever, D. Ceramic materials for thermal barrier coatings. *J. Eur. Ceram. Soc.* **2004**, *24*, 1–10. [CrossRef]
8. Zhou, Y.; Hashida, T. Thermal fatigue failure induced by delamination in thermal barrier coating. *Int. J. Fatigue* **2002**, *24*, 407–417. [CrossRef]
9. Trunova, O.; Beck, T.; Herzog, R.; Steinbrech, R.; Singheiser, L. Damage mechanisms and lifetime behavior of plasma sprayed thermal barrier coating systems for gas turbines—Part I: Experiments. *Surf. Coat. Technol.* **2008**, *202*, 5027–5032. [CrossRef]
10. Khan, A.N.; Lu, J. Behavior of air plasma sprayed thermal barrier coatings, subject to intense thermal cycling. *Surf. Coat. Technol.* **2003**, *166*, 37–43.
11. Czech, N.; Esser, W.; Schmitz, F. Effect of environment on mechanical properties of coated superalloys and gas turbine blades. *Mater. Sci. Technol.* **1986**, *2*, 244–249. [CrossRef]
12. Tamura, M.; Takahashi, M.; Ishii, J.; Suzuki, K.; Sato, M.; Shimomura, K. Multilayered thermal barrier coating for land-based gas turbines. *J. Therm. Spray Technol.* **1999**, *8*, 68–72.
13. Wu, B.; Chang, E.; Chang, S.; Chao, C. Thermal cyclic response of yttria-stabilized zirconia/CoNiCrAlY thermal barrier coatings. *Thin Solid Films* **1989**, *172*, 185–196. [CrossRef]
14. Miller, R.A.; Lowell, C.E. Failure mechanisms of thermal barrier coatings exposed to elevated temperatures. *Thin Solid Films* **1982**, *95*, 265–273. [CrossRef]
15. Schlichting, K.W.; Padture, N.; Jordan, E.; Gell, M. Failure modes in plasma-sprayed thermal barrier coatings. *Mater. Sci. Eng. A* **2003**, *342*, 120–130.
16. Tsipas, S.; Golosnoy, I.; Clyne, T.; Damani, R. The effect of a high thermal gradient on sintering and stiffening in the top coat of a thermal barrier coating system. *JTST* **2004**, *13*, 370–376. [CrossRef]
17. Zhou, B.; Kokini, K. Effect of surface pre-crack morphology on the fracture of thermal barrier coatings under thermal shock. *Acta Mater.* **2004**, *52*, 4189–4197. [CrossRef]
18. Kokini, K.; Takeuchi, Y.; Choules, B. Thermal crack initiation mechanisms on the surface of functionally graded ceramic thermal barrier coatings. *Ceram. Int.* **1996**, *22*, 397–401. [CrossRef]
19. Choules, B.D.; Kokini, K.; Taylor, T.A. Thermal fracture of ceramic thermal barrier coatings under high heat flux with time-dependent behavior.: Part 1. Experimental results. *Mater. Sci. Eng. A* **2001**, *299*, 296–304.
20. Choules, B.; Kokini, K.; Taylor, T. Thermal fracture of thermal barrier coatings in a high heat flux environment. *Surf. Coat. Technol.* **1998**, *106*, 23–29. [CrossRef]
21. Hutchinson, J.; Evans, A. On the delamination of thermal barrier coatings in a thermal gradient. *Surf. Coat. Technol.* **2002**, *149*, 179–184.
22. Donohue, E.M.; Philips, N.R.; Begley, M.R.; Levi, C.G. Thermal barrier coating toughness: Measurement and identification of a bridging mechanism enabled by segmented microstructure. *Mater. Sci. Eng. A* **2013**, *564*, 324–330. [CrossRef]

23. Dwivedi, G.; Viswanathan, V.; Sampath, S.; Shyam, A.; Lara-Curzio, E. Fracture toughness of plasma-sprayed thermal barrier ceramics: Influence of processing, microstructure, and thermal aging. *J. Am. Ceram. Soc.* **2014**, *97*, 2736–2744.

24. Viswanathan, V.; Dwivedi, G.; Sampath, S. Engineered multilayer thermal barrier coatings for enhanced durability and functional performance. *J. Am. Ceram. Soc.* **2014**, *97*, 2770–2778. [CrossRef]

25. Viswanathan, V.; Dwivedi, G.; Sampath, S. Multilayer, multimaterial thermal barrier coating systems: Design, synthesis, and performance assessment. *J. Am. Ceram. Soc.* **2015**, *98*, 1769–1777. [CrossRef]

26. Levi, C.G. Emerging materials and processes for thermal barrier systems. *Curr. Opin. Solid State Mater. Sci.* **2004**, *8*, 77–91. [CrossRef]

27. Jordan, E.H.; Xie, L.; Gell, M.; Padture, N.; Cetegen, B.; Ozturk, A.; Ma, X.; Roth, J.; Xiao, T.; Bryant, P. Superior thermal barrier coatings using solution precursor plasma spray. *J. Therm. Spray Technol.* **2004**, *13*, 57–65.

28. VanEvery, K.; Krane, M.J.; Trice, R.W.; Wang, H.; Porter, W.; Besser, M.; Sordelet, D.; Ilavsky, J.; Almer, J. Column formation in suspension plasma-sprayed coatings and resultant thermal properties. *J. Therm. Spray Technol.* **2011**, *20*, 817–828. [CrossRef]

29. Seshadri, R.C.; Dwivedi, G.; Viswanathan, V.; Sampath, S. Characterizing suspension plasma spray coating formation dynamics through curvature measurements. *J. Therm. Spray Technol.* **2016**, *25*, 1666–1683.

30. Guo, X.; Lu, Z.; Jung, Y.-G.; Li, L.; Knapp, J.; Zhang, J. Thermal property, thermal shock and thermal cycling behavior of lanthanum zirconate based thermal barrier coatings. *Metall. Mater. Trans. E* **2016**, *3*, 64–70. [CrossRef]

31. Zhang, J.; Guo, X.; Jung, Y.-G.; Li, L.; Knapp, J. Lanthanum zirconate based thermal barrier coatings: A review. *Surf. Coat. Technol.* **2016**, *323*, 18–29. [CrossRef]

32. Hsueh, C.H. Thermal stresses in elastic multilayer systems. *Thin Solid Films* **2002**, *418*, 182–188. [CrossRef]

33. Zhang, X.; Xu, B.; Wang, H.; Wu, Y. An analytical model for predicting thermal residual stresses in multilayer coating systems. *Thin Solid Films* **2005**, *488*, 274–282. [CrossRef]

34. Townsend, P.H.; Barnett, D.M.; Brunner, T.A. Elastic relationships in layered composite media with approximation for the case of thin films on a thick substrate. *J. Appl. Phys.* **1987**, *62*, 4438–4444. [CrossRef]

35. Tsui, Y.C.; Clyne, T.W. An analytical model for predicting residual stresses in progressively deposited coatings Part 1: Planar geometry. *Thin Solid Films* **1997**, *306*, 23–33. [CrossRef]

36. Xie, L.; Chen, D.; Jordan, E.H.; Ozturk, A.; Wu, F.; Ma, X.; Cetegen, B.M.; Gell, M. Formation of vertical cracks in solution-precursor plasma-sprayed thermal barrier coatings. *Surf. Coat. Technol.* **2006**, *201*, 1058–1064. [CrossRef]

37. Chen, W.; Wu, X.; Dudzinski, D. Influence of thermal cycle frequency on the TGO growth and cracking behaviors of an APS-TBC. *J. Therm. Spray Technol.* **2012**, *21*, 1294–1299. [CrossRef]

38. Liang, B.; Ding, C. Thermal shock resistances of nanostructured and conventional zirconia coatings deposited by atmospheric plasma spraying. *Surf. Coat. Technol.* **2005**, *197*, 185–192. [CrossRef]

39. Vaßen, R.; Kerkhoff, G.; Stöver, D. Development of a micromechanical life prediction model for plasma sprayed thermal barrier coatings. *Mater. Sci. Eng. A* **2001**, *303*, 100–109. [CrossRef]

Article

Crack-Resistance Behavior of an Encapsulated, Healing Agent Embedded Buffer Layer on Self-Healing Thermal Barrier Coatings

Dowon Song [1], Taeseup Song [1,*], Ungyu Paik [1], Guanlin Lyu [2], Yeon-Gil Jung [2,*], Baig-Gyu Choi [3], In-Soo Kim [3] and Jing Zhang [4]

1   Department of Energy Engineering, Hanyang University, Seoul 133-791, Korea; songdw@hanyang.ac.kr (D.S.); upaik@hanyang.ac.kr (U.P.)
2   School of Materials Science and Engineering, Changwon National University, Changwon, Gyeongnam 641-773, Korea; lyuguanlin@naver.com
3   High Temperature Materials Research Group, Korea Institute of Materials Science, 797 Changwondaero, Changwon, Gyeongnam 641-831, Korea; choibg@kims.re.kr (B.-G.C.); kis@kims.re.kr (I.-S.K.)
4   Department of Mechanical and Energy Engineering, Indiana University–Purdue University Indianapolis, Indianapolis, IN 46202-5132, USA; jz29@iupui.edu
*   Correspondence: tssong@hanyang.ac.kr (T.S.); jungyg@changwon.ac.kr (Y.-G.J.); Tel.: +82-2-2220-2333 (T.S.); +82-55-213-3712 (Y.-G.J.); Fax: +82-55-262-6486 (Y.-G.J.)

Received: 3 May 2019; Accepted: 29 May 2019; Published: 31 May 2019

Abstract: In this work, a novel thermal barrier coating (TBC) system is proposed that embeds silicon particles in coating as a crack-healing agent. The healing agent is encapsulated to avoid unintended reactions and premature oxidation. Thermal durability of the developed TBCs is evaluated through cyclic thermal fatigue and jet engine thermal shock tests. Moreover, artificial cracks are introduced into the buffer layer's cross section using a microhardness indentation method. Then, the indented TBC specimens are subject to heat treatment to investigate their crack-resisting behavior in detail. The TBC specimens with the embedded healing agents exhibit a relatively better thermal fatigue resistance than the conventional TBCs. The encapsulated healing agent protects rapid large crack openings under thermal shock conditions. Different crack-resisting behaviors and mechanisms are proposed depending on the embedding healing agents.

Keywords: crack healing; encapsulation; healing agent; thermal barrier coating; thermal durability

---

1. Introduction

Thermal barrier coatings (TBCs) are used to enhance the energy efficiency and durability of hot components of gas turbines or aerospace engines [1–5]. Typical TBCs are fabricated on the substrate of an Ni-based superalloy. MCrAlY (M = Ni and/or Co) is usually deposited to form a bond coat layer, which can enhance the bonding strength between the metallic substrate and ceramic top coat and protect the substrate from oxidation and corrosion [5–7]. Then, yttria-stabilized zirconia (YSZ) is typically used as a top coat material because of its excellent thermomechanical properties, such as low thermal conductivity (≈ 2.3 W/(m·K) at 1000 °C), and high coefficient of thermal expansion (CTE), which is similar to the bond coat (top: $\approx 11 \cdot 10^{-6}$/°C, bond: $\approx 14 \times 10^{-6}$/°C) [8–13].

During the actual operating service, TBCs are exposed to severe conditions with the following complex phenomena [14,15]: thermomechanical stresses, erosion, corrosion by foreign objects, diffusion, oxidation, phase transformation, and sintering. In particular, abrupt thermomechanical stress during starting up and shutting down is one of the key factors for damage accumulation, which can lead to formation and propagation of cracks and ultimately result in the failure of the TBCs [16–18]. Because of these harsh environmental factors, heavy costs are incurred for repairing, refurbishing, or replacing the hot components.

Several attempts have been made to enhance the thermal durability of TBCs. From the coating design perspective, Taylor [19] developed dense vertically cracked (DVC) TBCs, which greatly improved the strain tolerance. Graded and multilayer coatings were also proposed to reduce residual stress and enhance the cohesion and structural stability [20,21]. On the other hand, evaporation technologies such as electron beam physical vapor deposition methods emerged in the 1980s [22], forming columnar and intercolumnar microstructures of the top coat, which can noticeably enhance strain tolerance [23]. Padture et al. [24] demonstrated the feasibility of the solution precursor plasma spray (SPPS) as a new processing method because SPPS coatings have unique microstructures that contain features of both conventional plasma-sprayed TBCs and DVC TBCs. Similarly, suspension plasma spraying was suggested as a new method that employed suspension of submicron powders as a feedstock, resulting in fine grains and pores with dense microstructures as well as a high segmentation crack densities [25,26].

Recently, Derelioglu et al. [27] suggested the concept of self-healing TBCs, in which B-alloyed $MoSi_2$ was introduced as a potential healing agent. During thermal exposure, $MoSi_2$ was decomposed and oxidized, forming new solid bonding with the matrix material and filling the cracks. The self-healing concept and potential of $MoSi_2$ as a healing agent were proved. Furthermore, the healing agents were encapsulated by a sol-gel method to prevent their loss during coating fabrication, showing enhancement of oxidation resistance [28]. Chen et al. [29] developed self-shielding healing particles, which produced an oxygen impermeable Al_2O_3 shell, and identified crack-healing behavior during thermal cycling tests. Ouyang et al. [30] introduced a SiC-based healing layer on the surface of the top coat, and showed the filling of the surface cracks and improved oxidation and spallation resistance. Suggested healing agents from above previous studies contain Si in common, which can flow and fill the cracks due to fluidity of glass SiO_2 after oxidation [27]. So, Si is considered a potential candidate as a new healing agent. During operation, Si can be oxidized, which causes volume expansion, flowing, and filling of the crack gaps. Moreover, the oxidized SiO_2 can be dissolved into the ZrO_2 matrix [31], and it finally forms $ZiSiO_4$ when the solubility limits are reached above 1100 °C [32,33]. This new solid bonding mechanism is expected to enhance the interfacial stability between the splats, rather than exist as empty space.

The purpose of this research is to investigate the crack-resisting behavior of Si and encapsulated Si as potential healing agents. Specifically, the healing agents are encapsulated by a sol-gel-based glassification process to prevent premature oxidation and unintended reaction. The thermal durability is evaluated, and crack-healing behavior is investigated with artificial cracks. The crack-resisting behavior and mechanism of the healing agent are analyzed and elaborated.

2. Experimental Procedures

2.1. Healing Agent Powder Encapsulation Process

To produce a protective shell for the Si healing agents, the binary glassification process from our previous studies was employed [34–36]. This method involved the formation of a glass phase, which was synthesized through the sol-gel reaction and glassification between silicate and sodium alkoxide, resulting in a glassificated SiO_2 shell around the particle surface [36]. The detailed encapsulation process is described in Figure 1. Prior to the encapsulation process, the healing agent—silicon powder (Si, 325 mesh, 99% trace metal basis, Sigma-Aldrich, Saint Louis, MO, USA)—was dispersed in methyl alcohol (methanol, CH_3OH, 99.5%, Samchun Chemicals, Seoul, Korea) using an ultrasonic bath (Branson 3510, Branson Ultrasonics Corporation, Danbury, CT, USA) for 30 min at 60 °C. The binary precursor solution was composed of tetraethyl orthosilicate (TEOS, $Si(OC_2H_5)_4$, 98%, Sigma-Aldrich) and sodium methoxide solution (NaOMe, CH_3ONa, 25 wt% in methanol, Sigma-Aldrich) as SiO_2 and Na_2O precursors, respectively.

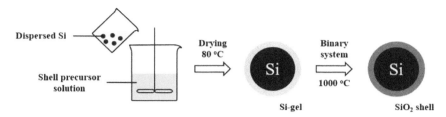

Figure 1. Schematic diagram of the encapsulation process for healing agents.

The composition of the binary precursor solution followed our previous studies [34–36] with the molar ratio of 0.18:1.5 of TEOS and NaOMe, which was stirred for just a few minutes at room temperature. Then, the dispersed healing agent was added to the solution, and the mixture was left in an oven at 80 °C for 24 h to undergo the hydrolysis reaction. The resulting gel was vacuum-filtered using filter paper (F1001, CHMLAB, Barcelona, Spain) and washed to remove unreacted precursors with deionized water. Finally, to produce a uniform glassificated SiO_2 shell, the coated Si powders were heat-treated at 1000 °C for 60 min in air.

The morphology of the encapsulated healing agents was investigated using scanning electron microscopy (SEM, JSM-5610, JEOL, Tokyo, Japan). In particular, to observe the cross-section of the microscale powder, the encapsulated powder was cold vacuum mounted by resin and finely polished with 1 μm diamond paste and polishing cloth. The polished area was Au-coated by a sputtering system (108 Auto Sputter Coater, Cressington, UK), which prevented charging during SEM observation. The composition was also analyzed by an energy dispersive spectrometer (EDS, Oxford Instruments, Abingdon, UK) and X-ray diffractometer (XRD, Mini Flex II, Rigaku, Japan) using Cu Kα radiation (λ = 1.5418 Å) with the operation condition of a step size 0.02° and a scan speed of 3°/min. The particle sizes of healing agents before and after encapsulation were analyzed by laser diffraction (Mastersizer 2000 Hydro 2000S, Malvern Instruments, Herrenberg, Germany). The encapsulated particles were gently ground to prevent the encapsulation shell from crushing to submicron particles, then each sample (100 mg) was dispersed in deionized water using an ultrasonic bath.

2.2. Coating Fabrication

In this study, the healing agents' embedded buffer layer was introduced between the bond coat and conventional top coat as a crack-resisting layer, following the coating designs in Figure 2. Three types of coating specimens were prepared: each structure of a conventional TBC with a YSZ top coat (sample A), a crack-healing TBC with healing agents embedded in a buffer layer (sample B), and a crack-healing TBC with encapsulated healing agents (sample C), which are described in Figure 2A–C, respectively. A disk-shaped Ni-based superalloy (Nimonic 263, a nominal composition of Ni–20Cr–20Co–5.9Mo–0.5Al–2.1Ti–0.4Mn–0.3Si–0.06C, in wt%, Thyssen Krupp VDM, Werdohl, Germany) was used as a substrate, with dimensions of 25 mm in diameter and 5 mm in thickness. The substrate was sandblasted using Al_2O_3 powder (particle size: ≈ 420 μm) before bond coat fabrication, and the bond coat was deposited by high-velocity oxygen fuel (Diamond Jet-2600 DJM, Sulzer Metco Holding AG, Winterthur, Switzerland) methods with the thickness of 150–200 μm using AMDRY 9954 (Oerlikon Metco AG, Pfäffikon, Switzerland, nominal composition of Co–32Ni–21Cr–8Al–0.5Y in wt% and particle size of 11–63 μm). The buffer layer and top coat were fabricated by atmospheric plasma spray (APS, 9MB coating system, Sulzer Metco Holding AG) methods for thicknesses of 100–150 and 400–450 μm, respectively. METCO 204 C-NS (Oerlikon Metco AG, 8 wt% Y_2O_3 doped in ZrO_2, particle size of 45–140 μm) feedstock was used for the top coat material. For the buffer layer, YSZ feedstock was blended with each normal Si and encapsulated Si powder. The healing agent and YSZ with a volume ratio of 10:90 were mechanically mixed through ball milling for 24 h. All employed top and bond coat fabrication parameters as suggested by the manufacturer; see Table 1.

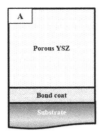 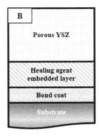 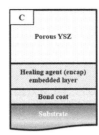

Figure 2. Schematic diagram of coating designs: (**A**) a conventional thermal barrier coating (TBC) (sample A), (**B**) a crack-healing TBC with a buffer layer (sample B), and (**C**) a crack-healing TBC with encapsulated agents (sample C). YSZ = yttria-stabilized zirconia.

Table 1. Parameters of air plasma spraying.

Parameter	Gun Type	Current (A)	Primary Gas, Ar (L/min)	Secondary Gas, H$_2$ (L/min)	Powder Feed Rate (g/min)	Spray Distance (mm)	Gun Speed (mm/s)
Top coat	METCO-3MB	480	23.596	5.663	40	80	4

2.3. Thermal Durability Evaluation and Analysis

Cyclic Thermal Fatigue (CTF) and Jet Engine Thermal Shock (JETS) tests were performed for the prepared specimens to investigate the crack-resisting behavior under thermal durability tests. First, for the CTF tests, the specimens were held in the furnace with a dwell time of 40 min at 1100 °C to impose a thermal fatigue condition and then naturally cooled in air for 20 min as one cycle [37]. The CTF tests were performed until the TBCs failed. The failure criterion was defined as more than 50% spallation area of the top coat. The JETS test was conducted to evaluate the thermal shock resistance using a system designed with a jet engine motif; the top coat surface was exposed for 25 s to a direct flame with a temperature of about 1400 °C, directly quenched by N$_2$ gas for 25 s, and then followed by natural cooling for 1 min as one cycle [38]. The JETS tests were performed with the target of 2000 cycles, and the failure criteria were defined as a spallation area of more than 20% of the top coat or any cracking specifically at the interface between top and bond coats. At least three samples were tested for each thermal durability test. The microstructure before and after thermal durability tests was observed using SEM and EDS.

To investigate the crack-resisting behavior in detail, the as-coated specimens were cut and polished using SiC paper, and they were finely polished with 1 and 3 μm diamond pastes and polishing sheets. The polished cross-sectional area was artificially cracked using a microindenter (HM-114, Mitutoyo Corp., Kawasaki, Japan) with a Vickers tip with the loading level of 10 N for 30 s. The artificial cracks were located above the interface between the top and bond coats within the buffer layer. Then, they were heat-treated at 1000 °C for 100 h, and their healing reaction and detailed crack-resisting behavior were analyzed by SEM and EDS.

3. Results and Discussion

3.1. Protection of Healing Agents and Resistance Against Premature Oxidation

The microstructure of the Si healing agent powder before and after encapsulation is shown in Figure 3. Figure 3A,B shows the normal Si and encapsulated Si powder surface morphologies, respectively. Each number indicated the components' intensity of Si, O, and Na from EDS mapping. Compared with the normal Si powder, the encapsulated powder had a relatively smooth surface morphology, which was evidence of a successful glassification process [36]. This morphology of glassificated shell implied that some agglomerated healing particles were covered by the glass shell immediately. The EDS mapping image shows that the encapsulated powder contained Na, which consisted of the shell from the glassification process. Further, encapsulated powders were mounted and fine-polished to observe the cross-sectional microstructure and more detailed shell morphology. Figure 3C shows the obtained microstructure and EDS mapping analysis. Encapsulated Si powder (light area) was surrounded by mounting resin (dark gray), showing unremarkable differences in the morphologies. The existence of the oxygen intensity indicated that the encapsulation process successfully produced the sub-micron-scale SiO_2 shell (see Figure 3C-1,C-2). This suggested that the healing agents had a glassificated shell, which could protect the healing agent from premature oxidation during coating fabrication. Figure 4 shows the XRD analysis of the healing agents before and after the encapsulation processes. The cubic phase Si was observed in both specimens. After the encapsulation processes, a small cristobalite SiO_2 peak was observed as a shell component. The results of microstructural and phase analyses indicated that both crystalline and amorphous SiO_2 shells were well glassificated in the encapsulation process.

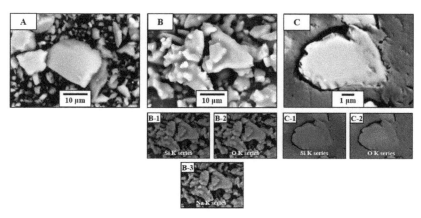

Figure 3. Powder morphology and component distribution of healing agent: (**A**) normal Si powder, (**B**) Si powder encapsulated by a binary system, and (**C**) magnified cross section of Si powder encapsulated by a binary system. Each number indicates energy dispersive spectrometer (EDS) mapping results of Si (**B-1**,**C-1**), O (**B-2**,**C-2**), and Na (**B-3**), respectively.

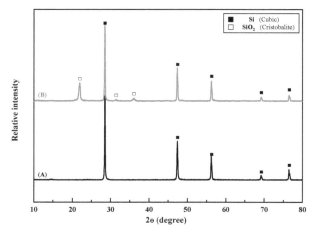

Figure 4. X-ray diffractometer (XRD) analysis results of Si powder encapsulated by a binary system: (**A**) normal Si, and (**B**) Si powder encapsulated by a binary system.

The particle size of the healing agents was analyzed for both the normal and encapsulated powders, the results of which are shown in Figure 5. The cumulative mass of the particles are shown in the Supplementary Table S1. Both samples showed similar size distributions, even after the encapsulation process. The encapsulated sample B showed that it contained more particles, with a particle size below 4 μm and above 20 μm, which resulted from the grinding after encapsulation and agglomeration, respectively. Similar particle size distributions indicated that the encapsulation process produced only a sub-micron-scale shell as well as the agglomerated particles, which corresponded to the microstructural observations in Figure 3B,C. In the APS process, the Si healing agent can be more easily oxidized than YSZ because it has a lower melting point and plasma-spray-forming temperature (10,000–15,000 K), resulting in the loss of its function [39]. However, the successfully produced submicron shell can protect healing agents, so it was expected that premature oxidation could be prevented. With the above discussion, the encapsulated healing agent was capable of being employed in the actual coating of specimens.

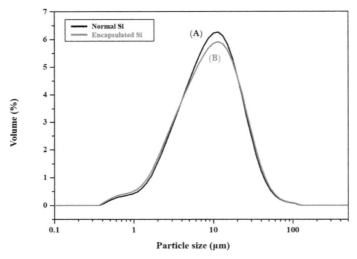

Figure 5. The particle size distribution of (**A**) normal Si, and (**B**) Si powder encapsulated by a binary system.

3.2. Thermal Durability Evaluation

All specimens were fabricated with the coating design shown in Figure 2. The cross-sectional microstructure of the as-coated specimens is shown in Figure 6. Each healing agent was embedded differently within the buffer layer, depending on the encapsulation process.

In Figure 6A-1,A-2, the conventional YSZ (sample A) showed a typical TBC microstructure fabricated by the APS method, showing splat boundaries, microcracks, and pores. All samples showed a sound bond coat and an interfacial condition without noticeable growth of a thermally grown oxide (TGO) layer.

The Si healing agent without encapsulation (sample B) had the morphology of an undulating shape and was embedded between the YSZ splats in the form of particles (Figure 6B-1,B-2). However, fewer Si healing agents were observed than the blended volume ratio in the as-prepared coating, which resulted from the evaporation of Si because of its low melting point [40].

The microstructure of the encapsulated healing-agent-embedded specimen (sample C) is shown in Figure 6C-1,C-2. The healing agents were embedded in the shape of the particles, which were similar to sample B. However, some of the healing agents were observed in the agglomerated condition, resulting from the encapsulation process (shown in Figure 6C-2). EDS-point mapping analysis of Figure 6C-1 is attached in Supplementary Figure S1 to prove the existence of the healing agent within the buffer layer. There was a relatively large number of embedded healing agents in comparison to normal Si (See Figure 6B-1,C-1. This result indicated that the encapsulation shell and larger particle size, as a result of agglomeration, reduced their evaporation [40].

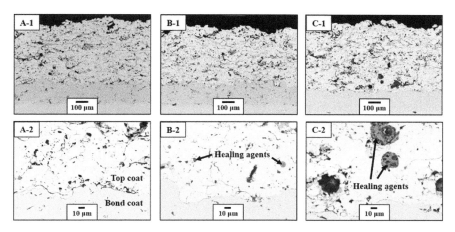

Figure 6. Cross-sectional microstructures of as-coated samples: (**A-1,A-2**) a conventional TBC (sample A), (**B-1,B-2**) a crack-healing TBC with a buffer layer (sample B), and (**C-1,C-2**) a crack-healing TBC with encapsulated agents (sample C). Each number indicates the magnification of (100×) and (500×), respectively.

Figure 7 shows the magnified microstructures of samples B and C with the component analysis around the healing agents. In Figure 7A, the healing agents in sample B were located between the YSZ splats, filling the empty splat boundaries. However, the encapsulated Si was in the shape of agglomerated powder as a kind of a cluster, which formed during heat treatment of the encapsulation process. The agglomerated healing particle consisted of pores, Si (light gray), partially oxidized Si (SiO_x, gray), and shell component SiO_2 (dark gray), which were based on the EDS-point analysis in Supplementary Figure S2. These results confirmed that the glassificated shell covered the healing agents well and protected them from premature oxidation during the APS process. The effects of healing agent distribution and morphology on the thermal durability and crack-healing behavior were investigated according to the encapsulation.

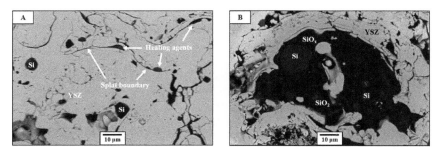

Figure 7. Magnified microstructure around the healing agent in as-coated samples: (**A**) sample B, and (**B**) sample C.

Figure 8 shows the cross-sectional microstructure around the delaminated area after CTF tests. During thermal cycling, different thermo-mechanical properties between the matrix and healing agent could develop stress, so only 10 vol% of healing agents was blended with YSZ to minimize the development of stress, which was founded in other previous studies [27,29].

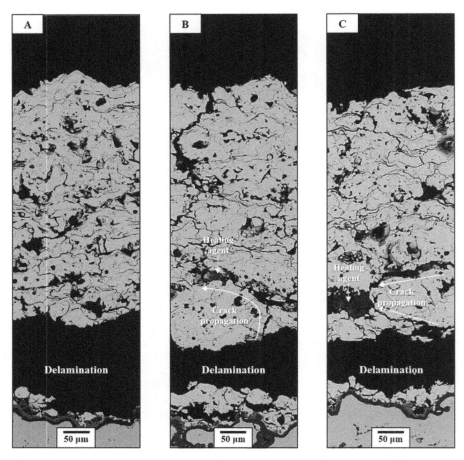

Figure 8. Cross-sectional microstructures after CTF tests: (**A**) sample A, (**B**) sample B, and (**C**) sample C.

Samples A, B, and C were delaminated after 1067, 1143, and 1103 cycles of CTF tests on average, respectively. Healing-agent-embedded TBCs (samples B and C) showed comparable thermal fatigue resistance to conventional YSZ. The continuous growth of TGO and some spinel oxides was observed at the interface between the top and bond coats, showing similar, common interfacial conditions. In sample A, small microcracks and pores were generated compared with the as-coated condition, while relatively thickened and enlarged cracks were generated within both buffer layers in samples B and C. Most of the cracks just above the bond coat grew horizontally because of the stress caused by CTE mismatch, which resulted in delamination, while the propagation of some cracks was inhibited by the healing agents. During the temperature change, the stress from CTE mismatch dominantly accelerated the thickening, linkage, and coalescence of cracks, resulted in the propagation of cracks. However, the healing agents inhibited propagation of these cracks because of their existence, which functioned as a ductile particle elaborated with an extrinsic toughening mechanism [41]. During thermal exposure, the healing agents were oxidized to SiO_2, which had a glass transition temperature of about 1200 °C. Then, the shell components were glassificated and acted as ductile particles, resulting in the enhancement of fracture toughness by plastic deformation [42,43]. Although they showed similar thermal fatigue resistance, the slightly enhanced thermal durability in sample B can be explained by increased toughening probability, which resulted from a relatively uniform distribution and the fine size of the healing agents. However, sample C with encapsulated Si showed a slight decrease in thermal fatigue lifetime compared to the normal Si. This was because the concentration of agglomerated Si particles rather limited its healing function. To achieve noticeable enhancement of thermal fatigue lifetime, these limitations were countered by optimization of encapsulation process or postprocessing for uniform powder without agglomeration.

The cross-sectional microstructures after the JETS tests are shown in Figure 9. All the specimens survived 2000 cycles of JETS tests. The noticeable delamination or failure of TBCs was not observed in common. Even though they had similar lifetime performances, they had quite different microstructural degradation behaviors. In common, the bond coats showed sound conditions without evident oxidation and TGO growth, while severe TGO growth (including spinel phase) was observed after the CTF test. The most severe microstructural degradation was observed in sample A, which showed large crack formations because of the repeated thermal shocks. Vertical cracks initiated from the surface because of rapid volume shrinkage during N_2 quenching, and they grew into large cracks through preexisting splats or pores under repeat of thermal shock, which was observed similarly in previous work [44]. Large horizontal cracks were generated near the interface because there was thermal stress from CTE mismatch between the top and bond coats, which could result in the failure of TBCs. Crack formation around the surface of the top coat was similarly observed in samples B and C. However, a different crack propagation was observed near the interface. Horizontal cracks formed and propagated to the healing agents during the JETS test. Although horizontal cracks were not clearly observed, the sub-micron-healing agent in sample B did not show noticeable crack-resisting behavior. This was because the crack scale had obviously larger openings and propagations than microscale Si healing particles, which embedded in the form of particles. On the other hand, the embedded Si particle, while agglomerated as healing agents in sample C, inhibited the rapid crack opening and propagation as a ductile particle under thermal shock conditions, which was not fully oxidized because of the relatively short thermal exposure period compared with the CTF test. Detailed crack-resisting mechanisms during the tests are elaborated on in Section 3.3.

3.3. Crack-Resisting Mechanisms

Figure 10 shows the cross-sectional microstructure around the indentation imprints, which induced artificial cracks within the crack-healing buffer layer in sample B. The crack propagation-resisting behavior related to healing agents was investigated. The typical self-healing system was designed to seal nano- or microcracks before the occurrence of extensive damage. However, in the air-plasma sprayed TBC system, there were preexisting defects such as splat boundaries and microcracks, so crack-filling behavior against the opened defects was mainly investigated [27]. In Figure 10A–C, the dotted rhombus box indicated indentation imprints (about 50 μm diagonal), and emerged cracks were indicated by white arrows. Crack-filling behavior was observed in Figure 10E,F by the healing agents, which showed volume expansion because of oxidation. The formation of $ZrSiO_4$ (zircon) evidenced new solid bonds between the YSZ matrix and Si healing agents, which could enhance the interfacial stability as well as heal the cracks by filling (see the magnified image in Figure 10D and EDS-point and mapping analysis in Supplementary Figure S3). Moreover, crack growth, like coalescence and/or linkage, was inhibited by the embedded healing agents, which can be observed within the YSZ splat boundaries in Figure 10G,H.

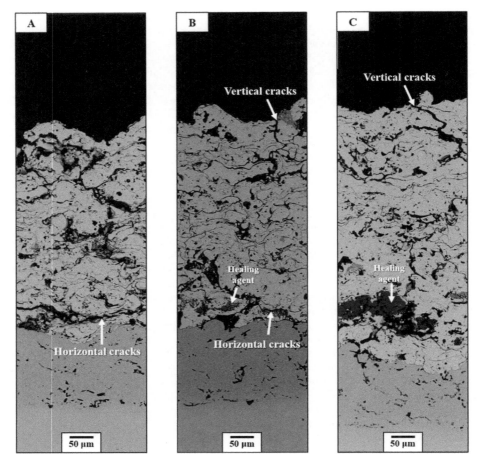

Figure 9. Cross-sectional microstructures after JETS tests: (**A**) sample A, (**B**) sample B, and (**C**) sample C.

The cross-sectional microstructure of sample C is shown in Figure 11 to investigate the crack-resisting behavior of encapsulated healing agents. In Figure 11A–C, the dotted rhombus box and white arrows indicated the indentation imprints (about 50 μm diagonal) and emerged cracks around the healing agents, respectively. In the magnified microstructure of Figure 11D, solid bonding was formed, the behavior of which was similar to the unencapsulated healing agents in sample B. The cracks around the healing agents were filled and propagated no further, especially around the unagglomerated particles (Figure 11E,F). However, some small microcracks were not fully filled around the agglomerated healing agents because the protective shell accommodated the volume expansion by oxidation. Even though the microcracks were partially filled, it could still prevent severe crack propagation that could lead to catastrophic failure [45]. In Figure 11G, large cracks were initiated because of the abrupt stress resulting from the CTE mismatch and TGO growth between the top and bond coats. The volume expansion of healing agent could generate stress, but the agglomerated healing agents contained some pores as a kind of a cluster, which accommodated some extent of stress (see the Figure 11F). Therefore, it was considered that stress by expansion was not dominant compared to the stress by CTE mismatch and TGO growth. As shown in Figure 11H,I, the microcracks and splat boundary were thickened from the interface. However, these cracks, which can finally cause delamination, stopped growing by branching into small cracks within the agglomerated healing agents, observed commonly in sample C.

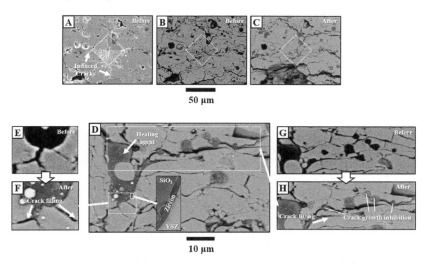

Figure 10. Microstructure around the indentation imprints in sample B before and after heat treatment. Microstructures of the as-coated sample are shown in (**A**), (**B**), (**E**), and (**G**), and those after heat treatment are shown in (**C**), (**D**), (**F**), and (**H**).

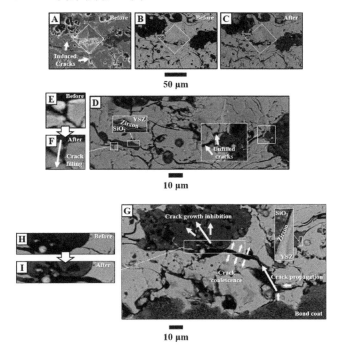

Figure 11. Microstructure around the indentation imprints in sample C before and after heat treatment. Microstructures of the as-coated sample are shown in (**A**), (**D**), and (**G**), and those after heat treatment are shown in (**B**), (**C**), (**E**), (**F**), and (**H**).

The crack-resisting behavior of Si healing agents can be elaborated on with the following three mechanisms: (i) healing agents that are located between splat boundaries form zircon as a new solid bonding, which enhances the resistance of tensile stress and results in less delamination of TBC; (ii) healing agents, with their partially unmelted shapes, can reduce the near-crack-tip stress as ductile particles and fill small cracks, preventing microcrack opening; and (iii) agglomerated healing agents above the interface between the top and bond coats can inhibit large crack propagation by branching into small cracks within the healing agents, although they cannot stop small crack openings through crack filling.

Based on the results above, repeating out-of-plane tensile stress can accumulate damage and cause coalescence and linkage of discontinuities such as microcracks and splat boundaries. Sample B has a relatively uniform distribution of healing agents with a fine particle size, so the healing agent can effectively stop the crack opening and form new solid bonding all over the buffer layer, which results in thermal durability and, especially, thermal fatigue resistance. On the other hand, large crack propagations, because of the abrupt stress from rapid temperature changes during the JETS test, were blocked by the agglomerated healing agent above the interface in sample C. This elaborates on the enhanced thermal shock resistance of sample C, as it has a relatively more sound microstructure than sample B without noticeable large cracks after the JETS tests.

However, even though the healing agents filled some cracks and blocked the crack opening successfully, they cannot fully fill the microcracks around them nor can they fill large cracks because of their poor fluidity [46,47]. This can be overcome by increasing the fluidity or decreasing the viscosity at the operating temperature by doping some appropriate contents or modifying the encapsulation process [27]. Furthermore, the optimization of particle size distribution and volume ratio of healing agents will be studied in future work.

4. Conclusions

In this work, a novel TBC system with a buffer layer embedded with Si-based crack-healing agents has been developed and evaluated. Using thermal durability tests, the crack-resisting behaviors and mechanisms of Si, and encapsulated Si, and the related mechanisms are presented. The main contributions are as follows.

- An encapsulation process is developed to cover the healing agents, preventing them from premature oxidation or evaporation during coating fabrication.
- The TBCs with a crack-healing buffer layer show comparable thermal durability in both the CTF and JETS tests.
- Crack-resisting mechanisms are elaborated on depending on the distribution and shape of healing agents through the observation of crack-healing behaviors.

Supplementary Materials: The following are available online at http://www.mdpi.com/2079-6412/9/6/358/s1, Figure S1: EDS mapping analysis around the healing agents in as-coated samples from Figure 6C-1; Figure S2: EDS point-analysis around the healing agents in as-coated samples from Figure 7A,B; Figure S3: EDS point- and mapping analysis around the healing agents after heat treatment from the magnified image in Figure 10C; Table S1: Particle diameters at 10%, 50%, and 90% of the cumulative mass of (A): normal Si, and (B) encapsulated Si from Figure 5.

Author Contributions: Conceptualization, D.S., T.S. and Y.-G.J.; Methodology, D.S., T.S., G.L., Y.-G.J. and J.Z.; Formal analysis, D.S. and G.L.; Investigation, D.S., T.S., G.L., Y.-G.J., B.-G.C., I.-S.K. and J.Z.; Writing-Original Draft Preparation, D.S.; Writing-Review and Editing, D.S., T.S., U.P., Y.-G.J., B.-G.C., I.-S.K. and J.Z.; Supervision, T.S., U.P. and Y.-G.J.; Project Administration, T.S., U.P. and Y.-G.J.; Funding Acquisition, T.S., U.P. and Y.-G.J.

Funding: This research was funded by "Human Resources Program in Energy Technology (No. 20194030202450)" and "Power Generation & Electricity Delivery grant (No. 20181110100310)" of the Korea Institute of Energy Technology Evaluation and Planning (KETEP); a granted financial resource from the Ministry of Trade, Industry & Energy, Korea; and by Fundamental Research Program of the Korean Institute of Materials Science (KIMS, No. PNK5620).

Conflicts of Interest: The authors declare no conflict of interest.

References

1. Miller, R.A. Current status of thermal barrier coatings—An overview. *Surf. Coat. Technol.* **1987**, *30*, 1–11. [CrossRef]

2. Padture, N.P.; Gell, M.; Jordan, E.H. Thermal barrier coatings for gas—Turbine engine applications. *Science* **2002**, *296*, 280–284. [CrossRef]

3. Evans, A.G.; Mumm, D.; Hutchinson, J.; Meier, G.; Pettit, F. Mechanisms controlling the durability of thermal barrier coatings. *Prog. Mater. Sci.* **2001**, *46*, 505–553. [CrossRef]

4. Clarke, D.; Levi, C. Materials design for the next generation thermal barrier coatings. *Annu. Rev. Mater. Res.* **2003**, *33*, 383–417. [CrossRef]

5. Strangman, T.E. Thermal barrier coatings for turbine airfoils. *Thin Solid Films* **1985**, *127*, 93–106. [CrossRef]

6. Haynes, J.A.; Ferber, M.; Porter, W. Thermal cycling behavior of plasma—Sprayed thermal barrier coatings with various MCrAlX bond coats. *J. Therm. Spray Technol.* **2000**, *9*, 38. [CrossRef]

7. Zhou, C.; Wang, N.; Wang, Z.; Gong, S.; Xu, H. Thermal cycling life and thermal diffusivity of a plasma—Sprayed nanostructured thermal barrier coating. *Scr. Materialia* **2004**, *51*, 945–948. [CrossRef]

8. Cao, X.; Vassen, R.; Stoever, D. Ceramic materials for thermal barrier coatings. *J. Eur. Ceram. Soc.* **2004**, *24*, 1–10. [CrossRef]

9. Vaßen, R.; Kerkhoff, G.; Stöver, D. Development of a micromechanical life prediction model for plasma sprayed thermal barrier coatings. *Mater. Sci. Eng. A* **2001**, *303*, 100–109. [CrossRef]

10. Hasselman, D.; Johnson, L.F.; Bentsen, L.D.; SYED, R.; LEE, H.L.; SWAIN, M.V. Thermal diffusivity and conductivity of dense polycrystalline Zr0. *Am. Ceram. Soc. Bull* **1987**, *66*, 799–806.

11. Hayashi, H.; Saitou, T.; Maruyama, N.; Inaba, H.; Kawamura, K.; Mori, M. Thermal expansion coefficient of yttria stabilized zirconia for various yttria contents. *Solid State Ion.* **2005**, *176*, 613–619. [CrossRef]

12. Cheng, J.; Jordan, E.; Barber, B.; Gell, M. Thermal/residual stress in an electron beam physical vapor deposited thermal barrier coating system. *Acta Mater.* **1998**, *46*, 5839–5850. [CrossRef]

13. Pan, D.; Chen, M.; Wright, P.; Hemker, K. Evolution of a diffusion aluminide bond coat for thermal barrier coatings during thermal cycling. *Acta Mater.* **2003**, *51*, 2205–2217. [CrossRef]

14. Czech, N.; Esser, W.; Schmitz, F. Effect of environment on mechanical properties of coated superalloys and gas turbine blades. *Mater. Sci. Technol.* **1986**, *2*, 244–249. [CrossRef]

15. Tamura, M.; Takahashi, M.; Ishii, J.; Suzuki, K.; Sato, M.; Shimomura, K. Multilayered thermal barrier coating for land—Based gas turbines. *J. Therm. Spray Technol.* **1999**, *8*, 68–72. [CrossRef]

16. Sumner, I.; Ruckle, D. Development of improved—Durability plasma sprayed ceramic coatings for gas turbine engines. In Proceedings of the 16th Joint Propulsion Conference, Hartford, CT, USA, 30 June–2 July 1980.

17. Chang, G.C.; Phucharoen, W.; Miller, R.A. Behavior of thermal barrier coatings for advanced gas turbine blades. *Surf. Coat. Technol.* **1987**, *30*, 13–28. [CrossRef]

18. Chang, G.; Phucharoen, W.; Miller, R. Finite element thermal stress solutions for thermal barrier coatings. *Surf. Coat. Technol.* **1987**, *32*, 307–325. [CrossRef]

19. Taylor, T.A. Thermal barrier coating for substrates and process for producing it. U.S. Patent 5,073,433, 17 December 1991.

20. Duvall, D.; Ruckle, D. Ceramic thermal barrier coatings for turbine engine components. In Proceedings of the ASME 1982 International Gas Turbine Conference and Exhibit, London, UK, 18–22 April 1982.

21. Musil, J.; Fiala, J. Plasma spray deposition of graded metal—Ceramic coatings. *Surf. Coat. Technol.* **1992**, *52*, 211–220. [CrossRef]

22. Schulz, U.; Leyens, C.; Fritscher, K.; Peters, M.; Saruhan-Brings, B.; Lavigne, O.; Dorvaux, J.-M.; Poulain, M.; Mévrel, R.; Caliez, M. Some recent trends in research and technology of advanced thermal barrier coatings. *Aerosp. Sci. Technol.* **2003**, *7*, 73–80. [CrossRef]

23. Johnson, C.; Ruud, J.; Bruce, R.; Wortman, D. Relationships between residual stress, microstructure and mechanical properties of electron beam—Physical vapor deposition thermal barrier coatings. *Surf. Coat. Technol.* **1998**, *108*, 80–85. [CrossRef]

24. Padture, N.; Schlichting, K.; Bhatia, T.; Ozturk, A.; Cetegen, B.; Jordan, E.; Gell, M.; Jiang, S.; Xiao, T.; Strutt, P. Towards durable thermal barrier coatings with novel microstructures deposited by solution—Precursor plasma spray. *Acta Mater.* **2001**, *49*, 2251–2257. [CrossRef]

25. Kassner, H.; Siegert, R.; Hathiramani, D.; Vassen, R.; Stoever, D. Application of suspension plasma spraying (SPS) for manufacture of ceramic coatings. *J. Therm. Spray Technol.* **2008**, *17*, 115–123. [CrossRef]

26. Guignard, A.; Mauer, G.; Vaßen, R.; Stöver, D. Deposition and characteristics of submicrometer—Structured thermal barrier coatings by suspension plasma spraying. *J. Therm. Spray Technol.* **2012**, *21*, 416–424. [CrossRef]

27. Derelioglu, Z.; Carabat, A.; Song, G.; van der Zwaag, S.; Sloof, W. On the use of B-alloyed MoSi2 particles as crack healing agents in yttria stabilized zirconia thermal barrier coatings. *J. Eur. Ceram. Soc.* **2015**, *35*, 4507–4511. [CrossRef]

28. Carabat, A.; Meijerink, M.; Brouwer, J.; Kelder, E.; van Ommen, J.; van der Zwaag, S.; Sloof, W. Protecting the MoSi2 healing particles for thermal barrier coatings using a sol-gel produced Al2O3 coating. *J. Eur. Ceram. Soc.* **2018**, *38*, 2728–2734. [CrossRef]

29. Chen, Y.; Zhang, X.; van der Zwaag, S.; Sloof, W.G.; Xiao, P. Damage evolution in a self-healing air plasma sprayed thermal barrier coating containing self-shielding $MoSi_2$ particles. *J. Am. Ceram. Soc.* **2019**, *102*, 16313. [CrossRef]

30. Ouyang, T.; Fang, X.; Zhang, Y.; Liu, D.; Wang, Y.; Feng, S.; Zhou, T.; Cai, S.; Suo, J. Enhancement of high temperature oxidation resistance and spallation resistance of SiC-self-healing thermal barrier coatings. *Surf. Coat. Technol.* **2016**, *286*, 365–375. [CrossRef]

31. Scott, H. Phase relationships in the zirconia-yttria system. *J. Mater. Sci.* **1975**, *10*, 1527–1535. [CrossRef]

32. Veytizou, C.; Quinson, J.-F.; Valfort, O.; Thomas, G. Zircon formation from amorphous silica and tetragonal zirconia: Kinetic study and modelling. *Solid State Ion.* **2001**, *139*, 315–323. [CrossRef]

33. Nozahic, F.; Monceau, D.; Estournès, C. Thermal cycling and reactivity of a $MoSi_2/ZrO_2$ composite designed for self-healing thermal barrier coatings. *Mater. Des.* **2016**, *94*, 444–448. [CrossRef]

34. Kim, E.-H.; Lee, W.-R.; Jung, Y.-G.; Lee, C.-S. A new binder system for preparing high strength inorganic molds in precision casting. *Mater. Chem. Phys.* **2011**, *126*, 344–351. [CrossRef]

35. Kim, E.-H.; Cho, G.-H.; Jung, Y.-G.; Kim, I.-S.; Jo, C.-Y.; Lee, J.-S. Adhesion phenomena between particles according to the content of organic binder in core for thin-wall casting. *J. Nanosci. Nanotechnol.* **2014**, *14*, 8048–8052. [CrossRef]

36. Jung, Y.-G.; Tumenbayar, E.; Choi, H.-H.; Park, H.-Y.; Kim, E.-H.; Zhang, J. Effects of alumina precursor species in a ternary—Phase binder system on the strength of sand mold. *Ceram. Int.* **2018**, *44*, 2223–2230. [CrossRef]

37. Park, H.-M.; Jun, S.-H.; Lyu, G.; Jung, Y.-G.; Yan, B.-I.; Park, K.-Y. Thermal durability of thermal barrier coatings in furnace cyclic thermal fatigue test: Effects of purity and monoclinic phase in feedstock powder. *J. Korean Ceram. Soc.* **2018**, *55*, 608–617. [CrossRef]

38. Park, K.-Y.; Yang, B.-I.; Jeon, S.-H.; Park, H.-M.; Jung, Y.-G. Variation of thermal barrier coating lifetime characteristics with thermal durability evaluation methods. *J. Therm. Spray Technol.* **2018**, *27*, 1436–1446. [CrossRef]

39. Laha, T.; Agarwal, A.; McKechnie, T.; Seal, S. Synthesis and characterization of plasma spray formed carbon nanotube reinforced aluminum composite. *Mater. Sci. Eng. A* **2004**, *381*, 249–258. [CrossRef]

40. Koch, D.; Mauer, G.; Vaßen, R. Manufacturing of composite coatings by atmospheric plasma spraying using different feed-stock materials as YSZ and mosi 2. *J. Therm. Spray Technol.* **2017**, *26*, 708–716. [CrossRef]

41. Ritchie, R.O. Mechanisms of fatigue—Crack propagation in ductile and brittle solids. *Int. J. Fract.* **1999**, *100*, 55–83. [CrossRef]

42. Ponnusami, S.A.; Turteltaub, S.; van der Zwaag, S. Cohesive-zone modelling of crack nucleation and propagation in particulate composites. *Eng. Fract. Mech.* **2015**, *149*, 170–190. [CrossRef]

43. Ojovan, M.I. Glass formation in amorphous SiO_2 as a percolation phase transition in a system of network defects. *J. Exp. Theor. Phys. Lett.* **2004**, *79*, 632–634. [CrossRef]

44. Song, D.; Paik, U.; Guo, X.; Zhang, J.; Woo, T.-K.; Lu, Z.; Jung, S.-H.; Lee, J.-H.; Jung, Y.-G. Microstructure design for blended feedstock and its thermal durability in lanthanum zirconate based thermal barrier coatings. *Surf. Coat. Technol.* **2016**, *308*, 40–49. [CrossRef]

45. Nozahic, F.; Estournès, C.; Carabat, A.L.; Sloof, W.G.; Van Der Zwaag, S.; Monceau, D. Self-healing thermal barrier coating systems fabricated by spark plasma sintering. *Mater. Des.* **2018**, *143*, 204–213. [CrossRef]

46. Seward, T.P., III; Vascott, T. *High Temperature Glass Melt Property Database for Process Modeling*; Wiley-American Ceramic Society: Westerville, OH, USA, 2005.
47. Fluegel, A. Glass viscosity calculation based on a global statistical modelling approach. *Glass Technol.-Eur. J. Glass Sci. Technol. Part A* **2007**, *48*, 13–30.

Article

Hot Corrosion Behavior of BaLa$_2$Ti$_3$O$_{10}$ Thermal Barrier Ceramics in V$_2$O$_5$ and Na$_2$SO$_4$ + V$_2$O$_5$ Molten Salts

Hui Liu [1,*], Jin Cai [2] and Jihong Zhu [1]

[1]   School of Mechanical Engineering, Northwestern Polytechnical University, Xi'an 710072, China;
      Jh.zhu_fea@nwpu.edu.cn
[2]   College of Aerospace Engineering, Shenyang Aerospace University, Shenyang 110136, China;
      saucai@sau.edu.cn
*   Correspondence: cr_si@nwpu.edu.cn; Tel.: +86-24-2438-2359; Fax: +86-24-2432-6643

Received: 12 March 2019; Accepted: 10 April 2019; Published: 29 May 2019

Abstract: BaLa$_2$Ti$_3$O$_{10}$ ceramics for thermal barrier coating (TBC) applications were fabricated, and exposed to V$_2$O$_5$ and Na$_2$SO$_4$ + V$_2$O$_5$ molten salts at 900 °C to investigate the hot corrosion behavior. After 4 h corrosion tests, the main reaction products resulting from V$_2$O$_5$ salt corrosion were LaVO$_4$, TiO$_2$, and Ba$_3$V$_4$O$_{13}$, whereas those due to Na$_2$SO$_4$ + V$_2$O$_5$ corrosion consisted of LaVO$_4$, TiO$_2$, BaSO$_4$ and some Ba$_3$V$_4$O$_{13}$. The structures of reaction layers on the surfaces depended on the corrosion medium. In V$_2$O$_5$ salt, the layer was dense and had a thickness of 8–10 μm. While in Na$_2$SO$_4$ + V$_2$O$_5$ salt, it had a ~15 μm porous structure and a dense, thin band at the bottom. Beneath the dense layer or the band, no obvious molten salt was found. The mechanisms by which the reaction layer forms were discussed.

Keywords: thermal barrier coating (TBC); BaLa$_2$Ti$_3$O$_{10}$; molten salt corrosion; corrosion mechanisms

1. Introduction

Thermal barrier coatings (TBCs) are extensively used in turbine engines, which can protect engine hot-components against thermal attack and corrosion, giving rise to enhanced engine efficiencies and performances [1–3]. Usually, a typical TBC system is composed of a ceramic topcoat and a metallic bond coat [4–6]. The top coat is important, which provides thermal insulation to the substrate, and is commonly made of yttria partially stabilized zirconia (YSZ) [1,2,7–9]. Up to now, many techniques have been developed to produce YSZ coatings [10–13].

In a marine environment or engines use low-quality fuel, molten salts have severe damage to YSZ TBCs, especially at a temperature range of 600–1000 °C [14–18]. Molten salts infiltrate into the TBCs, and react with YSZ grains to form YVO$_4$, leading to the depletion of yttria stabilizer in the TBC. During engine heating-cooling cycles, phase transformation of the TBC occurs, causing the coating to spall much faster than if no molten salt exists. Many researchers have studied the corrosion mechanisms of YSZ TBCs resulting from molten salt [18–22]. Some strategies have been proposed to improve the hot corrosion resistance of YSZ coatings, such as doping CeO$_2$, Al$_2$O$_3$, Ta$_2$O$_5$ and RE$_2$O$_3$ (RE = rare earth element) into the system [18,21–24].

Increasing engines operating temperature leads to enhanced power output and efficiency [1–3]. However, YSZ TBCs suffer from phase transformation and reduced thermal insulation above 1200 °C, which causes them unlikely to meet the long-term requirements for advanced engines. Moreover, even lower thermal conductivity of TBCs is practically required for better thermal insulation. Therefore, alternative TBC materials to YSZ suitable for high-temperature applications are strongly needed. For the application at higher temperatures, a similar threat to new TBCs posed by molten salts still exists. Thus, there is a strong need to understand the hot corrosion behavior of TBC candidates in molten slats.

Recently, the hot corrosion behavior of some newly developed TBC materials in molten salts has been reported. Ouyang et al. have studied the hot corrosion behavior of $Gd_2Zr_2O_7$ and $Yb_2Zr_2O_7$ ceramics in V_2O_5 molten salt at various temperatures [16,25]. Cao et al. have investigated the corrosion products of $LaTi_2Al_9O_{19}$ ceramic resulted from V_2O_5 salt attack, and proposed their formation mechanisms [17]. Recently, Guo et al. have systematically studied the hot corrosion behavior and mechanisms of some TBC candidates in molten salts, such as Ba_2YbAlO_5, $(Gd_{0.9}Sc_{0.1})_2Zr_2O_7$, Gd_2O_3-Yb_2O_3 co-doped YSZ and rare earth phosphate [26–29]. They reported that these novel TBC materials reveal better corrosion resistance than YSZ. Specially, $LaPO_4$ and $NdPO_4$ are found to highly resist to molten salt corrosion; exposed to high temperatures, the molten salt reacts with the ceramics to form an $RE(P,V)O_4$ (RE = Nd, La) solid solution, which leads to limited damage to the original microstructure [29]. $BaLa_2Ti_3O_{10}$ has been considered as a promising TBC candidate material [30], however, how it behaves in molten salts is not found in the open literature.

In order to understand the corrosion resistance of $BaLa_2Ti_3O_{10}$, its hot corrosion behavior in V_2O_5 and Na_2SO_4 + V_2O_5 salts for 4 h at 900 °C is investigated. In this study, the emphasis is placed on analyzing the corrosion products resulting from the reactions between $BaLa_2Ti_3O_{10}$ and the molten salts by using dense pellets, and the associated corrosion mechanisms are also discussed.

2. Experimental Procedures

$BaLa_2Ti_3O_{10}$ powders were produced by a solid-state reaction method. The raw materials contained $BaCO_3$, TiO_2 and La_2O_3 powders, which were dissolved in ionized water in an appropriate quantity. Then, the powders were ball mixed using zirconia media at a speed of 400 rpm for 10 h, followed by drying at 160 °C for 10 h. Afterward, the mixed powders were calcined at 1500 °C for 24 h. The bulk samples for hot corrosion tests were fabricated from the powders, which were cold pressed at ~250 MPa and then sintered at 1500 °C for 10 h.

The corrosion media were V_2O_5 and 50 mol% Na_2SO_4 + 50 mol% V_2O_5 (Na_2SO_4 + V_2O_5) salts. Prior to hot corrosion tests, pellets were ground by 800 grit sandpaper. Then, the samples were ultrasonic cleaned in ethanol and dried at 120 °C. The salts were uniformly spread on surfaces of samples, and its content was determined by weighting the samples before and after the salt coverage using an analytical balance. The salt concentration was ~10 mg/cm^2. Then, the salt covered samples were heated at 900 °C for 4 h in a furnace, followed by cooling in the furnace.

Phase structures of the corroded samples was identified by X-ray diffraction (XRD; Rigaku Diffractometer, Tokyo, Japan), with 2θ range of 10°–80° at a scanning rate of 0.1°/s. Surface morphologies were obtained by SEM (TDCLS4800, Hitachi Ltd., Tokyo, Japan), the composition analysis was performed using EDS (IE 350), and cross-sectional images were taken by SEM (TDCLSU1510, Hitachi Ltd.).

3. Results and Discussion

Figure 1 shows the XRD patterns of the as-prepared $BaLa_2Ti_3O_{10}$ pellet and the samples after hot corrosion. $BaLa_2Ti_3O_{10}$ bulk basically consists of a monoclinic phase. It is possible to observe that the peaks are sharp, suggesting good crystallization of the sample. After V_2O_5 salt corrosion, $LaVO_4$ (PDF#50-0367), $Ba_3V_4O_{13}$ (PDF#36-1466) and TiO_2 (PDF#99-0090) phases are detected by XRD on the sample surface. In the case of Na_2SO_4 + V_2O_5 salt corrosion, the corrosion products are $LaVO_4$, $Ba_3V_4O_{13}$, TiO_2 and $BaSO_4$, and some $BaLa_2Ti_3O_{10}$ diffraction peaks are also detected, as indicated in Figure 1. The corrosion products resulting from the two type of slats are different, which will be further confirmed by SEM and EDS analysis in the following section.

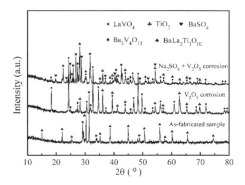

Figure 1. XRD patterns of BaLa$_2$Ti$_3$O$_{10}$ powders and the samples after hot corrosion in V$_2$O$_5$ and Na$_2$SO$_4$ + V$_2$O$_5$ salts at 900 °C for 4 h.

Figure 2a shows the surface image of the as-fabricated BaLa$_2$Ti$_3$O$_{10}$ pellet. Obvious BaLa$_2$Ti$_3$O$_{10}$ grains are observed. After hot corrosion in V$_2$O$_5$ salt, corrosion products are observed on the sample surface, as can be seen in Figure 2b. When observing the corrosion products at a higher magnification, one could find three different shapes, i.e., plate-shaped (marked as A), rod-shaped (marked as B) and particle-shaped (marked as C), as shown in Figure 2c. EDS analysis result listed in Table 1 indicates that A consists of Ba, V and O elements. In combination with the above XRD result, it is possible to determine that A is Ba$_3$V$_4$O$_{13}$. B is composed of Ti and O, and C contains La, V and O. Further analysis confirms that B and C are TiO$_2$ and LaVO$_4$, respectively.

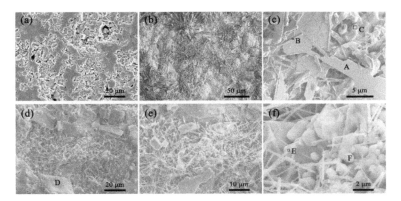

Figure 2. Surface morphologies of the as-fabricated BaLa$_2$Ti$_3$O$_{10}$ pellet (**a**), and the samples after V$_2$O$_5$ corrosion (**b**,**c**) and Na$_2$SO$_4$ + V$_2$O$_5$ corrosion (**d**–**f**).

Table 1. Compositions of compounds A–F in Figure 2 (in at.%).

Corrosion Products	Ba	La	Ti	V	S	O
A	15.87	–	–	21.56	–	62.57
B	–	–	31.58	–	–	68.42
C	–	16.38	–	17.63	–	65.99
D	16.45	–	–	–	18.53	65.02
E	–	–	33.16	–	–	66.84
F	–	17.57	–	18.46	–	63.97

After hot corrosion in Na_2SO_4 + V_2O_5 salt, the pellet surface is also completely covered with corrosion products, as shown in Figure 2d. The plate-shaped compounds (D) have Ba, S and O elements, without any evidence of V, as shown in Table 1, and they could be identified to be $BaSO_4$. Enlarging the image of the surface, one could find many rod-shaped and particle-shaped compounds, as presented in Figure 2e. These two different shaped compounds are marked as E and F, respectively in Figure 2f. As listed in Table 1, compound E contains Ti and O, and F has La, V and O, which could be confirmed to be TiO_2 and $LaVO_4$, respectively.

Figure 3a shows the cross-sectional image of the $BaLa_2Ti_3O_{10}$ sample after hot corrosion in V_2O_5 salt at 900 °C for 4 h. A continuous, dense reaction layer forms on the sample surface. Beneath the layer, the bulk keeps structure integrity, where no molten salt trace could be observed. This indicates that this layer has a positive function on suppressing the molten salt penetration. In the enlarged image (Figure 3b), it is possible to find that the layer is highly adhered to the bulk, with a thickness of 8–10 μm. Note that there are two sub-layers in the reaction layer. The upper sub-layer is light-contrasted and has some cracks, while the lower sub-layer is grey-contrasted and reveals a dense structure. EDS analysis was conducted on regions A–C in Figure 3c, and the results are presented in Table 2. The elements in Regions A and B are identical, including La, Ti, Ba, V and O. In combination with the above XRD result and the surface SEM analysis, it could be confirmed that the two sub-layers are composed of $Ba_3V_4O_{13}$, $LaVO_4$ and TiO_2. The different contrast of the two sub-layers might be attributed to the difference in the $Ba_3V_4O_{13}$ content. In region C, Ba, La, Ti and O elements are detected, with no evidence of V, implying that it has not been attacked by V_2O_5 molten salt.

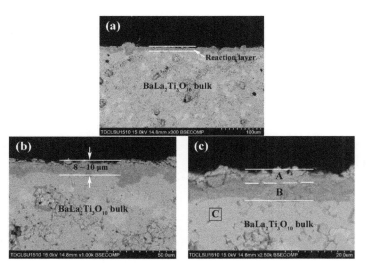

Figure 3. Cross-sectional images of $BaLa_2Ti_3O_{10}$ ceramic after hot corrosion in V_2O_5 salt at 900 °C for 4 h. (a–c) show the images with different magnifications.

Table 2. Compositions of compounds A–G in Figures 3 and 4 (in at.%).

Corrosion Products	Ba	La	Ti	V	S	O
A	8.17	5.12	8.38	15.29	–	63.04
B	8.95	3.68	7.31	18.17	–	61.89
C	6.31	12.58	20.74	–	–	60.37
D	10.13	6.99	7.53	8.13	9.86	57.36
E	9.34	5.48	7.25	16.46	–	61.47
F	7.18	13.54	20.35	–	–	58.93
G	6.05	13.26	18.78	–	–	61.91

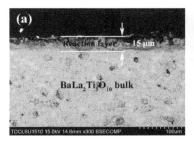 

Figure 4. Cross-sectional images of BaLa$_2$Ti$_3$O$_{10}$ ceramic after hot corrosion in Na$_2$SO$_4$ + V$_2$O$_5$ salt at 900 °C for 4 h. (**a**,**b**) show the images with different magnifications.

Figure 4 shows the cross-sectional image of the BaLa$_2$Ti$_3$O$_{10}$ sample after hot corrosion in Na$_2$SO$_4$ + V$_2$O$_5$ salt at 900 °C for 4 h. Being quite different from the case of V$_2$O$_5$ corrosion, the reaction layer resulting from Na$_2$SO$_4$ + V$_2$O$_5$ corrosion exhibits a porous structure and has a larger thickness (~15 μm). At the bottom of the layer, a continuous, grey-contrasted thin band could be observed. Beneath this band, no molten salt trace could be observed, and the bulk keeps structure integrity, suggesting that the molten salt infiltration has been arrested. Figure 4b shows the reaction layer at a higher magnification. EDS analysis results of regions D–G are presented in Table 2. Region D contains La, Ti, Ba, S, V and O elements. Combining with the above XRD result and the surface SEM analysis, this region is determined to consist of BaSO$_4$, LaVO$_4$ and TiO$_2$. Region E contains Ba, La, Ti, V and O elements. Regions F and G have a close chemical composition, including Ba, La, Ti and O elements. This suggests that they are BaLa$_2$Ti$_3$O$_{10}$ bulk.

Based on the above observations, it could be find that molten salts penetration in BaLa$_2$Ti$_3$O$_{10}$ thermal barrier ceramics could be arrested, and the inner regions of the samples are free from the attack by molten salts. The rationale behind this is the formation of a dense layer on the sample surface resulting from the reaction between BaLa$_2$Ti$_3$O$_{10}$ and the molten salts. The reaction could be understood in terms of the breakdown of the chemical bonds in the crystal by molten salts attack [17,31]. From the viewpoint of crystallography, BaLa$_2$Ti$_3$O$_{10}$ crystal could be seen as a tri-perovskite [La$_2$Ti$_3$O$_{10}$] layer separated by a Ba layer along c-axis [30]. Since the Ba insertion layers are poorly bonded, they are easier to be attacked by molten salts compared with [La$_2$Ti$_3$O$_{10}$] layers. It is thus possible that Ba-O bonds in BaLa$_2$Ti$_3$O$_{10}$ would first break in the presence of the molten salts, resulting in the formation of Ba contained corrosion products. Due to the consumption of Ba, La and Ti are enriched in the crystal, which provides a great chance for the molten salt to destroy La-O and Ti-O bonds. As a result, corrosion products of LaVO$_4$ and TiO$_2$ are formed.

Note that the reaction layer on the sample surfaces has different thickness and structure in the two molten salts, which may be related to the type of the corrosion products. In the case of V$_2$O$_5$ molten slat corrosion, the corrosion products are Ba$_3$V$_4$O$_{13}$, LaVO$_4$ and TiO$_2$, and the reaction could be expressed as follow:

$$3BaLa_2Ti_3O_{10}(s) + 5V_2O_5(l) \rightarrow Ba_3V_4O_{13}(s) + 6LaVO_4(s) + 9TiO_2(s) \qquad (1)$$

These reaction products have high melt temperatures and exist as solid states in this study. During the corrosion test, there are two processes, i.e., the penetration of the molten salts into the sample and its reaction with the sample. A reaction layer is formed on the sample surface when the reaction has a higher rate than that of the molten salts penetrating into the porous structure. The reaction layer resulting from V$_2$O$_5$ molten slat attack has a dense structure, which could effectively inhibit further penetration of the molten salt. Thus, it is reasonable to accept that V$_2$O$_5$ attacked BaLa$_2$Ti$_3$O$_{10}$ pellet has a thin reaction layer.

When the mixture of Na_2SO_4 and V_2O_5 salts are presented, they react with each other at high temperatures. At 900 °C, the reaction could be represented by the following expression [32]:

$$Na_2SO_4(l) + V_2O_5(l) \rightarrow 2NaVO_3(l) + SO_3(g) \tag{2}$$

Then, the formed products react with $BaLa_2Ti_3O_{10}$. Note that there may exist another possibility, i.e., V_2O_5 or Na_2SO_4 reacts with $BaLa_2Ti_3O_{10}$ separately before the reaction Equation (2) occurs. We mixed Na_2SO_4 and $BaLa_2Ti_3O_{10}$ powders together at a weight ratio of 1:1, and annealed them at 900 °C for 4 h. XRD measurements were performed on the as-mixed powders and the sample after heat treatment, and the results are shown in Figure 5. In the XRD pattern of the as-mixed powders, only $BaLa_2Ti_3O_{10}$ and Na_2SO_4 phases can be detected. By comparison, one could find that the annealed powders exhibit similar XRD pattern appearance to that of the as-mixed powders, and no peak from $BaSO_4$ could be detected. This indicates that Na_2SO_4 and $BaLa_2Ti_3O_{10}$ do not react with each other at 900 °C.

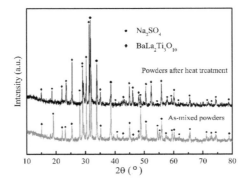

Figure 5. XRD patterns of the as-mixed $BaLa_2Ti_3O_{10}$ and Na_2SO_4 powders and the mixed powders after heat treatment at 900 °C for 4 h.

After the formation of $NaVO_3$ and SO_3, the following reaction could occur:

$$BaLa_2Ti_3O_{10}(s) + 2NaVO_3(l) + SO_3(g) \rightarrow BaSO_4(s) + 2LaVO_4(s) + 3TiO_2(s) + Na_2O(s) \tag{3}$$

It has been reported NaVO3 has better fluidity than V2O5 at liquid state [33–35], thus it has a larger tendency to infiltrate to the sample along cracks/pores, causing the formation a thicker reaction layer, as shown in Figure 4b. Note that the reaction layer on $BaLa_2Ti_3O_{10}$ surface resulting from Na_2SO_4 + V_2O_5 molten slat attack is porous, which could be explained in terms of the participation of SO_3 gas during the reaction process. Some unreacted gas escapes from the bulk, leaving pores and resulting in a decrease in the SO_3 content with the increase of the depth. At a certain depth, no SO_3 exists and only NaVO3 reacts with $BaLa_2Ti_3O_{10}$. The reaction could be described as follow:

$$3BaLa_2Ti_3O_{10}(s) + 10NaVO_3(l) \rightarrow Ba_3V_4O_{13}(s) + 6LaVO_4(s) + 9TiO_2(s) + 5Na_2O(s) \tag{4}$$

This causes the formation of a dense reaction layer, as shown in Figure 4b. The absence of $BaSO_4$ in this layer provides an evidence for this consideration. In the case of Na_2SO_4 + V_2O_5 slat corrosion, the dense reaction layer is formed at a deeper region from the sample surface. Thus, though $BaLa_2Ti_3O_{10}$ TBC candidate has good resistance to Na_2SO_4 + V_2O_5 slat corrosion, it does not perform as good as that in V_2O_5 slat.

4. Conclusions

Hot corrosion behavior of $BaLa_2Ti_3O_{10}$ thermal barrier oxide in V_2O_5 and $Na_2SO_4 + V_2O_5$ molten salts at 900 °C were investigated. After 4 h corrosion tests, a reaction layer formed on the sample surface, the phase constitution and structure of which depend on the type of the molten salt. In V_2O_5 molten salt, the layer consisted of $LaVO_4$, TiO_2 and $Ba_3V_4O_{13}$, with a dense structure and having a thickness of 8–10 μm. While in $Na_2SO_4 + V_2O_5$ molten salt, it contained $LaVO_4$, TiO_2 and $BaSO_4$, mainly exhibiting a porous structure, which could be attributed to the participation of SO_3 gas during the formation process of the reaction layer. At the bottom of the porous layer, there existed a dense, thin band, consisting of $Ba_3V_4O_{13}$, $LaVO_4$ and TiO_2. Beneath the dense layer or the band, no molten salt trace existed in the samples, indicating that further infiltration of the molten salts has been arrested. Based on this study, it could be concluded that though $BaLa_2Ti_3O_{10}$ ceramic as TBC candidate has good resistance in both salts, it shows better resistance to V_2O_5 salt corrosion.

Author Contributions: Conceptualization, J.Z.; Methodology, H.L. and J.C.; Validation, H.L. and J.Z.; Formal Analysis, H.L. and J.Z.; Investigation, H.L.; Data Curation, H.L.; Writing—Original Draft Preparation, H.L.; Writing—Review and Editing, J.C. and J.Z.; Supervision, J.Z.

Funding: This research was funded by National Key Research and Development Program (No. 2017YFB1102800), National Natural Science Foundation of China (Nos. 11722219, 11432011, 11620101002).

Conflicts of Interest: The authors declare no conflict of interest.

References

1. Vaßen, R.; Jarligo, M.O.; Steinke, T.; Mack, D.E.; Stöver, D. Overview on advanced thermal barrier coatings. *Surf. Coat. Technol.* **2010**, *205*, 938–942. [CrossRef]
2. Guo, H.; Gong, S.; Zhou, C.; Xu, H. Investigation on hot-fatigue behaviors of gradient thermal barrier coatings by EB-PVD. *Surf. Coat. Technol.* **2001**, *148*, 110–116. [CrossRef]
3. Padture, N.P. Advanced structural ceramics in aerospace propulsion. *Nat. Mater.* **2016**, *15*, 804–809. [CrossRef]
4. Qiao, M.; Zhou, C. Hot corrosion behavior of Co modified NiAl coating on nickel base superalloys. *Corros. Sci.* **2012**, *63*, 239–245. [CrossRef]
5. Zhang, B.Y.; Meng, G.H.; Yang, G.J.; Li, C.X.; Li, C.J. Dependence of scale thickness on the breaking behavior of the initial oxide on plasma spray bond coat surface during vacuum pre-treatment. *Appl. Surf. Sci.* **2017**, *397*, 125–132. [CrossRef]
6. Han, B.; Ma, Y.; Peng, H.; Zheng, L.; Guo, H. Effect of Mo, Ta, and Re on high-temperature oxidation behavior of minor Hf doped β-NiAl alloy. *Corros. Sci.* **2016**, *102*, 222–232. [CrossRef]
7. Guo, H.B.; Vaßen, R.; Stöver, D. Atmospheric plasma sprayed thick thermal barrier coatings with high segmentation crack density. *Surf. Coat. Technol.* **2004**, *186*, 353–363. [CrossRef]
8. Curry, N.; VanEvery, K.; Snyder, T.; Markocsan, N. Thermal conductivity analysis and lifetime testing of suspension plasma-sprayed thermal barrier coatings. *Coatings* **2014**, *4*, 630–650. [CrossRef]
9. Wang, Q.; Guo, L.; Yan, Z.; Ye, F. Phase composition, thermal conductivity, and toughness of TiO_2-doped, Er_2O_3-stabilized ZrO_2 for thermal barrier coating applications. *Coatings* **2018**, *8*, 253. [CrossRef]
10. Xu, Z.H.; Zhou, X.; Wang, K.; Dai, J.W.; He, L.M. Thermal barrier coatings of new rare-earth composite oxide by EB-PVD. *J. Alloy. Compd.* **2014**, *587*, 126–132. [CrossRef]
11. Dong, H.; Han, Y.; Zhou, Y.; Li, X.; Yao, J.T.; Li, Y. The temperature distribution in plasma-sprayed thermal-barrier coatings during crack propagation and coalescence. *Coatings* **2018**, *8*, 311. [CrossRef]
12. Li, C.; Guo, H.; Gao, L.; Wei, L.; Gong, S.; Xu, H. Microstructures of yttria-stabilized zirconia coatings by plasma spray-physical vapor deposition. *J. Therm. Spray Technol.* **2015**, *24*, 534–541. [CrossRef]
13. Gao, L.; Wei, L.; Guo, H.; Gong, S.; Xu, H. Deposition mechanisms of yttria-stabilized zirconia coatings during plasma spray physical vapor deposition. *Ceram. Int.* **2016**, *42*, 5530–5536. [CrossRef]
14. Huang, H.; Liu, C.; Ni, L.; Zhou, C. Evaluation of microstructural evolution of thermal barrier coatings exposed to Na_2SO_4 using impedance spectroscopy. *Corros. Sci.* **2011**, *53*, 1369–1374. [CrossRef]

15. Liu, Z.G.; Ouyang, J.H.; Zhou, Y.; Zhu, R.X. Hot corrosion of V_2O_5-coated $NdMgAl_{11}O_{19}$ ceramic in air at 950 °C. *J. Eur. Ceram. Soc.* **2013**, *33*, 1975–1979. [CrossRef]

16. Li, S.; Liu, Z.G.; Ouyang, J.H. Growth of $YbVO_4$ crystals evolved from hot corrosion reactions of $Yb_2Zr_2O_7$ against V_2O_5 and $Na_2SO_4 + V_2O_5$. *Appl. Surf. Sci.* **2013**, *276*, 653–659. [CrossRef]

17. Zhou, X.; Xu, Z.; He, L.; Xu, J.; Zou, B.; Cao, X. Hot corrosion behavior of $LaTi_2Al_9O_{19}$ ceramic exposed to vanadium oxide at temperatures of 700–950 °C in air. *Corros. Sci.* **2016**, *104*, 310–318. [CrossRef]

18. Habibi, M.H.; Wang, L.; Liang, J.; Guo, S.M. An investigation on hot corrosion behavior of YSZ-Ta_2O_5 in $Na_2SO_4 + V_2O_5$ salt at 1100 °C. *Corros. Sci.* **2013**, *75*, 409–414. [CrossRef]

19. Zhong, X.H.; Wang, Y.M.; Xu, Z.H.; Zhang, Y.F.; Zhang, J.F.; Cao, X.Q. Hot-corrosion behaviors of overlay-clad yttria-stabilized zirconia coatings in contact with vanadate-sulfate salts. *J. Eur. Ceram. Soc.* **2010**, *30*, 1401–1408. [CrossRef]

20. Jamali, H.; Mozafarinia, R.; Shoja-Razavi, R.; Ahmadi-Pidani, R. Comparison of hot corrosion behaviors of plasma-sprayed nanostructured and conventional YSZ thermal barrier coatings exposure to molten vanadium pentoxide and sodium sulfate. *J. Eur. Ceram. Soc.* **2014**, *34*, 485–492. [CrossRef]

21. Loghman-Estarki, M.R.; Razavi, R.S.; Edris, H.; Bakhshi, S.R.; Nejati, M.; Jamali, H. Comparison of hot corrosion behavior of nanostructured ScYSZ and YSZ thermal barrier coatings. *Ceram. Int.* **2016**, *42*, 7432–7439. [CrossRef]

22. Loghman-Estarki, M.R.; Razavi, R.S.; Jamali, H. Effect of molten V_2O_5 salt on the corrosion behavior of micro- and nano-structured thermal sprayed SYSZ and YSZ coatings. *Ceram. Int.* **2016**, *42*, 12825–12837. [CrossRef]

23. Nejati, M.; Rahimipour, M.R.; Mobasherpour, I. Evaluation of hot corrosion behavior of CSZ, CSZ/micro Al_2O_3 and CSZ/nano Al_2O_3 plasma sprayed thermal barrier coatings. *Ceram. Int.* **2014**, *40*, 4579–4590. [CrossRef]

24. Liu, H.F.; Xiong, X.; Li, X.B.; Wang, Y.L. Hot corrosion behavior of Sc_2O_3-Y_2O_3-ZrO_2 thermal barrier coatings in presence of $Na_2SO_4 + V_2O_5$ molten salt. *Corros. Sci.* **2014**, *85*, 87–93. [CrossRef]

25. Liu, Z.G.; Ouyang, J.H.; Zhou, Y.; Xia, X.L. Hot corrosion behavior of V_2O_5-coated $Gd_2Zr_2O_7$ ceramic in air at 700–850 °C. *J. Eur. Ceram. Soc.* **2009**, *29*, 2423–2427. [CrossRef]

26. Guo, L.; Zhang, C.; He, Q.; Yu, J.; Yan, Z.; Ye, F.; Dan, C.; Ji, V. Microstructure evolution and hot corrosion mechanisms of Ba_2REAlO_5 (RE = Yb, Er, Dy) exposed to $V_2O_5 + Na_2SO_4$ molten salt. *J. Eur. Ceram. Soc.* **2018**, *38*, 3555–3563. [CrossRef]

27. Zhang, C.; Li, M.; Zhang, Y.; Guo, L.; Dong, J.; Ye, F.; Li, L.; Ji, V. Hot corrosion behavior of $(Gd_{0.9}Sc_{0.1})_2Zr_2O_7$ in V_2O_5 molten salt at 700–1000 °C. *Ceram. Int.* **2017**, *43*, 9041–9046. [CrossRef]

28. Guo, L.; Zhang, C.; Li, M.; Sun, W.; Zhang, Z.; Ye, F. Hot corrosion evaluation of Gd_2O_3-Yb_2O_3 co-doped Y_2O_3 stabilized ZrO_2 thermal barrier oxides exposed to $Na_2SO_4 + V_2O_5$ molten salt. *Ceram. Int.* **2017**, *43*, 2780–2785. [CrossRef]

29. Guo, L.; Zhang, C.; He, Q.; Li, Z.; Yu, J.; Liu, X.; Ye, F. Corrosion products evolution and hot corrosion mechanisms of $REPO_4$ (RE = Gd, Nd, La) in the presence of $V_2O_5 + Na_2SO_4$ molten salt. *J. Eur. Ceram. Soc.* **2019**, *39*, 1496–1506. [CrossRef]

30. Guo, H.; Zhang, H.; Ma, G.; Gong, S. Thermo-physical and thermal cycling properties of plasma-sprayed $BaLa_2Ti_3O_{10}$ coating as potential thermal barrier materials. *Surf. Coat. Technol.* **2009**, *204*, 691–696. [CrossRef]

31. Chen, X.; Cao, X.; Zou, B.; Gong, J.; Sun, C. Corrosion of lanthanum magnesium hexaaluminate as plasma-sprayed coating and as bulk material when exposed to molten V_2O_5-containing salt. *Corros. Sci.* **2015**, *91*, 185–194. [CrossRef]

32. Habibi, M.H.; Yang, S.; Guo, S.M. Phase stability and hot corrosion behavior of ZrO_2-Ta_2O_5 compound in Na_2SO_4-V_2O_5 mixtures at elevated temperatures. *Ceram. Int.* **2014**, *40*, 4077–4083. [CrossRef]

33. Gitanjaly, H.; Singh, S.; Prakash, S. Role of CeO_2 coating in enhancing high temperature corrosion resistance of Ni-base superalloys as an inhibitor. *Mater. High Temp.* **2010**, *27*, 109–116. [CrossRef]

34. Rocca, E.; Aranda, L.; Moliere, M.; Steinmetz, P. Nickel oxide as a new inhibitor of vanadium-induced hot corrosion of superalloys-comparison to MgO-based inhibitor. *J. Mater. Chem.* **2002**, *12*, 3766–3772. [CrossRef]

35. Ramachandran, C.S.; Balasubramanian, V.; Ananthapadmanabhan, P.V. On the cyclic hot corrosion behavior of atmospheric plasma sprayed lanthanum zirconate based coatings in contact with a mixture of sodium sulphate and vanadate salts: A comparison with the traditional YSZ duplex and NiCrAlY coated samples. *Vacuum* **2013**, *97*, 81–95. [CrossRef]

 *coatings*

Article

A Novel Method for nZEB Internal Coverings Design Based on Neural Networks

José A. Orosa [1,*], Diego Vergara [2], Ángel M. Costa [1] and Rebeca Bouzón [1]

[1] Department of Energy, Universidade da Coruña, Paseo de Ronda, 51, 15011 A Coruña, Spain;
    angel.costa@udc.es (Á.M.C.); rebeca.bouzon@udc.es (R.B.)
[2] Department of Mechanical Engineering, Catholic University of Ávila, C/Canteros, s/n, 05005 Avila, Spain;
    diego.vergara@ucavila.es or dvergara@usal.es
* Correspondence: jarosa@udc.es or jose.antonio.orosa@udc.es; Tel.: +34-981-167-000 (ext. 4320)

Received: 4 April 2019; Accepted: 25 April 2019; Published: 27 April 2019

Abstract: Research from the International Energy Agency about indoor ambiences and nearly zero energy buildings (nZEB) in the past has been centred on different aspects such as the prediction of indoor conditions as a function of the weather using laboratory material properties for simulations and real sampled data for validation. Thus, it is possible to use real data for defining behavioural groups of indoor ambiences as a function of real vapour permeability of internal coverings. However, this method is not suitable for modelling it and predicting its behaviour under weather changes, which is of interest to improve the method of selection and use of building construction materials. In this research, artificial intelligence procedures were employed as the first model of permeable coverings material behaviour to provide a newer understanding of building materials and applications for the generation of new control procedures between the mechanical and electronic point of view of building construction materials.

Keywords: ANNs; passive methods; building energy; internal covering

1. Introduction

In the last decade, several research papers have attempted to evaluate and model the effect of building materials overheat and mass transfer processes [1,2]. Taking into account that the construction of nearly zero energy buildings (nZEB) requires innovative design processes based on an integrated design approach facilitated by multidisciplinary work teams [3], different research groups under the organisation of the International Energy Agency (IEA) shared real sampled laboratory data [4], new software resources like HAM tools [5] and real in-situ sampled data to validate the previous ones [6]. Thus, the aim of the present research was to validate software resources based on real sampled data to simulate and potentially predict and improve indoor conditions in buildings by using buildings construction materials as mechanical control systems in the future.

Accurate prediction of temperature and relative humidity in indoor ambiences is difficult to obtain unless a realistic understanding of the existing buildings is available. In this sense, the real properties of building materials once placed in the structure and its effect on indoor conditions as a consequence of its real behaviour must be analysed in detail for future optimisation.

The effect of internal coverings on indoor ambiences was reflected by statistical analysis in previous research works [6–11]. Specifically, in previous studies carried out by the same research group of the present paper [6–10], authors sampled indoor conditions of 25 office buildings in a year in a humid region of the Northwest Spain. The main results revealed how internal coverings exert a clear effect on indoor ambiences during non-occupancy period due to low air changes during the longer period at night. Furthermore, analysis of variance (ANOVA) revealed more interesting results that an average indoor relative humidity controlled by these passive methods reaches a more comfortable ambience with a lower need of energy for conditioning during the first hour of occupation [8,9].

As a consequence of these results, internal coverings were considered to be of special interest to act as permeable or impermeable barrier materials for use as building construction materials in order to control thermal comfort, energy saving and, in general, indoor conditions. The real sampled data demonstrated how this effect must be considered, although it was nearly depreciated during years in most of heat and mass transfer software resources—like, for instance, EnergyPlus—due to the difficulty understanding and define this process. Furthermore, the main results founded in previous papers of our research group [6–10] emphasize the importance of simulating and modelling real sampled data rather than just employing laboratory results as a consequence of the modifications that are experimented by these materials until its final placement.

On the other hand, artificial neuronal networks (ANNs) were described recently as the last step in data mining [12–16]. In particular, most times, statistical studies do not let us get a model of real processes despite the fact its main variables were previously statistically related. ANNs are the clearest solution to model and predict these non-linear processes with promising future applications.

In previous works [6–10], different indoor ambiences of 25 office buildings were classified based on both its internal coverings materials and the statistical studies of real sampled data of its indoor ambiences. In the present study, this hygroscopic behaviour of coverings materials will be modelled in a more exactly way by Multi-output Gaussian Process Regression Artificial Neural Networks (MGPR ANNs) once trained and tested with the aim to be employed in future indoor ambience predictions. Moreover, this more accurate model will help to improve office buildings envelope redesign [17] to control the heat and mass transfer process between indoor air and wall construction materials and, in consequence, it will serve as a guide to improve the existing indoor conditions [18–22].

2. Materials and Methods

2.1. Office Buildings

The present research is the second phase of a previous work in which solution to the prediction problem of indoors conditions based on real properties of building construction materials were discussed [6,7]. The office buildings used in this study were located in the city of A Coruña, which is identified as an extremely humid region in the Northwestern Spain. Their building construction characteristics, like in previous works, can be defined as identical as these buildings were constructed at the same time and with the same design criteria.

All these offices were destined to be bank offices placed in the ground floor of each respective building. In all these offices two main zones can be identified (Figure 1a): (i) clients' zone and (ii) employees' zone. In the employees' zone there are three employees during all the working period that goes from 8:00 till 14:00. Most of the day, the workers use to enter few minutes before to prepare for the morning's work, and from 16:00 till 19:00. Therefore, the unoccupied period was considered to be 19:00–09:00 h. On the other hand, an average value of three clients is estimated in the clients' zone during the working hours waiting to be attended. In this sense, this working period can be identified as a humidity generation period of time of 7 h.

It must be emphasised that these offices did not have any kind of air conditioning systems, except for mechanical ventilation which was rarely employed during the day under extreme occupation conditions and, more importantly, there were a high number of infiltrations due to the natural ventilation through the doors when they were open as a consequence of the transit of clients. In consequence, during this occupation period, the air changes in the office were high and humidity is released to outdoors. Once the office closes, the air changes are reduced, and the effect of wall constructions materials starts to work by controlling indoor ambience relative humidity based on the permeability level of the internal covering material employed in each office until the office will open again in the next morning.

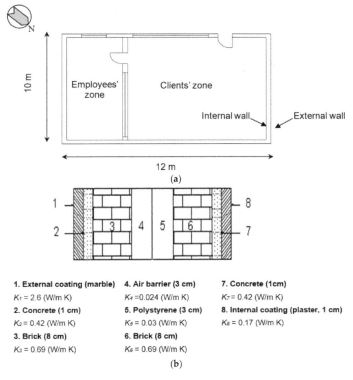

Figure 1. Walls' distribution: (**a**) office buildings zones; (**b**) detail of layers' distribution in a standard wall and their thermal conductivities (*K*).

In particular, a typical wall structure can be defined as being composed of an external covering, concrete, brick, air barrier, polystyrene, brick, concrete, and internal covering, as it is shown in the walls' distribution in Figure 1. The only difference in the buildings was in the type of internal coverings used, as those ranged from paper, wood, paint and plastics, all of which differed in their water vapour permeability (k_d) levels. In this sense, the levels of water vapour permeability in real buildings were not defined in that works in a quantitative way due to One Way ANOVA just let us define the similarity in indoor ambiences behaviours for a significance level of 0.05. As a consequence of this simple modification, different indoor temperature and relative humidity were identified with important effects on the thermal comfort and energy consumption. In particular, this effect was really intense during the first hours of occupation of the office buildings.

In previous studies [6–10], the external covering was of marble, while the internal coverings were of plastic, paint, wood, or paper, which were accordingly classified based on the real permeability levels (1/200, 1/100, 1/45, and 1/30 g·m/MN·s, respectively) obtained in laboratory test. In our case study, these same office buildings were employed with the same external covering of marble. This marble surface can be considered as do not act in moisture transfer through the wall due to its polished surface.

2.2. Sampled Variables and Mathematical Models

In the present case study, based on previous research works on heat and mass transfer processes of wall construction materials [6–10], the evolution with time of the indoor and outdoor partial vapour pressure was selected as the study variable. As explained earlier, indoor conditions of temperature and relative humidity were sampled with Tinytag Plus 2 dual channel dataloggers with thermistor and capacitive sensors were also installed to record temperature and relative humidity values with accuracies +/−0.2 °C and +/−3% of relative humidity, respectively [23].

These data loggers were placed in both employees' zone and clients' zone section of the office building with a sampling frequency of ten minutes for a period of one year. At the same time, based on weather information from nearer weather stations, it was possible to define the simultaneous indoor and outdoor conditions of temperature, relative humidity and pressure in each office building. Based on these moist air variables, it was possible to determine the partial vapour pressure inside and outside the office building.

Likewise, it must be remembered that moisture cumulated in building construction materials is released or adsorbed in only the first 4 h, as it was determined by Hameury and Lundstrom based on real sampled data of indoor ambiences [24]. Therefore, the unoccupied period can be considered a long period of time where, as revealed in previous research [6–9], the moisture transfer equation depended on the partial vapour pressure. Based on this, it was possible to define a clear relation between partial vapour pressure and moisture transfer equation during the night time, as detailed in Equation (1).

$$q_M = -k_d(u, T)\nabla P_v - \rho_o D_w(u, T)\nabla u + v_{air}\rho_v + K\rho_w g \tag{1}$$

where q_M is the mass flux (kg/(m²·s)), k_d is the vapour permeability (kg/(s·m·Pa)), u is the moisture content ($kg_{water}/kg_{Dry\ air}$), P_v is the partial pressure of water vapour (Pa), ρ_0 is the dry density of porous material (kg/m³), and D_w is the liquid moisture diffusivity (m²/s).

Thus, it was possible to assume that, for long periods of time, despite the fact that during the first 4 h of the unoccupied period the air changes were reduced and materials actuated realising or adsorbing humidity, the partial vapour pressure depends on the first term of the Fick's law, as shown in Equation (1).

After the main data was obtained, it was possible to train an ANN with various input variables and only one output variable for future optimization. Thus, it was possible to train the network with the outdoor temperature and relative humidity as well as define indoor vapour pressure values.

2.3. Neural Nets Predictions and Software Resources

An artificial neural network (ANN) or neural network toolbox (NNT) receives numeric inputs, performs different computation processes with them and provides an output. To reach this objective, a neural network takes to connect units defined as nodes (neurons) arranged in layers. The first layer receives the input data and transmits this to the next hidden layers until reaching the final output value.

Based on these principles, an NNT is employed as an alternative to traditional statistical procedures and it is usually employed as a function of approximation to define complex relationships under great reliability when the output value is a single variable. Since in previous works [6–9] it was possible the aggrupation of 25 office buildings based on a statistical similarity of its indoor moist air evolution as a function of weather conditions or, what is the same, 25 office buildings with the same internal covering permeability level (permeable, semi-permeable and impermeable internal covering material), now it should be possible to find the same results by means NNT. What is more, if now we train some indoor ambiences of one representative office building of each internal covering permeability level as a function of weather conditions by means of NNT, it would be a really interesting tool for redesign indoor ambiences in future office buildings.

Different considerations during the NNT configuration were done to reach this objective:

- Selection of NNT: There are different types of nets such as Multi-Layer Feedforward Network (MLF), Generalized Regression Neural Nets (GRN) and Probabilistic Neural Nets (PN). In an MLF net, the user must define the topology (number of layers and nodes), while, in a GRN/PN net, there is no need to make topology decisions and two hidden layers are employed. It must be remembered that the net topology is the selection of the number of layers and the number of nodes in the layer that determines the network capacity to learn the relationship between independent and dependent variables. At the same time, the main literature conclusions [25–28] about network topology are that a single hidden layer with few nodes is sufficient for most cases. Considering that this was the first of its kind study, a probabilistic neural network (GRN/PN) was selected to reach a precision level during the training and testing processes, as shown in Figure 2.

- Control algorithm: it is important to highlight that the error, which is measured as the mean square difference between the actual output value and the output value obtained from the net while training the numerical prediction, is employed as the control parameter to stop the training process.
- Prevention of over-training: NNT needs to prevent over-training. Over-training is when the net not only learns the general relations between variables and is very near to the particular case employed during the training. In this sense, as a normal validation procedure a part of the training data—usually 20% of the sampled data—is employed to test the net once it is trained.
- Input variables: the minimum number of input values to train a network was considered. As the sampling process of temperature and relative humidity during the unoccupied period of the offices was about 10 min, the number of values obtained for each variable during few other nights can be considered sufficient to train and test a neural net.

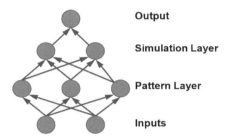

Figure 2. Example of Generalized Regression Neural Nets (GRN) net.

Finally, once main considerations for our training procedure were done, Matlab Simulink Neural Network Toolbox (R2015b) [29] was selected as software resource to develop this task due to its so specific toolbox and configuration for this so simple initial case study.

3. Results

3.1. ANN Selection and Training

As explained earlier, 25 neural networks were trained and tested based on indoor and outdoor sampled data during the extreme winter and summer seasons to develop future predictions of indoor ambiences as a function of the daily weather. In particular, a GRN/PN network was selected as a dependent variable of the indoor partial vapour pressure and an independent variable for the outdoor partial vapour pressure.

As the frequency of 10 min gave about 80 samples per day during the unoccupied period, more than 1 week was needed to obtain a minimum training data of 300 samples. Finally, 75% of the data were employed to train the network and 25% were employed to validate the same.

The stopping criteria were the minimum absolute number of errors obtained in most of the indoor vapour pressure predictions. In particular, the maximum absolute error allowed was fixed in 6 during the training and 9 during the testing (standard deviation ±8%), which represents an actual nearly null percentage of incorrect predictions [25–28] as a clear example of the power of ANNs to model this process. Finally, all this training process required about 1 h per office building, in a Hewlett Packard Intel i5-4200U computer.

3.2. Validation Results

Like in past studies [6–10], extreme office buildings were analysed because their behaviour can be identified easily as a consequence of the real permeability level. As a consequence, indoor ambiences in these different offices were trained in the previous section and now simulated by the obtained ANNs models to be tested. Results showed a good agreement between the sampled and predicted curves of indoor partial vapour pressure as a function of outdoor weather conditions (outdoor partial vapour pressure), as reflected in Figures 3–6.

In such figures, more than 700 values of the outdoor weather conditions are employed to test the NNT and represented by a red line, its respective sampled indoor conditions by a blue line, and the predicted values obtained by the NNT are shown in a green line. On the horizontal axis, part of the number of samples of indoor and outdoor conditions with a time frequency of ten minutes are shown.

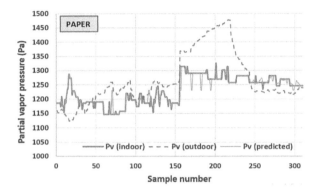

Figure 3. Partial vapour in office buildings using paper as an internal covering material.

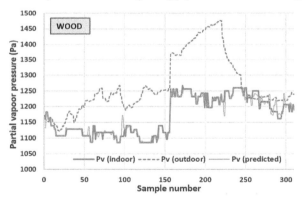

Figure 4. Partial vapour in office buildings with wood as an internal covering material.

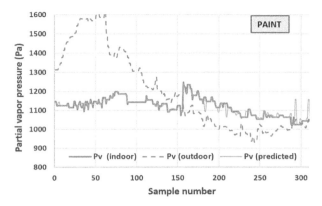

Figure 5. Partial vapour in office buildings with paint as an internal covering material.

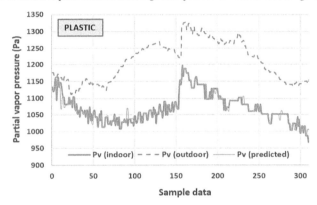

Figure 6. Partial vapour in office buildings with plastic as an internal covering material.

3.3. Internal Coverings Behaviour Characterisation

Once a neural net is trained for each of the interesting office buildings in accordance with a previous study—in which a testing laboratory bedroom was the subject of simulated outdoor weather conditions to analyse indoor ambience behaviour [4], in the present case study, partial vapour pressure was changed from 1200 to 1400 Pa and to 1000 Pa as outdoor weather conditions, and the predicted indoor conditions were compared with the effects obtained in the testing chamber. This procedure will allow one to understand the real behaviour of internal coverings in a transient process as it happens in real buildings and not in testing chambers.

Once each of the office building was modelled and tested with a neural network, past results obtained in [6–10] were applied to analyse the predicted values of internal vapour pressure for each office as a function of its internal covering effect. So, in Figures 7 and 8 it can be observed how the same sampled per hour weather conditions were employed as input data for each one neural network after trained. Because of this, a new output value for each different internal covering is represented in the unoccupied period (Figure 7) and occupied period (Figure 8). In this way, it can be observed in such figures the predicted effect over indoor ambiences partial vapour pressure of each internal covering under the same outdoor weather conditions.

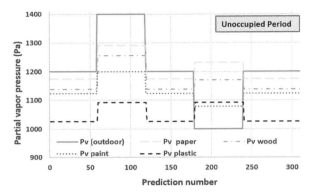

Figure 7. Artificial neural networks (ANNs) prediction of indoor and outdoor partial vapour pressure during the unoccupied period.

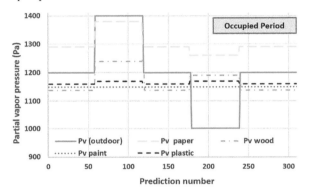

Figure 8. ANNs prediction of indoor and outdoor partial vapour pressure during the occupied period.

4. Discussion

In the past, the authors found that permeable covering tended to control indoor partial vapour pressure during the unoccupied period as a consequence of low air changes [6–10]. In this regard, permeable covering materials such as paper and wood reach a lower maximum humidity in the summer and a higher minimum humidity in the winter than impermeable ones [6]. As a consequence, permeable coverings are considered as very resourceful internal covering material for seeking thermal comfort and, at the same time, for improving the energy saving [8,9].

From these works it was concluded that, as a consequence of long periods of inoccupation—which can be considered to be longer than 4 h, permeable internal coverings can serve to control indoor ambiences to comfortable levels, thereby resulting in lower energy consumption for air conditioning the indoor ambiences during the first hour of occupation.

As explained earlier (Figures 3–6), NNT can be trained to predict indoor partial vapour pressure as a function of outdoor weather conditions. From these trained networks, the effect of permeable internal coverings can be analysed during the winter season for different experimental values of the outdoor weather conditions.

Furthermore, as the networks were trained for unoccupied and occupied periods, the respective effects could be analysed separately (Figures 7 and 8, respectively). Figure 7 depicts examples of outdoor winter weather conditions for this region (Galicia, a humid region of the Northwest Spain), which presents lower partial vapour pressure than that in summers. In this figure, the red line indicates a partial pressure evolution from 1200 to 1400 Pa and from 1200 to 1000 Pa. As a consequence of this evolution, during the unoccupied period, permeable materials like paper (represented by a yellow line) allow indoor partial vapour pressure to reach the higher value of nearly 1300 Pa and, when this outdoor value is reduced to 1000 Pa, the permeable coverings tended to release the cumulated moisture to indoor ambience and increase the partial vapour pressure till 1225 Pa, which is in clear agreement with the main results obtained in previous research works [6–10].

At the same time, in accordance with its permeability level, the remaining internal coverings act in a similar or less intense manner. For wooden materials (represented in green line), a similar behaviour as of paper was seen, albeit with a lower peak of indoor partial vapour values.

On the other hand, more impermeable materials such as paint demonstrated no sensitivity to the outdoor weather conditions and maintained its initial value during all experiments. An example of the behaviour of relay impermeable materials by impermeable materials like plastic is represented by a black dashed line (see Figure 7). As can be seen, when the outdoor weather condition changes, these materials exert lower partial vapour pressure on the indoor ambiences. This effect is in contraposition with the comfort conditions and the related energy consumption to condition this ambience; which is in in clear agreement with previous papers [6–10].

If the effect of these same outdoor weather conditions is analysed during the occupation period when the air changes are much higher, the effect of internal covering cannot be clearly detected and may be neglected (see Figure 8). From this figure, it can be can conclude that most of the offices tended to maintain their partial vapour pressure to an average value of 1100 Pa, and, only permeable materials showed an average value during this occupation period. In particular, indoor ambiences of offices with paper (yellow) or wooden (green) internal coverings showed an evolution influenced by outdoor weather conditions. This result is in agreement with previous research works [6–10].

According to the need of the technicians to understand the proposed procedure to relate indoor and outdoor conditions and internal coverings properties and, in particular, with the aim to define an adequate mathematical model that could be employed for engineers and architects, different simulations were needed to obtain this relation to our particular buildings, like in previous studies [30,31]. In this sense, NNT results revealed that it was possible to define an adequate three-dimensional model obtained, like in previous research works [31], by curve fitting of data previously obtained from software resources like Energy Plus or by neuronal networks for different internal covering materials (see Figures 9 and 10). This behaviour was simulated under an outdoor partial vapor pressure of 800–1200 Pa to show the expected indoor partial vapor pressure.

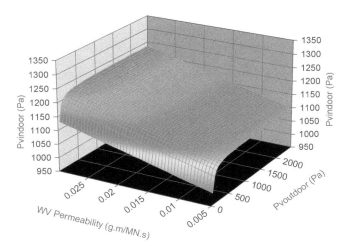

Figure 9. Indoor vapour pressure as a function of outdoor conditions and permeability during the unoccupied period.

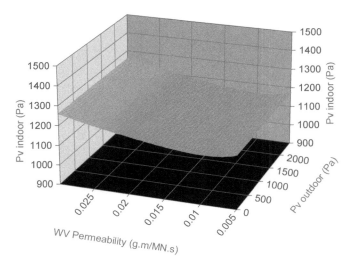

Figure 10. Indoor vapour pressure as a function of outdoor conditions and permeability during the occupied period.

Owing to both the need for an initial permeability value for each internal covering material to develop a final model that considers this variable and the values reflected in previous research works from test laboratories about the permeability level of the same materials [6–10], previously defined values were employed as the second input variable for the curve-fitting process. In this case, the determination factor was $r^2 = 0.806$ and the model obtained was reflected in Equation (2).

$$P_{v\_indoor} = 1072.1 - \frac{5494.6}{P_{v\_outdoor}} + 5460.7 \times k_d \tag{2}$$

where P_{v_indoor} is the indoor water vapor pressure (Pa), $P_{v\_outdoor}$ is the outdoor water vapor pressure (Pa) and k_d is the internal coverings water vapor permeability (g·m/MN·s).

It is interesting to highlight that, if the obtained Equation (2) is employed in an inverse way, it is possible to define the real permeability value in these real buildings through the sampled indoor and outdoor partial vapor pressure. Therefore, it could be a new and original methodology to determine the real effect of internal coverings and to determine how it was changing through the time due to materials' waste and damage.

Considering that this process occurs during long periods of time and in accordance with the moisture transfer equation (Equation (2)), only the first term must be modelled in this process as a consequence of the study period is concluded. In this sense, the second term of Equation (2) shows the effect of cumulated moisture in internal coverings. This effect will control indoor ambiences during a maximum of 4 h, after which its control capability remains only a function of the water vapour permeability, the first term of Equation (2).

On the other hand, the three-dimensional model of the occupied period revealed a horizontal plane that shows an indoor ambience experimenting a nearly null influence of the permeability level of internal coverings as a consequence of a great number of air changes during the working hours. This result is in clear agreement with that in previous works [6–10], and, as a result, it cannot be defined a clear difference between material behaviours when the number of air changes in an indoor ambience is high. In conclusion, indoor ambience is a function of outdoor weather conditions.

Our results suggest that neuronal networks allow the definition of an accurate model that can be employed in prediction studies unlike traditional statistical studies. In this sense, a map of the relationship between indoor and outdoor partial vapor pressure was obtained. Furthermore, this chart depicts an example of a new methodology to define hygroscopic material properties after they are placed in their final construction position, which can be considered as the first step toward future indoor ambience simulation and optimization.

Finally, this method, based on sampled data and a new generation of data mining techniques is just an example of application to improve indoor ambiences towards thermal comfort improvement and energy saving optimization. Furthermore, future applications of this procedure will help to improve indoor ambiances based on the amount and type of internal covering employed in an indoor ambience towards a natural control system of indoor ambience based on this building constants and passive methods.

Future works of this effect during the summer must be done to validate the effect of internal coverings materials, as it was concluded by previous researchers [32,33], and try to model this. Furthermore, final works about the effect of local thermal comfort and the energy peak during the first hours of occupation must be done and, furthermore, about the optimization of passive and active strategies in the early phase of a building's life cycle [30].

More other points of view can be considered at the time of selecting internal coverings, e.g., the prevention of fire expansion in office buildings. Anyway, based on the obtained experience, impermeable coverings are usually employed because plastic and glass are easier to be cleaned than paper and wood, which turns out to be a decisive aspect in the selection of coatings for public buildings.

5. Conclusions

The present research proposes a new methodology to predict the indoor ambience based on NNT procedure and using real-sampled data that would provide better insights to future research toward improving the system of predicting indoor ambiences and reaching a more detailed database of real material properties.

From this research, it can be concluded that it is possible to develop a predictive model of internal coverings' effect based on ANN and real-sampled data. This way, such a model becomes a useful tool to help predict the expected materials thermal behaviour. Furthermore, obtained ANN models showed that the control level of internal coverings is directly related to the vapor permeability, which is in clear agreement with previous statistical studies, thereby indicating the validity of this methodology.

In this case study, a common indoor partial vapor pressure model was obtained as a function of the permeability level of internal coverings and outdoor weather conditions during non-occupancy. Our results suggest that, as a consequence of the long period of non-occupation, the average effect of moisture release of materials can be neglected, and the model can be identified as the first term of the moisture transfer equation.

Simultaneously, the second model that reflects the same indoor conditions during the occupancy period as a function of material permeability level and outdoor weather conditions can be represented by a nearly horizontal plane. In other words, during this period, as a consequence of the high number of air changes, the permeability effect of internal coverings does not exert any effect on the indoor conditions.

Furthermore, as an example of the predictive accuracy of the ANN, our results showed that, during the winter unoccupied period, permeable materials tended to increase the internal partial vapor pressure and, on the contrary, impermeable internal coverings demonstrated the opposite behaviour. These results are in clear agreement with the main results obtained in our earlier studies [6–10].

Finally, for future research, the authors plan to focus on developing systems to improve thermal comfort and optimize energy saving on an average and during peak conditions, especially during the first hours of occupation. Furthermore, in-detail analysis of a new internal coverings design criteria based on these results is warranted.

Author Contributions: Conceptualization, J.A.O.; Methodology, J.A.O., Á.M.C. and R.B.; Software, J.A.O.; Validation, D.V., Á.M.C. and R.B.; Formal Analysis, J.A.O., D.V., Á.M.C. and R.B.; Data Curation, J.A.O. and D.V.; Writing—Original Draft Preparation, J.A.O.; Writing—Review and Editing, J.A.O. and D.V.

Funding: This research was funded by CYPE Ingenieros S.A. in their research project to reduce energy consumption in buildings and its certification, in collaboration with the University of A Coruña (Spain) and the University of Porto (Portugal) (Grant No. 64900).

Acknowledgments: The authors wish to express their deepest gratitude to the Sustainability Specialization Campus of the University of A Coruña for the administrative and technical support.

Conflicts of Interest: The authors declare no conflict of interest.

References

1. Padfield, T. The Role of Absorbent Building Materials In Moderating Changes of Relative Humidity. Ph.D. Thesis, The Technical University of Denmark, Kgs. Lyngby, Denmark, October 1998.
2. Hens, H. Indoor Climate in Student Rooms: Measured Values. IEA-EXCO Energy Conservation in Buildings and Community Systems Annex 41 "Moist-Eng" Glasgow Meeting. 2004. Available online: https://www.researchgate.net/publication/237716820_Indoor_climate_in_student_rooms_measured_values (accessed on 24 March 2019).
3. Cromwijk, J.; Mateo-Cecilia, C.; Jareño-Escudero, C.; Schröpfer, V.; Op't Veld, P. An introduction to a novel and rapid nZEB skill-mapping and qualification framework methodology. *Buildings* **2017**, *7*, 107. [CrossRef]
4. EBC Annex 41. Available online: http://www.iea-ebc.org/projects/project?AnnexID=41 (accessed on 27 April 2019).
5. Kalagasidis, A.S. Ham-Tools-An Integrated Simulation Tool for Heat Air and Moisture Transfer Analysis in Building Physics. Ph.D. Thesis, Chalmers University of Technology, Gothenburg, Sweden, January 2004.
6. Orosa, J.A.; Baaliña, A. Passive climate control in Spanish office buildings for long periods of time. *Build. Environ.* **2008**, *43*, 2005–2012. [CrossRef]
7. Orosa, J.A.; Baaliña, A. Improving PAQ and comfort conditions in Spanish office buildings with passive climate control. *Build. Environ.* **2009**, *44*, 502–508. [CrossRef]
8. Orosa, J.A.; Oliveira, A.C. Energy saving with passive climate control methods in Spanish office buildings. *Energy Build.* **2009**, *41*, 823–828. [CrossRef]
9. Orosa, J.A.; Oliveira, A.C. Reducing energy peak consumption with passive climate control methods. *Energy Build.* **2011**, *43*, 2282–2288. [CrossRef]
10. Orosa, J.A.; Oliveira, A.C.; Ramos, N.M.M. Experimental quantification of the operative time of a passive HVAC system using porous covering materials. *J. Porous Media Palgrave Macmillan* **2010**, *13*, 637–643. [CrossRef]
11. Mazzeo, D.; Oliveti, G.; Arcuri, N. A method for thermal dimensioning and for energy behavior evaluation of a building envelope PCM layer by using the characteristic days. *Energies* **2017**, *10*, 659. [CrossRef]
12. Chou, J.S.; Bui, D.K. Modeling heating and cooling loads by artificial intelligence for energy-efficient building design. *Energy Build.* **2014**, *82*, 437–446. [CrossRef]
13. Buratti, C.; Lascaro, E.; Palladino, D.; Vergoni, M. Building behavior simulation by means of artificial neural network in summer conditions. *Sustainability* **2014**, *6*, 5339–5353. [CrossRef]
14. Tian, Q.; Zhao, W.; Wei, Y.; Pang, L. Thermal environment prediction for metro stations based on an RVFL neural network. *Algorithms* **2018**, *11*, 49. [CrossRef]
15. Xu, X.; Feng, G.; Chi, D.; Liu, M.; Dou, B. Optimization of performance parameter design and energy use prediction for nearly zero energy buildings. *Energies* **2018**, *11*, 3252. [CrossRef]
16. Ngo, N.T. Early predicting cooling loads for energy-efficient design in office buildings by machine learning. *Energy Build.* **2019**, *182*, 264–273. [CrossRef]
17. Ballarini, I.; De Luca, G.; Paragamyan, A.; Pellegrino, A.; Corrado, V. Transformation of an office building into a nearly zero energy building (nZEB): Implications for thermal and visual comfort and energy performance. *Energies* **2019**, *12*, 895. [CrossRef]
18. Taleb, H.M. Using passive cooling strategies to improve thermal performance and reduce energy consumption of residential buildings in U.A.E. buildings. *Front. Archit. Res.* **2014**, *3*, 154–165. [CrossRef]

19. Nematchoua, M.K.; Tchinda, R.; Orosa, J.A.; Andreasi, W.A. Effect of wall construction materials over indoor air quality in humid and hot climate. *J. Build. Eng.* **2015**, *3*, 16–23. [CrossRef]

20. Khan, H.S.; Asif, M.; Mohammed, M.A. Case study of a nearly zero energy building in Italian climatic conditions. *Infrastructures* **2017**, *2*, 19. [CrossRef]

21. Orosa, J.A.; Oliveira, A.C. *Passive Methods as a Solution for Improving Indoor Environments*; Springer-Verlag London Limited: London, UK, 2012.

22. Ahmad, T.; Chen, H.; Guo, Y.; Wang, J. A comprehensive overview on the data driven and large scale based approaches for forecasting of building energy demand: A review. *Energy Build.* **2018**, *165*, 301–320. [CrossRef]

23. Gemini Data Loggers 2016. Available online: http://www.geminidataloggers.com (accessed on 24 March 2019).

24. Hameury, S.; Lundstrom, T. Contribution of indoor exposed massive wood to a good indoor climate: In situ measurement campaign. *Energy Build.* **2004**, *36*, 281–292. [CrossRef]

25. Karkalos, N.E.; Efkolidis, N.; Kyratsis, P.; Markopoulos, A.P. A comparative study between regression and neural networks for modeling Al6082-T6 alloy drilling. *Machines* **2019**, *7*, 13. [CrossRef]

26. Neto, F.C.; Geronimo, T.M.; Cruz, C.E.D.; Aguiar, P.R.; Bianchi, E.E.C. Neural models for predicting hole diameters in drilling processes. *Procedia CIRP* **2013**, *12*, 49–54. [CrossRef]

27. Singh, A.K.; Panda, S.S.; Pal, S.K.; Chakraborty, D. Predicting drill wear using an artificial neural network. *Int. J. Adv. Manuf. Technol.* **2006**, *28*, 456–462. [CrossRef]

28. Nalbant, M.; Gokkaya, H.; Toktas, I. Comparison of regression and artificial neural network models for surface roughness prediction with the cutting parameters in CNC turning. *Model. Simul. Eng.* **2007**, *2007*, 92717. [CrossRef]

29. MatlabWorks 2016. Create, Train, and Simulate Neural Networks. Available online: https://www.mathworks.com/products/neural-network.html (accessed on 26 April 2019).

30. Oh, J.; Hong, T.; Kim, H.; An, J.; Jeong, K.; Koo, C. Advanced strategies for net-zero energy building: Focused on the early phase and usage phase of a building's life cycle. *Sustainability* **2017**, *9*, 2272. [CrossRef]

31. Lu, S.; Wang, R.; Zheng, S. Passive optimization design based on particle swarm optimization in rural buildings of the hot summer and warm winter zone of China. *Sustainability* **2017**, *9*, 2288. [CrossRef]

32. Prabal-Talukdar, U.; Das, A.; Alagirusamy, R. Effect of structural parameters on thermal protective performance and comfort characteristic of fabrics. *J. Text. Inst.* **2017**, *108*, 1430–1441. [CrossRef]

33. Trník, A.; Vozár, L. Modeling of heat capacity peaks and enthalpy jumps of phase-change materials used for thermal energy storage. *Int. J. Heat Mass Transf.* **2017**, *107*, 123–132. [CrossRef]

Article

Contribution of High Mechanical Fatigue to Gas Turbine Blade Lifetime during Steady-State Operation

Sung Yong Chang [1,2] and Ki-Yong Oh [3,*]

[1] Power Generation Laboratory, Korea Electric Power Corporation Research Institute, Munjiro 105, Yuseong-gu, Daejeon 34056, Korea; sy.chang@kepco.co.kr
[2] School of Advanced Materials Engineering, Chung-Nam National University, 99 DaeHak-ro, Yuseong-gu, Daejun 34134, Korea
[3] School of Energy System Engineering, Chung-Ang University, 84 Heukseok-ro, Dongjak-gu, Seoul 06974, Korea
* Correspondence: kiyongoh@cau.ac.kr; Tel.: +82-2-820-5385

Received: 12 February 2019; Accepted: 22 March 2019; Published: 31 March 2019

Abstract: In this study, the contribution of high thermomechanical fatigue to the gas turbine lifetime during a steady-state operation is evaluated for the first time. An evolution of the roughness on the surface between the thermal barrier coating and bond coating is addressed to elucidate the correlation between operating conditions and the degradation of a gas turbine. Specifically, three factors affecting coating failure are characterized, namely isothermal operation, low-cycle fatigue, and high thermomechanical fatigue, using laboratory experiments and actual service-exposed blades in a power plant. The results indicate that, although isothermal heat exposure during a steady-state operation contributes to creep, it does not contribute to failure caused by coating fatigue. Low-cycle fatigue during a transient operation cannot fully describe the evolution of the roughness between the thermal barrier coating and the bond coating of the gas turbine. High thermomechanical fatigue during a steady-state operation plays a critical role in coating failure because the temperature of hot gas pass components fluctuates up to 140 °C at high operating temperatures. Hence, high thermomechanical fatigue must be accounted for to accurately predict the remaining useful lifetime of a gas turbine because the current method of predicting the remaining useful lifetime only accounts for creep during a steady-state operation and for low-cycle fatigue during a transient operation.

Keywords: degradation; high mechanical fatigue; hot gas path components; gas turbine lifetime; gas turbine blade

---

1. Introduction

Gas turbines form the heart of the electric power and aerospace industries, which has prompted a large amount of research into the use of material, mechanical el, and electrical engineering for increasing their efficiency [1–3]. Significant technological advances have led to increasing operating temperatures and pressures in recent decades, enhancing the efficiency of gas turbines to over 40%. These technological advances include coatings, heat treatments, a new superalloy permitting high operating temperatures, and a new cooling system [4–11]. Specifically, an F-class gas turbine, which operates at approximately 1300 °C and a pressure ratio of 16 during full-load conditions, was developed in the late 1990s and deployed to many thermal power plants. Gas turbines of the G and J classes, which operate at approximately 1500 and 1600 °C and a pressure ratio of 21 and 23, respectively, during full-load conditions, were also developed in the early 2000s and deployed to newly constructed thermal power plants. Power plants that deploy these high-efficiency gas turbines are currently operational and under construction.

As the operating temperature of gas turbines increases, the thermal barrier coating (TBC) laminated on the hot gas pass components (HGPCs) at the first and second stages of gas turbines [12] has received increased research attention. The blades and vanes of the third and fourth turbine stages of gas turbines are not coated because the metal superalloys used for these components can withstand the more moderate operating temperatures of the third and fourth stages without the TBC. The TBC not only permits increased gas temperatures and reduced cooling requirements but also improves fuel efficiency and reliability. It plays a critical role in protecting the substrate of the HGPCs at the first and second stages of gas turbines because the superalloy, which can withstand high temperatures of over 1500 °C, is still developing at this time. Hence, the TBC mitigates heat transfer from the coating surface of the HGPCs to the substrate of the HGPCs; the thermal gradient between the two is approximately 200 °C. Therefore, the role of the TBC suggests that the failure modes of HGPCs are different from those of the other components.

If the TBC on the HGPCs becomes damaged or cracked, the substrate starts to degrade because of creep and fatigue. In contrast to HGPCs, other components such as the third- and fourth-stage blades and vanes are affected by creep and fatigue during the entire operation, owing to lack of surface coating. Thus, coating failure accelerates HGPC degradation because the metal is directly exposed to high operating temperatures, suggesting that HGPC coatings should be carefully examined and promptly repaired.

To this end, power utility companies schedule periodic maintenance known as overhaul, during which all HGPCs are disassembled and examined by an expert system following standard maintenance guidelines for gas turbines [13–18]. The expert system evaluates the coating failure and damage of HGPCs according to three categories: normal, repair, or replace. Coating failure is one of the most important features of an overhaul because it results in a fatigue failure of the substrate. Note that creep effects on the substrate can be rejuvenated using heat treatment [19,20]; thus, fatigue damage to the metal after TBC failure is more important than creep. The overhaul procedure and failure mechanism of HGPCs clearly suggest that scheduling prompt operations and maintenances (O&M) can mitigate concerns regarding coating failure due to fatigue. Moreover, the proactive maintenance of and the accurate estimation of an HGPC lifetime is an effective way to secure the safety and reliability of HGPCs as well as decrease O&M costs. Note that power utility companies typically aim to reuse HGPCs after overhaul repairs as replacing them is more expensive.

A coating failure is mainly caused by fatigue resulting from two phenomena on the coating layers. One is rumpling caused by cyclic local volume changes [21,22] due to chemical reactions in the coating layer surfaces. Local volume changes are caused by aluminum depletion and the subsequent decomposition of the β-(Ni, Pt)Al phase in a bond coat. The other phenomenon is ratcheting [23] caused by significant variations in the operating temperature, which results in periodic thermal stress on the coating layers. This phenomenon leads to undulating interfaces between the TBC and the bond coat due to thermally grown oxide that produces undesirable cyclic failure modes when it is larger than a critical undulation amplitude [24]. In addition, creep causes the growth of an interdiffusion zone and aluminum depletion layer when coatings are exposed to constant and uniform high temperature [25–27]. However, these effects do not result in coating failures (i.e., the metal is not directly exposed to high operating temperatures owing to creep).

The effects of fatigue on gas turbine lifetime have been comprehensively studied to understand the degradation mechanisms and failure modes of HGPCs [28–31] and to assess their remaining useful lifetime (RUL) [32–34]. These studies enable one to accurately estimate the operational lifetime of HGPCs and their coating layers in a gas turbine. Hence, fatigue is nowadays considered together with creep to predict the RUL of HGPCs. Specifically, low-cycle fatigue during start, stop, and trip operations and creep during steady-state operations are accounted for by calculating the equivalent operating hours (EOHs) that determine the maintenance interval of a gas turbine. This approach assumes that creep only affects the gas turbine lifetime during a steady-state operation, owing to the constant and uniform temperature [13–18]. However, EOHs cannot fully explain the degradation of actual service-exposed blades and vanes during an overhaul. The gap between EOHs and the scrap rate that represents the RUL of a gas turbine suggests the need to elucidate the effect of both creep and fatigue on gas turbine degradation by evaluating service-exposed blades and vanes and the operating temperature.

This is the first study to characterize the contribution of fatigue to coating degradation using laboratory experiments and an analysis of service-exposed blades and vanes. In the laboratory experiments, the effect of creep on coating failure was quantified by analyzing the roughness changes in coupon specimens, which replicate the actual coatings of blades and vanes, exposed to 8000 h of operation in a range of high, constant temperatures. In the analysis of service-exposed blades and vanes, scrapped F-class service-exposed blades and vanes were analyzed using the evolution of roughness and operational data obtained from a supervisory control and data acquisition (SCADA) system. Several factors were considered to accurately predict the RUL of a gas turbine based on the aforementioned analyses.

2. Experiments

Two experimental approaches were employed to quantify the effects of isothermal heat exposure and fatigue on coating degradation. First, coupon specimens were prepared in the laboratory. These specimens were exposed to a range of uniform high temperatures to characterize the correlation between an isothermal heat treatment and the evolution of fatigue. Second, scrap blades and vanes were analyzed by observing the evolution of the roughness and analyzing the operational data obtained from a SCADA system, including the generated power and the inlet temperature of the gas turbine. Scrapped blades and vanes were deployed in an F-class gas turbine operating at a rotating speed of 3600 rpm and inlet temperature of 1293 °C (Figure 1). The specimens were cut from a cross section of the service-exposed blade airfoil 15 mm below the top of the blade tip. The specimens were fabricated with a diameter of 30 mm and thickness of 3 mm. The roughness due to rumpling and ratcheting, which is a sensitive metric for evaluating coating fatigue failure, was measured for a quantitative comparison.

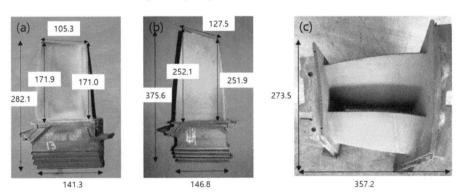

Figure 1. Service-exposed hot gas pass components (HGPCs): (**a**) first-stage blade, (**b**) second-stage blade, and (**c**) second-stage vane (unit: mm).

For the matrix of the coupon specimens in the laboratory experiments, a nickel-based directionally solidified IN738LC superalloy (nominal composition: 8.5 wt. % Co, 16 wt. % Cr, 3.4 wt. % Al, 3.4 wt. % Ti, 1.75 wt. % Mo, 2.6 wt. % W, 1.75 wt. % Ta, 0.85 wt. % Nb, 0.12 wt. % Zr, 0.012 wt. % B, 0.13 wt. % C, and the rest is Ni [35]) was cast. The specimens were cut to a diameter of 30 mm and thickness of 3 mm and prepared with the appropriate surface roughness for the adhesion of the bond and top coats by sand blasting; Sa, measured with Keyence VX-X260K (Keyence, Osaka, Japan), was less than 10.49 μm. Atmospheric plasma spray (APS, 9M, Oerlikon Metco, Westbury, NY, USA) and low-vacuum plasma spray (LVPS, Multicoat, Oerlikon Metco, Wohlen, Switzerland), 8 wt. % Y_2O_3-ZrO_3 and NiCoCrAlY, were applied onto the IN738LC coupons as a TBC and a corrosion-resistant bond coat, respectively. The thicknesses of the TBC and bond coat (310 and 230 μm, respectively) were designed to replicate those of actual HGPCs, and these vary in the range of 250–400 and 150–300 μm, respectively depending on the manufacturer, type of components, and location, even for the same component [36].

The heat treatment of the specimens was conducted at 1120 °C for 2 h and 840 °C for 24 h in sequence. The specimens were annealed for 8000 h in a furnace at a constant temperature of 850, 950, or 1000 °C at a heating rate of 5 °C/min to quantify the effect of isothermal heat exposure on the evolution of coating fatigue.

Eight of the service-exposed blades and vanes were used to elucidate the effect of high thermomechanical fatigue as well as low-cycle fatigue and isothermal heat exposure on the blades and vanes. The blades and vanes were coated with NiCoCrAlY and stabilized zirconia after being disassembled from a W501F gas turbine at a thermal power plant in Korea, referred to as "power plant A" hereafter because of confidentiality. The blades and vanes were attached to an F-class gas turbine and were determined as fully scrapped during the overhaul by the expert system. The operational history of the blades and vanes obtained from the SCADA system are summarized in Table 1.

Table 1. The operational history of the blades and vanes scrapped from power plant A.

Sample #	Type	Stage	Equivalent Stop (ES) (h)	Operating Hours (OH) (h)	Equivalent Operating Hours (EOH) (h)
1	Blade	1st	741	14,674	29,494
2	Blade	1st	755	13,546	28,646
3	Blade	1st	232	3,248	7,888
4	Blade	2nd	1249	20,000	44,980
5	Blade	2nd	232	3,248	7,888
6	Vane	2nd	238	947	5,707
7	Vane	2nd	232	3,248	7,888

The equivalent operating hours (EOH) in Table 1 are calculated as

$$EOH = 20 \times ES + OH \tag{1}$$

where ES and OH denote the equivalent stop and operating hours [13], respectively. The O&M guidelines of the manufacturers suggest that overhaul should be carried out to repair or replace HGPCs when an ES of 8000 h or an EOH of 24,000 h is met [14–18]. Hence, ES and EOH determines the RUL of components including HPGCs, and the period of overhaul considering two effects; ES accounts for the low-cycle fatigue during transient operations including start, stop, and trip operations, and OH accounts for the creep during steady-state operations. Note that Equation (1) is a phenomenological equation proposed by the manufacturers. The approach used by manufacturers to build Equation (1) and the values of ES and EOH that determine the RUL are strictly confidential. Hence, utility companies follow this guideline [14–18] to schedule the overhaul in general.

One important assumption in Equation (1) is that the operating temperature is constant and uniform during a steady-state operation; therefore, a steady-state operation does not contribute to fatigue. However, the failure mechanism of the HGPCs differs from that of other components, which suggests that the same formula cannot be deployed to calculate the EOH of HGPCs. As mentioned earlier, a coating failure from fatigue occurs first in HPGCs laminated using TBC and a bond coat. Once the coating is completely cracked or damaged, the metal underneath is degraded by creep and fatigue. Degradation is particularly significant in the first and second stages because the metal is exposed to high operating temperatures.

All coupon specimens and service-exposed blades/vanes were mounted and then polished with #800–#2000 SiC paper and then a vibratory polisher with alumina solutions to study their cross-sectional microstructures. The roughness of the bond coat was measured for all specimens by using an optical microscope (DM15000M, Leica, Wizlar, Germany) to quantify the fatigue due to a coating failure. Digital cross-sectional images of all the specimens were analyzed at ×100 magnification to calculate the roughness of the bond coat. Each image was vertically divided into 200 sections, each of which had a horizontal length of approximately 6 μm. Then, the standard deviation of the bond coat surface with respect to the mean value was measured, which is defined as the roughness hereafter, using the Leica Material workstation software (V3.6.2). Four digital images were obtained for each specimen at different locations. The standard deviations of the four digital images were averaged for an accurate estimation of the roughness of each specimen.

3. Results and Discussion

3.1. Contribution of Isothermal Heat Exposure to Fatigue

The thicknesses of the TBC and bond coat of the coupon specimens were measured 10 times via a scanning electron microscope (JSM-7001F, JEOL, Akishima, Tokyo; Figure 2) to verify that the coupon specimens were fabricated as designed. The accuracy and resolution of JSM-7001F were 0.1 and 0.01 μm, respectively. The mean thicknesses of the TBC and bond coat for one coupon specimen were 310.8 and 231.1 μm, respectively. Their respective standard deviations were 15.2 and 13.2 μm, respectively. The thicknesses of other specimens were of a similar order. A reference roughness (i.e., initial roughness) was also measured on one specimen without the isothermal heat treatment as 11.2 μm. This reference roughness (i.e., initial roughness) is shown as a green circle in Figure 3a. The initial roughness was in the preferred range of 8.9–11.4 μm for the plasma sprayed TBC performance [37], suggesting that coupon specimens could be employed to represent the coatings of blades and vanes deployed on F-class gas turbines.

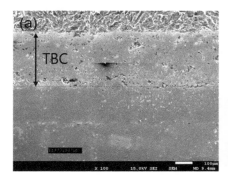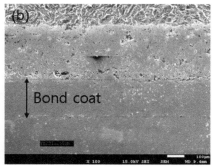

Figure 2. The scanning electron microscope images of a coated specimen: the measured thickness of (**a**) the thermal barrier coating (TBC) and (**b**) the bond coat.

The roughness of the bond coat on coupon specimens was measured to quantify the contribution of isothermal heat exposure to the evolution of fatigue. The evolution of roughness due to isothermal heat treatment is shown in Figure 3a. The square markers with a dashed line, the triangle markers with a solid line, and the circle markers with a dotted line denote the roughness at 850, 950, and 1000 °C (for 8000 h of exposure), respectively.

In Figure 3a, the roughness does not indicate any trends with isothermal heat exposure, suggesting that the isothermal heat treatment does not contribute to the rumpling and ratcheting that result in the fatigue failure of the bond coat. Specifically, an image of the bond coat surface exposed to 8000 h of heat treatment (Figure 3c) is not significantly different from that exposed to 500 h of heat treatment (Figure 3b) at a constant temperature of 1000 °C; the roughness values on the surface between TBC and the bond coat are 11.2 and 11.4 μm, respectively. It can be deduced that the isothermal heat exposure of the blades and vanes only contributes to the degradation caused by creep. In particular, the thermally grown oxide, which is caused by the degradation due to isothermal heat exposure, is negligible in Figure 3b because the coupon specimen is only exposed for 500 h. In contrast, the thickness of thermally grown oxide is 55.3 μm when the coupon specimen is exposed for 8000 h, as shown in Figure 3c. The thickness of the thermally grown oxide is averaged 10 times, and its standard deviation is 9.0 μm. Note that fatigue, which mainly causes coating failure, is of interest in this study. Hence, thermally grown oxide representing the evolution of creep is not analyzed in detail in this study. It can be deduced that the EOH calculated by Equation (1) is reasonable if HGPCs operate only under a constant operating temperature during a steady-state operation.

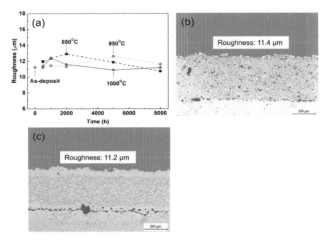

Figure 3. (**a**) The evolution of roughness on the surface between a TBC and bond coating for a variety of isothermal heat exposures and the post-processed optical microscope images representing a slight variation in the roughness on the surface between the TBC and bond coating exposed to (**b**) 500 h and (**c**) 8000 h at a constant temperature of 1000 °C.

3.2. Effects of Steady-State and Transient Operations on Fatigue

The roughness of service-exposed blades and vanes was analyzed to characterize the effect of steady-state and transient operations on the evolution of fatigue (Figure 4). The square markers with a dashed line, the triangle markers with a solid line, and the circle markers with a dotted line denote the roughness of first-stage blades, second-stage blades, and second-stage vanes, respectively.

Figure 4a shows the relationship between EOH and roughness. The roughness shows a linear dependence on EOH for all blades and vanes. Moreover, the slope of roughness with respect to EOH in the first stage is larger than that of blades and vanes exposed in the second stage, suggesting that the blades in the first stage are affected by a severe operating condition, namely a high operating temperature. These results indicate that an increase in roughness correlates directly with EOH and operating temperature. However, the limit of the result is that the contribution of a steady-state operation cannot be distinguished from that of a transient operation in these data.

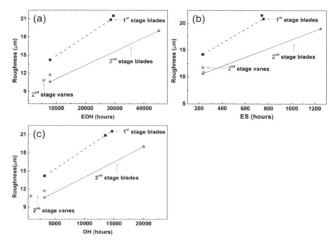

Figure 4. The controls on blade and vane roughness: The effect of (**a**) the equivalent operating hours (EOHs), (**b**) equivalent stop (ES), and (**c**) operational hours (OH) on the blade and vane roughness.

Figure 4b shows the contribution of transient operations, such as the start, stop, and trip operations, to fatigue. A low-cycle fatigue results in rumpling and ratcheting due to thermal shock loading [21,23]; therefore, the roughness should be proportional to ES. Overall, roughness should be proportional the roughness trends for all blades and vanes increase with ES. Moreover, the slope of roughness with respect to ES in the first stage is larger than that of blades and vanes exposed in the second stage, also suggesting that an increase in roughness is directly related to ES and the operating temperature. However, the roughness of the first-stage blade exposed to an ES of 741 h (sample 1) is larger than that exposed to ES of 755 h (sample 2). Although the ES of sample 1 is smaller than that of sample 2, the OH of sample 1 is larger than that of sample 2. Similarly, the roughness of the second-stage vane exposed to an ES of 232 h (sample 7) is larger than that exposed to an ES of 238 h; however, the OH of sample 7 is over three times larger than that of sample 6. These observations suggest a hypothesis that a steady-state operation can contribute to an increase in roughness: the longer the steady-state operation, the larger the roughness. However, the variation in the roughness of two vanes at the second stage is not significant, suggesting that the contribution of a steady-state operation to fatigue may be smaller than that of a transient operation.

Figure 4c shows the contribution of a steady-state operation duration to the evolution of roughness. Interestingly, the roughness of all blades and vanes increases with the number of operating hours. This result differs from the results of laboratory experiments with coupon specimens, where the roughness does not vary with the duration of the steady-state operation. There are two possibilities to explain the linear dependence of roughness on the steady-state operation. One is that power plants in Korea use a load-following mode and thereby control the power generation depending on the electricity demand. Hence, the effect of the transient response (i.e., the effect of ES) would be stochastically included in Figure 4c. The other possibility is that another reason exists for the increase in roughness during a steady-state operation. An in-depth analysis of the first hypothesis is not possible with service-exposed blades and vanes because the detailed operational history of the roughness evolution during transient and steady-state operations is not available. Regarding the second hypothesis, it is possible that the temperature is not constant during a steady-state operation. It is our view that both hypotheses contribute to the increased roughness in Figure 4c.

Figure 5 clearly shows an increase in the roughness for service-exposed blades and vanes due to fatigue. Figure 5a shows an image of the first-stage blade (sample 1 in Table 1), whereas Figure 5b shows an image of the second-stage blade (sample 4 in Table 1). The surfaces of the bond coats are rougher than those subjected to an isothermal heat treatment (Figure 3b,c) at 21.6 and 19.0 μm, suggesting again that roughness is a sensitive metric for evaluating the evolution of fatigue.

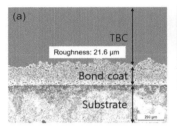 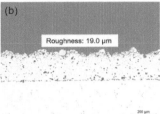

Figure 5. Post-processed optical microscope images of the bond coat surface representing a significant increase in the surface roughness compared to the fresh state (Figure 3b): (**a**) First-stage blade (sample 1 in Table 1) and (**b**) second-stage blade (sample 4 in Table 1).

To test the second hypothesis, the operating temperature of a gas turbine, which was measured from a different power plant, was analyzed. Note that the operational data is extremely difficult to obtain as these are confidential. The temperature of the steady-state operation was obtained from the SCADA system of a different power plant, referred to as "power plant B" hereafter because of confidentiality. This power plant deployed an F-class gas turbine manufactured by General Electric (GE). The total period of the obtained operational data was approximately 22 months, from 18 July 2008 to 27 May 2010. The data included the date, the generated power, and the inlet temperature at 1-h intervals. The inlet temperature of the gas turbine was calculated using the exhaust gas measured at an outlet of the gas turbine with an GE in-house code embedded in the SCADA system [19,38]. This code was developed to predict the temperature of HGPCs because the gas temperature around HGPCs is so high that it is difficult to measure. This data was fed into the SCADA system for optimal control of the power plant.

Figure 6a shows the inlet temperature with respect to the generated power. The generated power of over 150 MW is generally in a steady-state operation (inset of Figure 6a). However, the generated power in the other ranges also includes a steady-state operation because power plants in Korea have introduced a load-following mode. Hence, the inlet temperature during a steady-state operation should be separated from that during a transient operation by considering the inlet temperature over the generated power together with the operational trend. The temperature during a steady-state operation is generally in the range of 1250–1340 °C, whereas the temperature in the transient state changes over a wider range, from room temperature to 1340 °C. The maximum variation of the inlet temperature is approximately 140 °C at steady state, suggesting that temperature variations during a steady-state operation can also result in thermal stress, in addition to transient operations.

Figure 6b shows the temperature variations with 1-h intervals. Within this time interval, temperature variations above 140 °C generally occurred during transient states including the start, stop, and trip operations, whereas temperature variations below 140 °C occurred during the steady-state operation. This figure also demonstrates that the operating temperature varies even during a steady-state operation.

Figure 6c shows the temperature variations during a steady-state operation. The steady-state operation accounted for approximately 4600 h during the entire period of operation. The figure clearly shows that the inlet temperatures of the gas turbine during the steady-state operation are not constant, with a maximum variation of approximately 140 °C. Thus, it can be inferred that temperature variations during a steady-state operation contribute to rumpling and ratcheting and can contribute to thermal fatigue caused by thermal stress. Note that the coefficient of thermal expansion at a temperature of 1000 °C is 1.5 times greater than that at room temperature [39], suggesting that thermal stress during a steady-state operation also significantly affects coating degradation, although the steady-state temperature variations are significantly smaller than those during transient operations. This high thermomechanical fatigue (HMF) observed during a steady-state operation is defined as HMF hereafter.

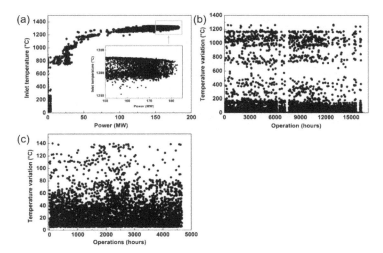

Figure 6. The temperature variation during operation: (**a**) The inlet temperature of a gas turbine against the generated power, (**b**) the variations of the inlet temperature during the entire operation, and (**c**) the variations of the inlet temperature during a steady-state operation.

In order to confirm the contribution of HMF to coating failure, additional operational data were analyzed, as presented in Table 2. These datasets were obtained from the first-stage blades in a different gas turbine in power plant B. Blade 1 and blade 2 were similarly serviced, whereas blade 3 and blade 4 were similarly serviced based on EOH. However, the scrap rate of blades 1 and 2 was different as well as that of blades 3 and 4, suggesting that EOH cannot fully account for the degradation mechanism of the HPGCs. Specifically, the scrap rate ratio of blade 4 to blade 3 was 1.10, whereas the EOH ratio of blade 4 to blade 3 was 1.01. The difference in the scrap rate could be explained by the fact that blade 4 experienced a severely transient operation (ES value in Table 2) compared to blade 3.

Table 2. The scrap rate and operational information of service-exposed blades in the gas turbines of power plant B.

Sample #	Operating Hours (OH) (h)	Equivalent Stop (ES) (h)	Equivalent Operating Hours (EOH) (h)	Scrap Rate (%)
Blade 1	10,908	376	18,428	50
Blade 2	9403	464	18,683	34
Blade 3	11,395	497	21,335	67
Blade 4	10,727	545	21,627	74

Similarly, blade 1 and blade 4 were both operated under steady state; blade 1 was used 1.6% more than blade 4. However, blade 4 was affected by long transient operation; hence, the scrap rate of blade 4 was higher than that of blade 1. These comparisons demonstrated that the thermal shock loading during a transient operation increased the coating failure and, hence, the scrap rate.

In contrast, although the EOH of blade 1 had a similar order of magnitude to that of blade 2, the scrap rate of blade 1 was higher than that of blade 2. A notable factor was that blade 1 was exposed to a shorter transient operation and a longer steady-state operation. This observation cannot be explained using the previous approach. The above comparison clearly suggests that thermal stresses from steady-state temperature fluctuations accumulate in the coatings and contribute to coating failure. Hence, accumulated thermal stress during a steady-state operation should be accounted for when estimating fatigue lifetime to accurately predict the RUL of a gas turbine.

Our analysis of the operational data clearly demonstrates that EOH cannot fully account for the lifetime of HGPCs in a gas turbine because the coatings laminated on the surfaces of the HGPCs have different failure mechanisms compared to other components. Hence, HMF during steady state should be considered to accurately predict coating failures of HGPCs, as proposed in Figure 7. The current approach accounts for only two phenomena: low-cycle fatigue during transient states and creep during steady states. However, HMF during steady states also contributes to coating fatigue. Hence, HMF during steady states should be combined with a low-cycle fatigue to calculate the accumulated fatigue as

$$\text{EOH} = \alpha \times \text{ES} + \beta \times \text{HMP} \tag{2}$$

where α and β denote the contribution factors of each effect.

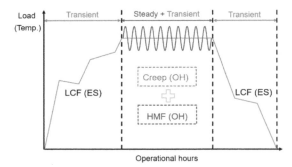

Figure 7. The proposed approach for predicting the remaining useful lifetime (RUL) and coating failure of blades and vanes in a gas turbine.

4. Conclusions

This study characterized the contribution of three factors relevant to the fatigue coating failure of HGPCs in gas turbines, which plays a critical role in the degradation of gas turbines, with the evolution of the surface roughness between the TBC and the bond coat; the factors are low-cycle fatigue during a transient operation, creep (isothermal heat exposure) during a steady state operation, and high thermomechanical fatigue during a steady state operation.

- The low-cycle fatigue during a transient operation correlated highly with the lifetime of HGPCs and linearly depended on transient operation. Hence, the current method that accounts for transient operation to evaluate the RUL of a gas turbine is reasonable.
- Isothermal heat exposure during a steady state operation slightly contributes to the RUL of HGPCs. Laboratory experiments with coupon specimens show that isothermal heat exposure does not increase roughness, although it contributes to the evolution of creep. Hence, the current method that accounts for creep during steady state to evaluate the RUL of a gas turbine should be modified.
- The high thermomechanical fatigue during a steady state operation significantly contributes to fatigue and results in coating failure as the temperature fluctuates up to 140 °C during a steady state operation, whereas the current method to evaluate the RUL of a gas turbine assumes that there is no temperature fluctuation during a steady state operation.
- The current method to evaluate the RUL of a gas turbine accounts for the high thermomechanical fatigue instead of the creep during a steady-state operation. In the future, the study should focus on calculating the thermal stress and strain during the transient state and steady state and on

evaluating the quantitative effect of HMF on coating degradation using additional long-term operational data at various operating conditions and results from laboratory experiments. A detailed phenomenological model of RUL that accounts for the effects of HMF will be developed and validated based on a quantitative analysis.

Author Contributions: Methodology, S.Y.C.; Writing—Original Draft Preparation, K.-Y.O.; Writing—Review and Editing, K.-Y.O.; Supervision, S.Y.C.

Funding: This research was supported by the National Research Foundation of Korea (NRF) grant funded by the Korea government (MEST) (No. 2017R1D1A1B03032746) and the Chung-Ang University Research Grants in 2019.

Conflicts of Interest: The authors declare no conflict of interest.

References

1. Sivakumar, R.; Mordike, B.L. High temperature coatings for gas turbine blades: A review. *Surf. Coat. Technol.* **1989**, *37*, 139–160. [CrossRef]
2. Heppenstall, T. Advanced gas turbine cycles for power generation: A critical review. *Appl. Therm. Eng.* **1998**, *18*, 837–846. [CrossRef]
3. Horlock, J.H. *Advanced Gas Turbine Cycles: A Brief Review of Power Generation Thermodynamics*; Elsevier: Amsterdam, The Netherlands, 2013.
4. Ghai, R.C.; Chen, K.; Baddour, N. Modelling thermal conductivity of porous thermal barrier coatings. *Coatings* **2019**, *9*, 101. [CrossRef]
5. Ye, D.; Wang, W.; Huang, J.; Lu, X.; Zhou, H. Nondestructive interface morphology characterization of thermal barrier coatings using terahertz time-domain spectroscopy. *Coatings* **2019**, *9*, 89. [CrossRef]
6. Guo, X.; Zhao, W.; Zeng, Y.; Lin, C.; Zhang, J. Effects of splat interfaces, monoclinic phase and grain boundaries on the thermal conductivity of plasma sprayed yttria-stabilized zirconia coatings. *Coatings* **2019**, *9*, 26. [CrossRef]
7. Lin, C.; Chai, Y.; Li, Y. Oxidation simulation of thermal barrier coatings with actual microstructures considering strength difference property and creep-plastic behavior. *Coatings* **2018**, *8*, 338. [CrossRef]
8. Manero, A.; Knipe, K.; Wischek, J.; Meid, C.; Okasinski, J.; Almer, J.; Karlsson, A.M.; Bartsch, M.; Raghavan, S. Capturing the competing influence of thermal and mechanical loads on the strain of turbine blade coatings via high energy X-rays. *Coatings* **2018**, *8*, 320. [CrossRef]
9. Dong, H.; Han, Y.; Zhou, Y.; Li, X.; Yao, J.-T.; Li, Y. The temperature distribution in plasma-sprayed thermal-barrier coatings during crack propagation and coalescence. *Coatings* **2018**, *8*, 311. [CrossRef]
10. Xiao, Y.; Ren, E.; Hu, M.; Liu, K. Effect of particle in-flight behavior on the microstructure and fracture toughness of YSZ TBCs prepared by plasma spraying. *Coatings* **2018**, *8*, 309. [CrossRef]
11. Daleo, J.A.; Ellison, K.A.; Boone, D.H. Metallurgical considerations for life assessment and the safe refurbishment and re-qualification of gas turbine blades. *J. Eng. Gas Turbines Power* **2002**, *124*, 571–579. [CrossRef]
12. Padture, N.P.; Gell, M.; Jordan, E.H. Thermal barrier coatings for gas-turbine engine applications. *Science* **2002**, *296*, 280–284. [CrossRef]
13. Janawitz, J.; Masso, J.; Childs, C. *Heavy-Duty Gas Turbine Operating and Maintenance Considerations*; GER: Atlanta, GA, USA, 2015.
14. *F-Class Combustion Turbine Life Management: Siemens V94.3A (SGT5-4000F)*; EPRI: Palo Alto, CA, USA, 2009; p. 1018614.
15. *Design Evolution, Durability, and Reliability of Alstom Heavy-Duty Combustion Turbines: Pedigree Matrices*; EPRI: Palo Alto, CA, USA, 2013; Volume 5, p. 3002001073.
16. *Design Evolution, Durability, and Reliability of Siemens Heavy-Duty Gas Turbines: Pedigree Matrices*; EPRI: Palo Alto, CA, USA, 2014; Volume 4, p. 3002006064.
17. *Design Evolution, Durability and Reliability of Mitsubishi Hitachi Heavy-Duty Gas Turbines: Pedigree Matrices*; EPRI: Palo Alto, CA, USA, 2014; Volume 7, p. 3002003863.
18. *Design Evolution, Durability and Reliability of General Electric Heavy-Duty Gas Turbines: Pedigree Matrices*; EPRI: Palo Alto, CA, USA, 2014; Volume 3, p. 3002003665.

19. Lvova, E.; Norsworth, D. Influence of service-induced microstructural changes on the aging kinetics of rejuvenated Ni-based superalloy gas turbine blades. *J. Mater. Eng. Perform.* **2001**, *10*, 299–313. [CrossRef]
20. Lvova, E. A comparison of aging kinetics of new and rejuvenated conventionally cast GTD-111 gas turbine blades. *Mater. Eng. Perform.* **2007**, *16*, 254–264. [CrossRef]
21. Tolpygo, V.K.; Clarke, D.R. Surface rumpling of A (Ni, Pt) Al bond coat induced by cyclic oxidation. *Acta Mater.* **2000**, *48*, 3283–3293. [CrossRef]
22. Panat, R.; Zhang, S.; Hsia, K. Bond coat surface rumpling in thermal barrier coatings. *Acta Mater.* **2003**, *51*, 239–249. [CrossRef]
23. He, M.Y.; Evans, A.G.; Hutchinson, J.W. The ratcheting of compressed thermally grown thin films on ductile substrates. *Acta Mater.* **2000**, *48*, 2593–2601. [CrossRef]
24. Im, S.H.; Huang, R. Ratcheting-inducted wrinkling of an elastic film on a metal layer under cyclic temperatures. *Acta Mater.* **2004**, *52*, 3707–3719. [CrossRef]
25. Anton, R.; Bkrkner, J.; Czech, N.; Stamm, W. Degradation of advanced MCrAlY coatings by oxidation and interdiffusion. *Mater. Sci. Forum* **2001**, *369*, 719–726. [CrossRef]
26. Viswanathan, R.; Cheruvu, N.S.; Chan, K.S. Coatings for Advanced Large Frame Combustion Turbines for Power Generation. In Proceedings of the ASME Turbo Expo 2003, Atlanta, GA, USA, 16–19 June 2003.
27. Kiruthika, P.; Makineni, S.K.; Srivastava, C.; Chattopadhyay, K.; Paul, A. Growth mechanism of the interdiffusion zone between platinum modified bond coats and single crystal superalloys. *Acta Mater.* **2016**, *105*, 438–448. [CrossRef]
28. Carter, T.J. Common failures in gas turbine blades. *Eng. Fail. Anal.* **2005**, *12*, 237–247. [CrossRef]
29. Mazur, Z.; Ramirez, A.L.; Islas, J.A.J.; Amezcua, A.C. Failure analysis of a gas turbine blade made of Inconel 738LC alloy. *Eng. Fail. Anal.* **2005**, *12*, 474–486. [CrossRef]
30. Vardar, N.; Ekerim, A. Failure analysis of gas turbine blades in a thermal power plant. *Eng. Fail. Anal.* **2007**, *14*, 743–749. [CrossRef]
31. Poursaeidi, E.; Aieneravaie, M.; Mohammadi, M.R. Failure analysis of a second stage blade in a gas turbine engine. *Eng. Fail. Anal.* **2008**, *15*, 1111–1129. [CrossRef]
32. Chan, K.S.; Cheruvu, N.S.; Leverant, G.R. Predicting Coating Degradation Under Variable Peak Temperatures. In Proceedings of the ASME Gas Turbine & Aeroengine Congress & Exhibition, Indianapolis, IN, USA, 7–10 June 1999.
33. Cheruvu, N.S.; Chan, K.S.; Viswanathan, R. Evaluation, degradation and life assessment of coatings for land-based combustion turbines. *Energy Mater.* **2006**, *1*, 33–47. [CrossRef]
34. Chan, K.S.; Cheruvu, S. Field Validation of a TBC Life-Prediction Model for Land-Based Gas Turbines. In Proceedings of the ASME Turbo Expo 2010, Scotland, UK, 14–18 June 2010.
35. Ellison, K.A.; Daleo, J.A.; Hussain, K. A New Method of Metal Temperature Estimation for Service-Run Blades and Vanes. In Proceedings of the 10th International Symposium on Superalloys 2000, Champion, IL, USA, 17 September 2000; pp. 759–768.
36. Smith, J.; Scheibel, J.; Classes, D.; Paschke, S.; Elbel, S.; Fick, K.; Carlson, D. Thermal barrier coating validation testing for industrial gas turbine combustion hardware. *J. Eng. Gas Turbines Power* **2016**, *138*, 031508. [CrossRef]
37. *Combustion Turbine Repair Guidelines: Hot Section Coatings, Hot Section Coatings*; EPRI: Palo Alto, CA, USA, 2010; Volume 7, p. 1022336.
38. Kniat, J. Means for Calculating Turbine Inlet Temperature of a Gas Turbine Engine. U.S. Patent 4055997A, 1 November 1977.
39. *Life Management System for Advanced F Class Gas Turbines: Siemens-Westinghouse W501F*; EPRI: Palo Alto, CA, USA, 2005; p. 1008319.

MDPI

St. Alban-Anlage 66

4052 Basel

Switzerland

Tel. +41 61 683 77 34

Fax +41 61 302 89 18

www.mdpi.com

Coatings Editorial Office

E-mail: coatings@mdpi.com

www.mdpi.com/journal/coatings

Lightning Source UK Ltd.
Milton Keynes UK
UKHW051815310822
408125UK00002B/108